Gemma

Gemma

A Novel by

Meg Tilly

Syren Book Company

Minneapolis

Most Syren Books are available at special quantity discounts for bulk purchases for sales promotions, premiums, fund-raising, and educational needs. For details, write

Syren Book Company
Special Sales Department
5120 Cedar Lake Road
Minneapolis, MN 55416

Published by
Syren Book Company
5120 Cedar Lake Road
Minneapolis, MN 55416

Printed in the United States of America on acid-free paper

ISBN-13: 978-0-929636-61-0
ISBN-10: 0-929636-61-9

LCCN 2006920903

Cover design by Kyle G. Hunter
Book design by Wendy Holdman

To order additional copies of this book see the form
at the back of this book or go to www.itascabooks.com

For Charlotte Sheedy
If it weren't for you, Gemma *would still be a short story, languishing in the top drawer of my desk.*

Gemma

CHAPTER ONE

Buddy, my mama's boyfriend, was waitin for me after school. Waitin in his ol' rusty blue pickup truck. Almost didn't see him. Almost walked right by, on account of nobody ever pickin me up at school before. "Hey, Gemma . . ." he called, and tooted his horn a bit. *Boop . . . boop . . .* Like that.

"Hey, Gemma . . ." And I'm lookin around, tryin to figure out who's callin my name. Doesn't sound like no kid from school. So I'm lookin around, can't see him, cause the sun's reflectin on his dirty ol' windshield, and yeah, I know his truck. I mean if somebody said, "I want you to pick out Buddy's truck," you know, if they had a car lineup or somethin, I'd be able to pick it out fine. Bam. No problem. "That's his truck right there," I'd say.

The thing is, I wasn't expectin him. It was out of *context*. That's why I didn't recognize it.

Pretty good, huh? That was pretty slick the way I slipped that in. *Context.* And I think I used it right. I try to use my spellin words durin the week, work them into my regular conversation.

Mrs. Watson, my teacher, she says that's what you gotta do. "Make friends with the words," she says. "Use them, feel them on your tongue, taste them. Let these new words I give you enhance your way of speaking."

Some of the kids laugh at her behind her back. Think she's weird, her way of talkin. But I like it, listenin to her, talkin so passionate, so earnest, her cheeks, sides of her neck gettin all flushed and red. "Language will set you free," she says. Says it in ringin tones, like she's a minister standin at the front of the church, preachin hell and redemption. "Language will set you free." She says it ferocious, like it's real important, a life and death matter to her that we understand. Like it'll save us from gangs and no money, and no food in the house cause your mom's out boozin again.

It's one of Mrs. Watson's favorite sayins. "Language will set you free." Says it maybe five times a day. Arm out, gesturin, hand all smudgy from the chalkboard. Or sometimes she pounds the desk when she says it, or a book she's holdin in her hand. And she really seems to believe it, so I don't know, maybe it will, maybe it won't, but just in case she's right, I work on my language, my spellin words, my vocabulary. I work on them hard, cause I wouldn't mind bein free.

And that's another thing. She gives us real weird writin assignments. Take today, for instance. She comes waltzin into the room. "Good morning, class." Nobody really answered. Nobody ever does. Not really, not even me. I would, cause I like her. Like and feel sorry for her all at the same time, cause to be honest, we aren't that great of a class. But even I didn't answer her, not really, cause I'm kinda cool. Not real cool, like "lots of friends cool." I'm more like a "loner cool." People don't mess with me, not too much, cause if they did, they know they'd get a face full of fist. I'm a wild card, so people leave me alone, sorta let me fly under the radar screen, like a stealth bomber, and I don't wanna mess with that, so I don't say hi, or good morning, don't want to look like a goody two-shoes, just shuffled my feet with the rest of the kids, like I was real bored or somethin. Even though I actually was kinda interested to see what she was gonna come up with today.

Didn't let on though, just mumbled a little bit of a good morning, that's about all I could get away with, and to be honest, it's pretty respectful, considerin what some of the other kids do. I mean, at least I was sittin in my seat, not screwin around in the back of the class, throwin things, swaggerin about, pants half fallin off my ass, pretendin not to see the teacher come in. At least I wasn't doin that.

Now maybe I don't say it loud, clear, in a, you know, a TV sitcom voice, but at least I say somethin. You know what I mean, at least I mumble "Good morning," cause I'm tellin you, it's more than most people do.

Not that I think "Good morning" is so important. Sayin it. Don't think it is. To say, "Good morning," when most of the time, for most of us, it isn't a very good morning at all. I'm not complainin, mornins are generally better than evenins, that's usually when the shit hits the fan. Generally mornins are better, as a rule, cause you got the whole day in front of you, shimmerin in front of you like a promise, like maybe today somethin fun's gonna happen, somethin good, somethin excitin. You got all that in front of you. So I have to say, I do like mornings the best, the way it smells, the way it looks, like it just woke up and maybe today things are gonna be okay.

But this custom of sayin "Good morning" every mornin, well it's just not truthful.

"The . . . Topic . . . Is . . ." Mrs. Watson, readin each word out loud as she wrote it, "Love . . ." and then when she'd finished writin the words out on the blackboard, she underlined them once, twice, so emphatically that a little bit of chalk powder fell, like a puff of smoke, from her stick of chalk.

Then she turned around and faced the class, and the expression on her face, it was almost like a dare. I like this about her class, that she's so into what she does. I look forward to her class, cause most teachers, they're just too tired to care anymore, too beaten down. I can see it in their faces sometimes, when all the kids are actin out, screwin around. I can see the weariness, see them wonderin why the hell they took this job. Tired out, pissed off, just goin though the motions like they're underwater swimmin.

And sometimes, I get worried for Mrs. Watson, that she's gonna get like that too, all tired out, sharp edged and bitter. So I try to be nice to her, nice on the sly, so she won't give up, lose hope, think we're all lost causes.

"The topic is love," she said again, just in case we didn't hear her the first time, hear the whole thing properly. She likes to repeat, Mrs. Watson, just in case.

"We're going to try something new today. *Free association*. I want you to write. Just pick up your pen and write. Don't worry about punctuation, or spelling, or telling a story. I just want you to write whatever comes into your mind, whatever pops into your head, write it down. The topic is love. You have twenty minutes, start writing."

She turned to her desk, like that was all that needed to be said, but nobody was writin, we were all starin at her like she was a freak show. Cause she's come up with some weird assignments, but this one's a doozy. And to be honest, I'm tryin to encourage her and all, but even I had no idea what to do with that one.

"Love . . ." Billy Robinson mimicked in a mamsey-pamsey voice. He started gaggin and his cronies were all snickerin, and then it's like his face all of a sudden gets mad, like Mrs. Watson assigned this exercise for the sole purpose of pissin him off. "What the hell kind of *shit* is that?"

"Exactly," Mrs. Watson said. Cause she's not scared of him, like some of the other teachers. She just beamed at him, nodded her head, like he'd just been real insightful, like he wasn't just bein a smart ass. Beamed at him like he was joinin in for once, like she was takin his question seriously. "Exactly." And then she looked at the rest of the class, actin as if we were having a philosophical discussion. "What is love? What does it mean to you? How does love, or the lack thereof, manifest itself in your life?" She smiled at us, nodded encouragingly. "Just pick up your pen and write. There is no right or wrong in this exercise. As long as you have written something on your paper, you'll get a good mark."

So I picked up my pen. She's the teacher after all.

The topic is love, I wrote. I underlined it. And then that was it. I just sat there, starin at it. Those words at the top of my page, and I dunno, I was stuck or somethin, couldn't think of anything to write. Nothin.

"The topic is love . . ." I say it under my breath, test the words on my tongue. "The . . . topic . . . is . . . love."

My pen's not writin, but my brain, my brain's flippin through memories like the speed dial on my mama's phone. It's just flippin through memories, all of my mom, none of my dad, but that's probably cause I don't know him, never met him, otherwise, he probably woulda been in there too.

And these images of my mom, they're not whole images spun out. It's not like they made sense. It was more like one of those kaleidoscope toys that you look into, but you weren't holdin it. Somebody was, and they were turnin it so the images were tumblin, morphin, changin shape too fast and I couldn't catch the tail of them. Just short little memories flyin past, just flashes of them. Short flashes, like a strobe light in the dark. And my brain, tryin to catch up, flippin through them like a recipe holder. Flippin through and discardin. Nope, can't write about that, or that, ho . . . ho . . . definitely not that! Bits and snatches of her, flyin past, like I'm rifflin through one of those little plastic recipe holders that normal households have, with recipes written down on index cards. Normal households that have a mother and a father, and the mother cooks and the children have cookies and cupcakes and things when they come home from school. Normal households with moms who have pretty beauty shop hairdos and they drive their kids to piano lessons and skatin lessons and things.

Like my friend I used to have, Angela McCauley. We were best friends for part of fifth grade, but that's neither here nor there. I'm not bemoanin the fact that we aren't friends now, could care less. That's not what I'm talkin about. The point of all this, what I'm gettin at is, she had a mother like that. Her mom had a pink recipe holder. It wasn't a pale pink, but it wasn't real bright either. Not hot pink or neon colored or anything tacky like that, it was more like the color of double bubble gum after it's been chewed for a while, just a few minutes. Sorta like that color.

And she had all kinds of recipes written down in it. She let me look at it once. Took it down from the shelf over the stove, let me hold it.

She had all kinds of recipes in there, some of them she'd tried, some of them she hadn't yet. All kinds of recipes. Ones friends had given her, ones she had clipped from the Good Housekeeping magazines she kept on her coffee table. She liked Good Housekeeping magazines. That's the kind of mother Angela's mom was. She liked doin motherly, homey things. And when me and Angela were friends, Angela would invite me home for lunch. And I'd go. Let me tell you, I'd leave my soggy peanut butter sandwich in my desk and walk with her to her house. Didn't matter, rain or shine, didn't matter to me if we got soakin wet, didn't matter one bit, cause I knew what would be waitin for us.

And Angela's clean-smellin mom would meet us at the door, and on rainy days, when we'd come in, all drippin wet and laughin, she'd fuss and worry that Angela wasn't wearin her coat done up, hadn't used her umbrella, things like that.

She noticed things like that, that Angela's hair was wet, for instance. And she'd give us towels to dry off and we'd stand there in her hallway and we'd rub our heads and I'd pretend like I was familiar with this, like my mom met me at the door and gave me towels too. And Angela would roll her eyes at me and I'd roll my eyes back at her as if to say, "Moms, what are you gonna do?" But I'd be savorin it. The fresh-washed towel, all soft and fluffy. Thick too. Not all scratchy and thin and mildewy smellin like ours. Not rancid with underarm smell and yesterday's throw-up.

No, these towels were thick and soft and fluffy. And I'd rub my hair, my face, bury my nose in, breathe in the smell, the softness, all that love. I'd rub and pretend that this was me, my life. That I'd woken up in the middle of a Beverly Cleary novel.

I'd rub my hair as long as I could and then when we were done dryin off, we'd head into the livin room.

And we'd sit in the livin room cross-legged on the floor and play Scrabble on their wood and glass coffee table. And I'd be real careful not to touch the glass part, not to leave fingerprints, so her mother wouldn't think me comin over was a whole pile of work. I'd make sure to only let my hands rest on the wood rim that held the glass in place, that and the Scrabble board. And it was cozy, us playing Scrabble while her mom bustled around the kitchen makin us pipin-hot Kraft macaroni and cheese.

I'd always say "yes please," and "no thank you" to her mom. Try and behave real good so her mama would like me and ask me back.

So that was good. That was all good, but then, you see, the problem was, at night. That was the problem. Cause I'd lie in bed, and I'd think about the day. And at first, you know, for the first couple of months I was happy. I liked bein Angela's friend, it was real comfortin, cause I'd think about her house, and her mom, and everything, and it made me happy. It was like a real good bedtime story. Made me feel all cozy and I'd go to sleep with a smile on my face.

But then one night, it flipped on me. I was runnin though my images, my memories, the smell of her mom, the house, the tick of the brass and glass clock on their mantle. I loved that clock. Thinkin about her mom in the kitchen with her yellow terry cloth slippers makin a *shush . . . shush* sound on the linoleum. I'm tellin you, I could almost taste that macaroni and cheese, and then, the damned thing flipped on me. It's like this little voice dropped down into my head from nowhere, and it said, "Yes, well, that's all fine and good, but be honest, Gemma, do you really like her?"

And me, my heart started racin. "What?" Cheeks gettin hot, stomach grippin up, gettin all embarrassed, even though no one could see me. "Who?"

"Angela." Like this voice is pissed off with me, like it thinks I'm the lowest of low. "What do you *like* about her, other than her mother and her life?"

"What are you talkin about?"

"Stop playin dumb! You find her *boring* and you know it. You're just usin her."

"What?" Actin indignant, but I know it's true.

"Borrowin her life, stealin little snatches, pretendin they're yours . . ."

And that was that. I had to stop bein her friend. Cause it really wasn't fair, her thinkin it was her I liked. Had to stop, wasn't fair. Foolin her like that.

It was real hard, but I stopped acceptin her invitations, stopped goin over. Think I hurt her feelins, but I just felt like too bad a person the other way, usin her like that. Her good nature.

So that's when I became a loner, not cause I'm a loser. I'm a loner cause I choose to be. Better than bein a usin, lyin *hypocrite*. Ahem . . . spellin word.

It was hard at first, eatin my sandwiches by myself, sittin on top of the jungle gym. Pretendin I didn't care. Actin like I didn't notice when Angela and her new best friend, stupid Patty Tomas, would walk past me, noses in the air, their permission slips to leave school property clutched in their hands. Walk out of the playground, laughin and talkin. Off they'd go to Angela's house for her warm mother and hot meals. It was hard at first, but now, no problem. Doesn't bother me at all.

Anyway, back to my mama. She doesn't do that kind of thing. The kind of things Angela's mom does. Not that my mom doesn't love me, she does. She just doesn't have time to show it, is all. I mean, it's hard raisin a kid, and I'm no walk in the park. I try to be good, but I don't know, seem to always be messin up somehow, makin her mad. And then there's work. She's gotta work, you know. How else are the bills gonna get paid? How else is she gonna keep a roof over our head? So she's gotta work.

Used to be a cocktail waitress at Shooters. Tips were good, but she got too old. "They like their flesh firm over there at Shooters," she says. "They like them young. Young and stupid." That's what my mama says, face all twisted up. "They don't want a washed-up hag like me hangin around, ruinin people's appetites. Assholes."

And I try to tell her, "Mama, you're pretty." Cause she is when she's not drinkin. Real pretty. But she doesn't listen to me, just takes another slug from her bottle and threatens to "go on over there, give 'em them what-for."

Anyway, she got another job, down at Joe's diner. But she's gotta work harder, longer hours and tips aren't so good. Apparently, the people that eat at Joe's are cheap, cheap, cheap.

I try to be in my bedroom, with my door closed, by the time she gets home from work. Try to stay outta her way, cause by closin time, she's usually not in too good a mood.

So see, if my mama had a nicer life, an easier one, she'd have lots of time to be all lovin and cozy. Lots of time. It's not that she doesn't love me, she does. She's just busy is all, worked to the bone. And if it was important, like real, real important, she'd make the time, and that's the truth.

I remember once, in second grade, I had a bad fever. Real bad. Apparently I fainted in the lunchroom and they called my mama, and she came to get me lickety-split, dropped work and everything. Drove to the school straightaway and took me to the doctor. And I guess what he told her was pretty bad, cause she let me sleep in her bed. I was sick, real sick, and no matter what they did, the fever wouldn't break. Gave me medicine, fed me pop-sicles, even got a shot in my butt. But nothin was workin and the doctor was worried they were gonna lose me. And my mama, she stayed home from work, watched over me, soothed my forehead with her cool hands. Had her metal mixin bowl and a washcloth with water in it, and when the huge black spiders, bigger than my fist, would be crawlin all over the place, up the walls, and I was the only one who could see them, she'd wring out the washcloth, sponge bathe me, and make them go away. The water cold, so cold, that my body would shake and shake and I'd have to grit my teeth to stop their clatterin. My head all fuzzy. I didn't tell my mama that I didn't want the popsicles. She kept tryin to feed me, cause she'd already bought them, and popsicles are expensive, cost good money. So I'd eat them, even though they were weighin heavy in my hand, and it was so hard to sit up. I'd try and eat them for her, cause she was tryin so hard.

She let me sleep in her bed for eleven days. Stayed home from work. Eleven whole days. Wish I could remember them better. Kind of passed in a blur. I try to force my brain to remember more. But it doesn't work . . . Just clutchin at images, bits and pieces, like the memories were scattered, torn by a windstorm.

But I do remember she let me sleep in her bed once. I do remember that.

And all of this, it was all flashin through my head, and I still hadn't written a damned word. I heard the other kids writin. Heard their pens draggin across the paper. Heard Dale Robinson saunter across the room. Didn't even have to look up. Knew it was him, his footsteps.

"Where are you going" Mrs. Watson said.

"The crapper," all innocent as can be. "Got a bad case of the runs." And his sidekicks giggled like he's God or something, cause everyone knows he doesn't have the runs. Isn't gonna come back for a good fifteen, twenty minutes. Gonna go sneak a smoke out back behind the gym.

He shuffled out, cause what could she say? "You can't go to the bathroom"?

And there I was, still starin at the page. Time was runnin out. Had to write somethin. Didn't want to get an F. Had to write somethin.

So I wrote "Love is pretty good at my house, the quality of it." And I wrote about goin home for lunch, and Kraft macaroni, and warm, soft, sweet-smellin towels.

I wrote about it, but I wrote about it like it was me. Like it was my mom. And I gotta say, it was fun, really lost myself in it. Almost believed what I was writin there for a moment. Almost did. Got this excited feelin in my belly, like maybe, when I got home, it would be true. Like maybe, in the writin of it, it was like a reminder to God or somethin. Like maybe he didn't realize, didn't remember that he'd made a mistake.

Anyway, crazy as it may seem, all day long, cause Mrs. Watson's class was the first class of the day, all day, on and off, I'd get excited all over again. Wantin to get home. Knowin it's not true, my story I wrote. Not tryin to be silly or anything, but the wishin part of me, wantin to get home just in case.

So I went through my day, a little trickle of anticipation dancin in my belly. Not a big excitement, more like the feelin when you find an old piece of candy in your pocket that you forgot you had, and now your mouth is waterin, waitin for recess. More like that level of excitement.

I mean, come on. I'm not a baby. I know magic isn't true. But sometimes it's fun, you know, fun to pretend.

So anyway, cause I had this hope, the day seemed to drag on, go so slow, and finally, when the final buzzer went, I was outta there like a flash. Like yeah, I got somewhere important to go. Out the front door like a bullet, but by the time I'd reached the bottom of the front steps, I'm like, "Who am I kiddin?" And all of a sudden I feel real stupid, like, "Why am I racin home?"

And then, to make matters worse, Buddy was waitin for me. Like what the hell's that about?

And that thing I was sayin, when I said I didn't see Buddy at first. It's not cause I have bad eyesight or anything. I didn't see him, cause I wasn't expectin to see him. Him or his dumb ol' truck. Nothin wrong with my eyes, I saw him fine once he got outta his truck.

"Hey, sugar . . ." he calls out, with that stupid southern drawl he thinks sounds so smooth. Makes me wanna punch him in the face. Hate it when he calls me that. "Sugar . . ." Hate it. Stupid smirk on his fat face. Stupid asshole.

"Give me some sugar . . ." he always says, late at night when he creeps into my room, my bed. "I need somah yo' sugar . . ." Stupid creep. "Your pussy's so sweet . . ." he says while he's gruntin over me like a filthy, sweaty pig. "I'm addicted to yo' pussy. It's your fault, you know. Your pussy's so sweet, it keeps me comin back for more." Says it like he thinks it's a compliment, like I should be pleased! He knows I don't like it! Hurts like hell and he knows it. Why else would he be holdin his stupid greasy hand over my mouth? Why else? I tell you why. He don't want my mama to hear me cryin, that's why. Don't want my screams wakin up the neighbors.

Thought I was gonna die, the first time he did it. Eight years old. Thought I was gonna die, split in two for sure. Mama outta town, vistin my granddaddy. Just me and Buddy, me and Buddy at home. One afternoon, Buddy, he comes home from work, and he's actin weird, been drinkin, smell it on his breath. He puts the music on. Turned on the hi-fi, pumped it up loud. Had the music pumped up loud, so you could feel the bass poundin right through the soles of your feet. Music so loud. Loud, loud, loud. Neighbors couldn't hear, nobody could hear, Buddy, holdin me down, doin bad things to me, me cryin, cryin out, but nobody could hear nothin.

Tried to tell my mama. Tried to tell her when she finally got back, but she wasn't up to talkin. Sometimes she gets that way after visitin Grandaddy. She just went into her bedroom with her bottle of Jack Daniels and took a good long nap. I didn't bother her, knew she was tired. But later, after she woke up, was rummagin through the refrigerator, tryin to find some eats, I tried again, followed her in, but she was still in no mood.

"Jesus Christ," she said, slammin the fridge door, nostrils flarin. "I get so tired of your goddamned whinin." Hands fisted on the ledge of her hips.

Thought I was whinin and I hadn't even told her the worst of it, any of it really. Hadn't gotten to the bad stuff yet, had just gotten out that I didn't want Buddy to babysit me anymore when she went to visit Granddaddy, that I didn't feel comfortable, didn't feel real safe with him . . . I wanted to tell her more, everything, but her face stopped me, the way she was lookin at me stopped me cold. "What am I supposed to do?" she said, mouth twisted. "Who am I supposed to leave you with? You tell me. Hmm? Do you see great mobs of people standin in line, clamorin to take care of you?"

I didn't have no answer.

"Do you?" she demanded, voice risin. She started lookin around the room, like she was lookin for volunteers. "I don't see anyone," she said. "I don't see anyone sayin 'Oh please, let me.' " All sarcastic like. "I don't see a single goddamned livin soul . . . I mean, please, correct me if I'm wrong, maybe I'm not seein so good. Do you see anyone volunteerin?" And of course I didn't, how could I, there was nobody else in the room. No right way to answer that one, so I just shut up, and Buddy stayed my babysitter. And when he heard from my mama that I was complainin, that wasn't good. He got me alone, slammed me up against the wall in the hallway, held me up, feet off the ground. Held me up by the front of my shirt, face up close, bad breath, stinkin me out. Told me to shut my yap. Did I want to be thrown in jail? "Yes, that's right, thrown in jail, cause that's what they do to little girls who seduce grown men. Flauntin your pussy like you do. If they knew about you, they'd lock you up in jail and throw away the key for good."

That's what they do, cause apparently, what I did with him is against the law and I can't tell anybody. Anybody at all, unless I want to spend the rest of my life rottin away in jail. And I don't wanna do that, I'd be scared of jail. I'd be real scared. So it's a good thing I guess, that I found out in time. Found out before I accidentally spilled the beans, told someone. Good thing I found out about the laws.

Anyway, it's bad enough I have to deal with him at home, but now he's waitin outside my school, sleazin up the place. Callin me sugar, people lookin. Hope they don't know what that means. Sugar.

"Hey, sugar . . ." Buddy says, comin round the front of his pickup truck, left thumb slung in the belt loop of his saggy old blue jeans, right arm free, loose, danglin. "How was school?" Like he cares, stupid jerk, comin round my school. He's got no right.

I keep walkin. Head in the air. Pretend I don't see

him. Keep walkin like he's got nothin on me. Keep walkin past like he's just a squashed fly on his windshield. Just speed up my steps a bit, move round back to the other side of the sidewalk, get a few kids between us. Speed up my steps a bit, casual, like I just remembered I'm late for somethin important. But he sped up too, caught me by the arm. Laughin like it's a game, but he's got my arm hard.

"Ain't lettin you get away as easy as that," he says, and hauls me off to his truck. Nothin I can do about it. Don't want to cause a fuss, don't want kids lookin anymore than they already are. Nothin I can do about it but make my feet walk in his direction.

"Bet you're wonderin why I picked you up from school," Buddy says, lookin over his shoulder, out the back window, steppin on the gas, swingin the truck out into the traffic, when even I, and I'm only twelve, can't drive, no matter, even I can see that there's not enough room. That silver car's comin way too fast. But he swings the truck out, turnin the steerin wheel hard, causin the silver car to slam on its brakes, lean on its horn. Which pisses Buddy off. "Fuck you!" he yells stickin his middle finger out the open window. "Fuck you!" Like they were the asshole. Like they were the screwup.

Then, like nothin happened, like he didn't just almost kill us for sure, he turns back to me. "Betcha can't guess?"

I am a bit curious why he picked me up from school, but I'm not about to give him the satisfaction. Cause that's the thing about Buddy, the thing you gotta watch out for. He always does this, pretends he's got a special treat for you, somethin real great, builds you all up, your expectations, and more likely than not, it's gonna be a big steamin slice of crap pie.

I don't say nothin, just look out the window. Keep to my side of the truck. Don't get too close to Buddy, cause you wouldn't think it, with that big belly hangin down over his jeans, you wouldn't think it, but Buddy can move pretty damned fast.

I can feel him lookin at me, don't turn, don't let on I can feel him.

"I got you a job," he says.

"A job?" I keep my voice casual, keep the eagerness out, just in case I heard him wrong. Could be his idea of a joke or somethin.

"You got me a job?" I say, and I'm sorta nervous, but, to be honest, this is kinda excitin too. I wouldn't mind a job, make a little money. The kids at school would be jealous. Don't know anybody my age that's got a job. Usually you gotta be fifteen, sixteen. Which is kinda a dumb rule, cause I'm a real hard worker. Shouldn't matter the age, they'd get their money's worth outta me.

"Yeah . . ." he says. "I got you a job." He looks at me. "And you want to do well at this job, right?"

And I say, "Yeah. Yeah!" I smile big so he'll know I mean it. Don't know why he's bein so nice all of a sudden. But a job would be cool. Real cool.

"Don't want to mess up, right?" he says, and I shake my head so he'll know I'm sincere, he keeps talkin. "Cause if you mess up, I'm gonna be real pissed. And you don't want to get me pissed, isn't that right?"

"Uh . . . huh . . ." And I nod my head. I don't know why, but my heart's poundin and my mouth is real dry. I mean,

I'm glad to have a job, but I'm kind of scared too. Buddy's not much fun when you mess up. "What . . . what do I gotta do?" I ask.

But he doesn't answer me. Not really, just laughs, not a nice laugh, not a friendly one, and says, "Sugar, you just do what you do best." And he's still laughin about that one as he jerks the steerin wheel hard, cross two lanes of traffic, and there we are, pullin into a Denny's parkin lot. And I think, "Oh, Denny's, maybe I'm gonna get to be a waitress."

I'd like that. That would be nice. Maybe I'd get a uniform and everything!

. ⬤ .

Hazen is sitting in Denny's restaurant. Got himself a booth in the corner, back against the wall, good vantage point of the door. Hands sweaty, the dregs of his coffee gone cold, got that tie-dye thing going with the sugar, the cream. He swirls it slowly, both hands wrapped around the mug, like it's still hot, drinkable, sits there, like he has every right. Takes a sip, something to do. Waiting for Buddy, just on the off chance, pretty sure actually, that he's not going to show. But he's waiting just in case.

The waitress with blue mascara slides by, fresh pot of steaming coffee. Hazen gestures her over. Not that he wants more. Stuff tastes like shit. Badly brewed. Already feeling jittery, drunk two cups of the stuff, but what the hell, he'll give Buddy ten more minutes and then call it a day. What a bullshitter.

Just getting ready to leave, settling up his bill, the waitress smelling like cheap talcum powder and last night's sex. Settling up his bill, when Buddy waltzes in, thirty minutes late. Hazen had thought he'd been stood up, played for a fool. The fucker was just blowing smoke up his ass. Telling him all about this Gemma chick he was banging. Saying what a great lay she was.

"You've never had it good until you've tried some of this," Buddy'd said. "The kid's twelve, talk about tight, best lay this side of the Rockies, and beautiful too. A regular little Lolita. Insatiable. Can't get enough, begs for the cock, twenty-four, seven." Said it with this satisfied smirk on his face that made Hazen want to call his bluff.

Hazen thought Buddy was just blowing smoke up his ass, but then in he walks, the kid in tow, and she is perfect. Absolutely perfect. Long blond hair, pale blond, the color of summer grass along the highway, a natural blond, and Hazen Wood wonders about her heritage. Swedish ancestors? Danish perhaps? Beautiful blond hair, a natural. Yes sir, she is perfect, just how Buddy had described her. High tight ass perched on lanky colt legs, legs not quite filled out. No tits, none visible anyway. Maybe just little buds, little swollen buds hiding beneath her T-shirt, the nipples just starting to swell. Absolutely perfect. Well worth it, the wait, the money.

- ◆ -

"This is Hazen," Buddy says, pushin me forward, givin me a slap on the ass. Like he owns me, like I'm a donkey or somethin. And this guy, this Hazen guy, is steppin forwards, smilin big for a mouth that looks like it's not used to smilin much.

"Hey there, little girl . . ." he says, which kind of offends me, cause I'm not little, I'm twelve, for Christsake. Would correct him on his assumption, but I don't want to be rude.

"Hi," I say. I'm feelin funny, don't know why. Don't like the way this Hazen guy is lookin at me. Lookin at me all greasy, oily-like. Freakin me out.

"Well, what do you think?" Buddy asks, me standin there, just standin there.

"Good. She'll do, she'll do real nice," says Hazen, smilin. Runs his forefinger down my arm, does it slow, like he's brandin me. Don't like it. Try to step back, but there's nowhere to go. Buddy's stepped in right behind me, right up close, crowdin me in. Nowhere to go, and I kinda suffer from claustrophobia, you know, like panic spells when people crowd me too close. I get dizzy, everything kinda slows down, rushes by, blurry like. Standin there in Denny's, Buddy pressin up against my back, this Hazen guy right in front, table, chairs, cuttin out my air. I can hear the kitchen noises, dishes, cutlery clinkin loud. Real loud, like they're amplified, and yet voices, muffled, foggy, like they're talkin through a vacuum hose. And they laugh, Buddy and Hazen, they both laugh, tunnel laugh, and then Hazen takes out his wallet, gets it outta his back pocket starts countin out money. "Twenty . . . forty . . . sixty . . . eighty . . . and . . . one hundred dollars." Gives the money, the hundred dollars to Buddy. And I'm wonderin what this has to do with my waitressin job. But Buddy doesn't explain. Just pockets the money, gives my ass a feel, then stuff my hand into this Hazen guy's sweaty, clammy one. His soft, pulpy, soggy hand, that feels like mashed, spit-out bananas. "She's all yours, man," Buddy says, smilin still. Smilin big. Then he makes a noise like a train whistle. "Whoohoo!" he says, pumpin his fist up and down in the air. "Go to town."

And while Hazen's puttin away his wallet, Buddy leans over me, smile gone now. No smile now, eyes like ice picks, chop right through me. "You be good," he says, hand slid under my hair, squeezin the back of my neck. Squeezin it hard, real hard, makin my eyes fill up. "Hazen's boss now, you hear? You do whatever he says, you hear? Whatever he says. He'll bring you home when you're done, and I don't wanna hear about you givin him any flak. You hear me?"

And I'm tryin to keep my head upright, tryin not to let on how much it's hurtin. How humiliatin it is, for him to be doin this kind of thing in public. "You hear?" Gives me a shake, speakin low, through his teeth, nobody but me, me and Hazen can hear him.

"I hear you," I say. "I hear you." And he gives me one last shake for emphasis, then lets me go, and his friend Hazen is laughin, shakin his head. "You got her trained good," he says admiringly, like I'm a dog or somethin. "You got her trained real good."

Next thing I know, Buddy's gone. Didn't fill out no application for no waitressin job. Don't know how to get home from here. Got no idea. Stuck here with Hazen, not sure why. Not sure, but I got a feelin. I got a sick kinda feelin in my belly. Stuck here with this Hazen guy, but I'll be damned if I'm gonna cry.

- ◆ -

He knew she wasn't a virgin. Hell, Buddy had told him so. He'd had her. And according to Buddy, he probably wasn't her first either.

Hazen knew she wasn't a virgin, but he couldn't help the brief stab of disappointment when he entered her. It's like his head knew that she wasn't, but the rest of him refused to believe it. She was warm, tight, small, real small, kinda dry, but spit had helped that along. Not much hair, just a little bit of peach fuzz, hell, her only being twelve and all. But he wasn't the first. He wasn't her first. And the sensation that was missing, the resistance, her gasp of pain, surprise, pleasure as he first forced his way into her, his keen disappointment made his penis go soft and flaccid. And his dick doesn't care how nice she feels, his dick is annoyed with him and his goddamned fairytale promises and starts sliding, oozing outta her.

"Shit!" he yells. "Shit!" And he rolls over onto his back, yanks the covers up over his waist, arms crossed, gripping the covers to him. He lies there trying to get his breathing under control.

"Paid a hundred bucks. A hundred lousy bucks, and you can't even make me keep it up," he says, glaring at the ceiling.

"I . . . I'm sorry . . . ," she whimpers, face puffy, tear-streaked. Hasn't stopped crying since she got there. Got to his apartment, got the bad news. Apparently Buddy hadn't told her what she was there for, what the deal was.

"No . . . no . . . no . . . ," she kept saying. "You don't understand . . ." She kept babbling on about her waitressing job. Her waitressing job at Denny's. Clutching at her clothes, like she had half a chance. Trying to keep her clothes on, trying to scramble out the door. Not that that bothered Hazen, the chase. Kind of funny, actually, how scared she was. No, that didn't bother him. It was the fact that she didn't feel quite how he imagined. That was the thing that made him get soft, shrivel up like a snail doused in salt.

He glares at the ceiling, doesn't look at her face, doesn't want to feel guilty, wishes she would stop her goddamned crying, enter into the fun a bit. Tries not to look at her face, but he can see it hovering in the periphery of his eye line, her long blond hair swinging forward, falling, obscuring her like a curtain, her naked body all wrapped around itself, legs, arms all tucked in, small, like she's trying to disappear. Tucked up around herself so small he could easily fit her in the half-sized oven he has in the kitchenette. Bake her up for dinner. He has to laugh at that. Might have lost his hard-on, but he still has a sense of humor.

She is rocking slightly, her body. "Can I go home now?" she's whispering, voice coming out all scratchy. "Can I go home?"

He doesn't answer, stupid bitch, little cock-teasing whore.

"Ask me nice," he finally says, not that he has any intention, paid a hundred bucks for Christsake, but he's interested to see what she'll do.

He can feel her thinking, holding her breath.

"Ask . . . me . . . nice." His voice slow, measured.

There's a slight pause.

She takes the bait.

"P . . . please . . . can . . . can . . . I go h . . . home now?" Her head tips up slightly from her knees, and he can tell that she is peeking at him from behind her hair. Sussing him out. It's a chess game now, pure and simple. And Hazen, all modesty aside, is a damned good chess player.

"P . . . please?" she's saying, she's pleading. This is good, the pleading thing, the dick likes this.

"Nicer than that," he says. "You gotta ask me way nicer than that if you want to get home. Push your hair away from your face. I want to see your face." Feels good to boss her, to be the boss for a change. Feels goddamned good.

Her hand, shivering, shaking slightly, pushes her hair back out of her face. "That's better," he says. "Now ask me again, and make it good."

"Pl . . . please . . . can . . ." But he cuts her off, smacks her across the side of the face. Not hard, just enough to snap her head back a little, jerk it up, snatch her breath in.

"Words! That's it? Goddamned words? That all you got to offer? That all you got, you little slut! You stupid whore! Hits her again, harder this time, full fist this time, full dynamite force. The power of him sends her flying off the bed, smashing into the wall like a comic book character. Smashing into the wall, crumpling down to the floor.

Then everything's still, like even the clocks have stopped.

"Little slut . . ." he says. But he says it kindly, more like a joke, anger gone. He can afford to be more compassionate now. Now that she's learned her lesson. It's not her fault she likes getting laid so much. Some kids are born that way, come out of the womb craving the cock. Some kids are just born that way, born to be whores.

"Come here . . ." he says, and she comes to him pale, shaky legged. "Sit," he says, patting the bed, and she sits down beside him, too scared now to cry, just shaking, whole body shaking. "I'm not going to hurt you," he says, stroking her long, blond, sunlight hair. "You don't have to be afraid. I'm not going to hurt you, baby, I just want you to show me a good time is all. It's only fair." Her hair, silky, soft. "I paid my money for a good time, that's your job, it's only fair. You're supposed to make it good for me, see? You're supposed to make it the best for me. That's what you do. That's what you whores do."

He pauses.

"I tell you what, you make it good for me, and I'll take you home. Plain and simple, that's the deal. You make it good for me, fuck me nice, and you can go home, okay?"

She doesn't answer. Needs a little more persuading, the gentle kind. She's in the palm of his hand now, she's listening now, no need to play rough. "Listen Gemma, that's why I paid all that money. I paid a hundred goddamned dollars. That's a lot of money. I don't just have that kind of money just floating around. It doesn't grow on trees. I had to work hard, damned hard for that money. Now I've paid that money, it's gone. I've given it to Buddy. Not that I mind. The minute I saw you I knew you were worth it. But Gemma, a hundred bucks, we're talking about a hundred dollars here, and a hundred dollars should buy a man a pretty damned good time. A fucking amazing time, as a matter of fact. Anything less is a rip-off. Anything else is a cheat." He takes his time, lets what he's said sink in.

"Now . . ." he says all friendly, after all, he's a reasonable man, this is just business. A simple business transaction. "Gemma, sweetheart, you wouldn't want to cheat me, would you? I'd get pissed off if you were trying to cheat me."

She shakes her head, breath all catchy.

"Do you have the hundred dollars? If you have the hundred dollars you can pay me back, go home now." She doesn't answer, just looks down at her hands she is twisting in her lap. Her hands, he notices, are disproportionate to her wrist, like they don't fit her body, like he tried to fuck her just before a growth spurt or something.

"Do you have the hundred dollars?" She shakes her head. "You don't?" He makes his voice surprised. "So what are you going to do?" He puts a little impatience in his voice, a little pressure, a little snap, and it works. He can feel the sting of it stiffen her body. Her hands shake, twisting, like she's wringing out a dirty dishrag. Face is twisted too, contorted, already starting to swell up, discolor where he smacked her.

"Well?"

A small moan comes out of her lips. Face like a moving picture show, all the color drained out. "I . . . I'll . . ." she whispers, head tipping down, like it is just too heavy for her neck to hold up anymore. "I'll . . ." She starts sobbing, sobbing in earnest, but her fingertips reach out, hesitant slightly, a shudder runs through her skinny frame, rattles through her and then she touches his cock. The tips of her fingers icy, on his hot skin, like she's been gripping a cold vodka on the rocks for the last half hour.

"That's good," he says. "That's more like it . . ."

And they go to it. He gives it to her good, the little whore. And it's amazing. Better than his dreams. It's a wild crazy night. She lets him do everything. Doesn't stop crying, but she lets him do everything. Everything, everywhere. Doesn't want to let him, cries out big time, screaming, had to slam his hand over her mouth. Guess Buddy never got around to that last place. She was a virgin there. Buddy never got around to there, but Hazen does. Hazen is thorough.

He does her hard. Doesn't let up until she is bloody

and ragged. He drives it in, hard and deep, shows her no mercy, and he cums. Oh god does he cum. Cums like a goddamned Fourth of July rocket.

- — -

Couldn't sleep after he drove her home. Dropped her off half a block from her house. Watched her climb stiff legged, up the front steps, disappear through the door.

Couldn't sleep. Was too revved up. Couldn't sleep. Just drove and drove and drove. Windows open, music blasting. Felt like howling at the moon. Couldn't sleep. Couldn't sleep. Didn't get to sleep until after four in the morning.

- — -

Buddy looked real worried when he saw my face. Never hits me in the face, just places where it don't show. Grabbed my arm as I was goin out the door for school, said he'd thought about it, thought it was only fair that we split the profits. After all, he said, we were partners in this. Business partners. Took out his wallet, counted out fifty bucks, gave it to me, slipped me a Kit-Kat bar too, finger to his lips, like we had a secret, him and me. "Shhh . . ." he said, voice low quiet, lookin over his shoulder to their bedroom where my mama was sleepin.

Took me out the front door, wasn't done talkin, walked me as far as the telephone pole yappin at me. Remindin me about the police, how I couldn't mention this to anybody. That if I told anybody what happened, the police would find out. They have spies everywhere. The police would find out and throw me in jail for sure.

"Little slut like you, seducin grown men, corruptin 'em.

Throw you in jail for sure before you ruin the rest of the state of California." He tells me this, face sweatin up, getting all greasy like a fried egg. And hey, it's not like I didn't know this already. I mean please, if he's told me once, he's told me a thousand times. What does he think I am? Retarded?

I walk to school, takes longer than usual, body sore. Hope nobody notices my face. Styled my hair over it, cause it's all swollen up like a jack-o'-lantern. I hate that Hazen guy. I really hate him. Hope I never see him again for the rest of my life. Stunk to high heaven. Really, I'm not joking, he stunk. Had to hold my breath.

It's lucky I know how. It's a skill of mine I developed. Don't think many people can do it. I first learned how to do it cause my mom smokes. Smokes like a chimney. So that's how I discovered, developed this particular talent. You see, what I do is I shut my nose in the back of my throat. I press my tongue up in the back like this and breathe through my mouth. No one can tell that I'm pluggin my nose. They just think I'm talking weird cause I have a cold or somethin. They don't know that they stink. I don't hurt their feelings and at the same time I protect myself against havin to smell them.

Stinky Hazen. That's what I shoulda called him. Stinky Hazen. Shoulda plugged my nose with my fingers, wiggled my butt at him and made fartin noises with my mouth. That's what I shoulda done. "Suck my cock." "Screw you . . . *Pplllatt.*" That's what I should have done. Would have served him right. Stupid asshole.

Face hurts pretty bad. Has that *waaah . . . waaah . . .* feelin, like my heart left my chest and is pulsin in my cheek, my jaw. My tongue's bad too. Kinda hard to talk cause I accidentally bit it when he whacked me. Other parts hurt too. Hurts more than when Buddy does me, bigger I guess. Hurts bad, but I'm too ladylike to mention them.

Stupid ol' jerk. Mean ol' dickhead. Mean as a stupid ol' one-eyed snake. Actually, I've never seen a one-eyed snake. Heard about them, but I've never actually seen one. Bet they're mean, on account of them havin only one eye. Bet the other snakes laugh at them, beat them up at recess. They do that at my school. Just gang up on kids, beat them up. Not me, don't beat me up. I'm like the one-eyed snake. I'm mean, real mean when I have to be. I got fists, and I know how to use 'em.

But there's this boy, José, I was gonna say friend, but he's not really my friend cause we never really talk to each other. But the boys are always pickin on him, makin fun of his stutter. Stand around him in a circle, wavin their arms, pushin him. Laughin their fool stupid heads off. Floppin their arms around like dead fish. Eyes buggin out, pretendin to stutter. Makin big gobs of spit fly all over him. Laughin, thinkin they're so cool, but they're not. They're just stupid ignorant jerks. And then, when they get tired of pushin him around, pretendin to stutter, when they get tired of that, sometimes they let him go, but more often than not, they end up beatin him up. Day after day, week after week. And the yard duty does nothin. Nothin. Just stands there talkin.

Grown-ups don't care. That's the fact of the matter. They just plain don't care. "Stop pulling my arm, missy," was all the yard duty supervisor said when I was tryin to tell her what was goin on with José. "Stop yanking on my arm. Didn't yo mama teach you no manners?"

I feel bad for José, I really do. But the reason I say he's not my friend isn't cause I don't like him, cause I do. Don't mind his stutter, think it sounds like a beat-up old car warmin up. You know how it is on cold winter mornins when the ground's all covered with frost. Pretend snow. A thin layer of white, so if you squint your eyes just so, it looks like it has, like it really has snowed. And you get that catch in your breath, even though you know it's not true, you get that catch in your breath, like maybe, just maybe, you went to sleep in Oakland, but you woke up in Alaska. Cold winter mornins, freezes everything to the bone, so when my mama turns the car engine on it complains, goes *Kachunk . . . kachunk . . .* That's what José's stutters like. Like a car engine that isn't warm yet. And he's got nice eyes, nice brown hair.

The reason I say he's not my friend is cause we've only talked once. Only once ever since he moved here, and I was the only one who talked.

But I gotta tell you, I knew from the minute he walked in the classroom they were gonna pick on him. New kid, hair all in place, neat, clean clothes, and I mean neat. I'm tellin you, someone in his house is in love with ironin, cause I swear, if you took his pants off, I bet even his underwear would have a nice neat crease right down the middle of them. A recipe for disaster. You just knew, him lookin so sweet, like a scared lost puppy, you just knew he was gonna get picked on. I mean come on, of course they're gonna.

The time I talked to him was about three weeks ago, back in September. See what happened is, I got behind him in the hall at after-lunch lineup. They'd pushed him around pretty bad at lunch. Shirt was all stretched outta shape where they'd been yankin on it. They'd been holdin him down, had gotten some dirt in an old pop bottle, holdin him down by the jungle gym. Pinned to the ground, one guy sittin on his chest, a guy on each arm. A bunch of them standin around like it's a rape or an orgy. Standin around laughin, spittin on him, while Billy Robinson tipped the pop bottle over him and poured a steady stream of dried-out dirt in José's face. Poured it on him just like he was peein on him. Standin over him, straddlin his face. Laughin, pourin it all over, gettin it in José's nose, his eyes, his mouth. José tryin to get away, skinny body twistin and turnin. Tryin not to cry, tryin not to, but I could see that he was, even from where I was standin. So I started throwin rocks at them. Hit Billy Robinson in the head. Musta hurt like hell, cause he bellowed like a wounded bull and got off of José like a bullet and started chasin me. It was real funny, cause with him chasin me, everybody else did too, like a big, long, choo-choo train. Follow the leader. I tell you, there's not an ounce worth of individual thought between the lot of them. And for me, no problem, don't worry about me. I just ran into the girls' bathroom. Waited for them to cool off and then sauntered on out as fine as could be.

Looked all over for José. Didn't know where he went to. I looked all over the playground, couldn't find him. And I'm real good at findin things. When my mama loses somethin, her wallet, her keys, pack of smokes, whenever she loses somethin important, she just sics me on it. I always find things for her in no second flat. So I'm tellin you, if I couldn't find José, he wasn't there. Musta left the playground, school property. Was worried he'd get in trouble for skippin, cause nobody's allowed to skip. But when the lunch bell rang, there he was, head lookin down towards his feet., hair fallin forward so nobody can catch his eye, make fun of him. He must hate this school.

Anyway, there he was, tryin to slip into the back of the line, slip in like a shadow. And, I don't know, I kinda did it wrong. Didn't mean to. Had been holdin onto my Kit-Kat bar all lunch hour. Got outta the line, walked to the back of the lineup where José was standin. Was going to give it to him casual. Like I wasn't hungry for it. "Hey," I was gonna say. "Want my Kit-Kat bar? I'm full."

Sounded good in my head, sounded just right. But I don't know, I did it all wrong, cause at first, it's like he didn't hear me, or didn't know I was talkin to him or somethin, so I said it a little bit louder. "Hey, José. Want my Kit-Kat bar?" My face gettin redder and redder by the second. And I was wishin I didn't have this stupid idea, cause he's not lookin happy, he's lookin embarrassed, like he thinks I feel sorry for him or somethin. And he shook his head, just a little twitch like I'm a fly he was tryin to flick off. And his face got this odd, stiff look, jaw all clenched up like Kit-Kat bars make him mad or somethin. But his eyes were doin the opposite. Like Kit-Kat bars make his eyes sad all over again, cause they started squeezin up and blinkin to hold back the fresh flood of hurt. And I said, "I'm not makin fun of you. I mean it. You can have it if you want." And I held it out to him. But stupid old Billy Robinson was listenin and he started laughin and sayin in this mamsey-pamsey voice.

"Oh . . . José gotta girlfriend?" Real nasty, and they all

started pickin on him again. Needless to say, after that fiasco José avoided me like the plague.

— ◆ —

Hazen slept in. Late to work, Gemma on the brain. Gotta see her. Called her school during his coffee break. Went down to the pay phone on the corner. Pretended to be a parent. Little Johnny had forgotten his lunch. When would his lunch hour be?

Hands sweating, the school secretary's voice tinny, faint, barely audible through the traffic noise, through the buzzing in his ears.

"What grade?" She's asking, she sounds impatient, like she's already asked him before.

"What grade?" He says palms slippery with sweat. Trying to think, trying to think.

And now she talks very slow, enunciating every syllable. "What . . . grade . . . is your . . . boy . . . in?"

"Oh . . ." his mind scrambles, trying to find a way to answer, to be plausible. She knows. He thinks. She knows. "Uh . . . Well, let me think . . . sh . . . he . . . sorry . . . uh . . . he turned twelve in July. Uh, July twenty-third."

There is a brief pause on the other end of the phone followed by a weary sigh. "You men," she says, disapproval prickling. And he can just see her. Some dried-up old gray-haired virgin, lips puckered up like she's sucking sour apples. Never been laid, taking her disappointment out on the world. "You're all the same. Don't even know your own child's grade. I bet you don't even know who his teacher is."

And he finds himself standing on the street corner, getting mad. Phone slammed up against his ear. Forefinger stuffed in the other. Finds himself getting incensed, even though his son is fictitious. Finds himself snapping. "How dare you judge me." Finds himself yelling, "What gives you the right? I am a good father. A damned good one. And right now all I want to know is when my son's class gets out for lunch so I can bring it by the school so he won't starve." His voice in his outrage had built to a roar, and the silence that followed was deafening.

"Very well . . ." She sniffed after a long pause. "How old is your son?"

"Twelve. He's twelve."

"Then he'd be in the *seventh* grade. Their lunch break is from eleven forty-five to twelve-thirty."

And she hangs up without saying good-bye, leaving him with an all-over body flush that he had not experienced since he'd peed his pants at school in third grade. An all-over body flush, a dead phone clutched to his ear, and a boner the size of Montana.

— ◆ —

He gets there early, parks his car across the street from the schoolyard. Feeds the meter a quarter, gets back in the car, and waits.

He feels her before he sees her. He was watching the front entrance and then it was like something tapped him on the shoulder, jerked his head around. And there she was, coming out a side door. She was alone. Her shoulders rounded slightly, her hair falling forward, covering her face. She is walking a little bowlegged. That's good. He thinks.

Maybe he hadn't been her first, but the way she's walking, she's not gonna forget him anytime soon. And that thought makes him feel good in the belly.

And then just as he felt her, it's like she feels him, cause all of a sudden she stops. Stops right where she is. Right in the middle of the playground, kids swarming on either side of her, but she stops and her eyes leave the pavement and find his from all the way across the playground, through the iron link fence, across the street to where his car is parked in front of Jamba Juice. All that way her eyes travel to lock with his. And he can see her chest rising up and down and her mouth moving like she's praying. And he can see that her face is slightly bruised from where he hit her. But more than that. More than all that, he can see, oh sweet Jesus in heaven, he can see that she wants him. Can see that from all the way over here in his car. And he watches her run away around the back of her school, face pale, hair fluttering behind her like a tattered flag. And he knows, he knows at this moment that he is to save her. Save her from the life she is leading, the crooked path she is on. Knows in that moment, that they are meant to be together, meant to get married. That he is to plant his seed into her again and again and watch her grow ripe and round with his seed. And he knows that God led him to her, because she is his destiny.

—◆—

You know that little kids' book "Alexander's Very Bad, Terrible, Horrible No Good Day." Well, that's the kind of day I'm havin. A terrible, horrible, no good day.

Mrs. Watson didn't believe my story about walkin into

a door. I mean, geeze, who can figure them out? Poor José gets the crap kicked out of him every day. Every day. And nothin. I come to school with one little black eye, a swollen cheek, and it's like they become the friggin FBI. Asks me a bunch of personal questions, which I have to say, is nobody's business but my own. Then sends me down to the principal's office, and the principal makes me talk to Mr. Jamison, the school counselor. Who smells like old ladies and mothballs. And he's actin all concerned. Asks me all kind of sly, sneaky questions. But I didn't tell him a thing. Knew what to say. Buddy has been over this material with me a million times. Didn't switch my story one iota, no way I'm goin to jail.

Did tell him my concerns about José, though. Did tell him that. Told him that what was happenin to that poor boy was criminal. Those were my very words. Don't know where they came from. Just came out of my mouth all articulate like. Was really cool. Was the kind of sentence you wish you would have said, when you think about the circumstances later. Lyin in bed, late at night, you can think up plenty of good things to say, but that'll do you no good. You didn't think of it when you had the chance. So that was satisfyin. Very satisfyin indeed. He said he'd check into it. Talk to the yard supervisor.

But other than that, this day is turnin into a real stinker. Old sicko is at my school. At *my* school! Sittin in his stupid old car, ruinin my lunch hour. Just sittin there gawkin. Givin me the creeps. I mean who asked him to ruin my lunch hour. Stupid jerk. Just tryin to freak me out. Stupid old creep. But I'm not gonna. Not gonna be scared. Not gonna give him the satisfaction. I'm just gonna stay here.

Stay back here behind the school. No problem. Doesn't bother me. I'll just play out here in the back.

· ➤ ·

He stays, waits, can't see her, but he stays in his car, touching himself through the lining of his pants pocket. Stroking himself, squeezing the tip hard when he gets to close to cuming. Watches the playground. The other kids moving and surging, running, playing, legs flashing, arms flailing, soft succulent necks, cheeks. And he watches, but they are more like the background, the rumble of a big crowd before the hockey players take the ice. And he watches them, not whole, just pieces scotch-taped together. An arm, a leg, the curve of the neck, the ass, the color of her hair, the length. He takes bits and pieces and sews them together in his mind to create her. And he wishes he didn't have to do this, but it can't be helped, she is hiding, playing coy, playing hard to get. He knows the game. That's okay, he has time, he can afford to indulge her.

The bell rings, and the children run towards the big double doors shrieking, laughing, playing tag. A massive movement from all corners of the playground, like a watercolor painting with too much water, all the colors blurring and smearing and running towards the bottom. And he watches close, eyes moving fast, cause he knows she's there somewhere, knows she's gotta go in. And then he finds her, wouldn't have if he wasn't watching carefully, he sees her, sneaking around the side of the building, and she is running, head down, her knees slightly bent. Trying to stick to, lose herself in the periphery of a group.

But he spots her, oh yes he spots her and all his plans of waiting. Waiting until he can safely jack off in the bathroom at work, all his plans go flying out of his dick. Cause there she is, so skinny and awkward. So beautifully young. There she is with her tight little child's ass that he had the night before, and he can't help himself, he just cums right there in broad daylight, right there in his car in front of Jamba Juice.

And it is good.

And when he is done, when he has finished pumping a full soggy fistful into his hand, he wishes she were here, so he could force her to taste it, rub it on her cheeks, her forehead, her chin. Not let her wash, make her go back to school with the proof of his love all over her face. And the very thought of it makes his heart start racing and his cock get all riled up again.

But he is late. Very late, so he starts up his car. Has to drive back to his apartment first, cause there is no way in hell he can go back to work without changing his pants.

Gets there, wipes his leg off with his underwear, sticks his mouth under the faucet, sucks up a few mouthfuls of water, cause his mouth is all rancid and dryer than chalk. Then he grabs new pants, does them up as he sprints to his car.

Tries to slide in late, but wouldn't you know it, the old bitch catches him. And he tells her he's sorry he's late. But oh no, that's not good enough for her. Stupid bitch doesn't let it go. Has to let the whole floor know about it. Has to scream it out in her loud strident voice. On and on about how incompetent he is. How he'd better watch his step. How *inconvenienced* she was. Having to answer her *own* phone for twenty-three minutes!

And he wants to take out his dick and piss on her shiny Gucchi pumps. Piss all over them. That would shut her up. But he doesn't. Just stands there, arms dangling. Neck, ears hot. Just stands there, eyes lowered. Just stands there, tuning her out saying an occasional "Yes ma'am . . . No ma'am." And "It won't happen again, ma'am." Just stands there, trying to keep the smile off of his face. Just stands there thinking about Gemma's hot twat and how good she felt last night.

- ◆ ·

He calls her after work. "Hi Gemma," he says. "It's me." She doesn't answer, but he knows she's there, cause he can hear her breathing. "Hazen." He tells her, but he knows he doesn't have to. He knows she knows who he is.

She still doesn't speak, but he's happy just to listen to her breath, shaky and rapid.

"I want to see you," he says

She hesitates. "I'm sorry . . ." she says, her voice more high pitched, younger than he remembers. "I'm . . . I'm sorry. I . . . I think you have the wrong number."

"Gemma," he says, "I need to see you."

"I . . . I think you've reached the . . . the public library," she says, her voice small, tentative.

And he starts to laugh, ready to reason with her, but she hangs up. The little bitch hangs up. And won't pick up even when he calls back again and again and again.

- ◆ ·

Stupid phone. Ringin all day. Stupid, asinine phone. I don't pay it no mind. I don't care. I don't pay it no mind. Doesn't bother me.

Oh hey! I got a brand-new turtle! I bought her with my money. Bought her, an aquarium, turtle food, and some little plastic greenery. Took all my money, but it was worth it. Been wantin a turtle for a long, long time. Walkin home from school, and as usual, I browsed through the pet store, wishin I could have a pet. Walkin through the Critters and Fins Pet Store, and then I saw her. *Bah-dah-bing* ... Love at first sight.

And I'm standin there, feelin all sorry for myself. "Oh poor me ... my mom can't afford for me to have a pet .. ." Whine, whine, whine. And then I realize ... Wait a minute ... I can. I have fifty whole bucks of my own. Fifty whole bucks to do whatever I want with. So I talked to the shop lady, and we figured out the whole thing, all the costs, includin tax, and the total cost was forty-eight dollars and fifty-six cents.

It was so cheap cause they were havin a sale that day. A sale on turtles, turtle food, turtle aquariums. They were even havin a sale on the special light thingy you need to keep them warm. "Full spectrum light." Fancy, huh? It produces special light rays just for them, to keep them healthy and warm and keep their shells hard. I mean wow, I didn't even know turtles needed that. They were havin a sale on all this. Just started. Which was amazingly lucky for me, cause I never would have been able to buy all that stuff otherwise. Yep, brand-new sale. She hadn't even gotten around to getting the sale sign up. The whole kit and caboodle for forty-eight dollars and fifty-six cents.

Well, that was a sign if I ever saw one. So I took my money, without a second thought, I took my fifty bucks outta my pocket, and bought my turtle right there on the spot.

Had to walk careful, had to glide my steps like a roller-blader in slo-mo. Didn't want to jostle her. Makin my feet skim the ground, don't care if I look funny, sidewalks can be tricky, potholes, red lights, curbs and things. Didn't want to trip. Had to walk real slow, smooth. Took me a long time to get home.

At first, my turtle was scared. Stayed in her shell. But after a while, when she saw how nice I fixed up her new home, that I made her a little swimmin pool out of a cereal bowl and got her a rock from outside, put it in the middle of her pool so she could rest between laps. That I moved all the furniture around in my room so that my dresser was out from under the window, cause I know how important it is for turtles not to get a draft. That's what the lady at the pet store told me. "Very important, cause they could catch cold and die." Interestin, huh? I didn't know turtles could catch cold. Anyway, after my turtle saw what I did to make it nice for her, after she saw that, she came out. First her little head, just the tippy tip of it, peekin out, and I held really still, didn't breathe. Still as a stone. So then the rest of her head came out, and then her legs, and her tiny little tail poked out the back. And she nosed forward, cranin her head this way and that, takin in her fabulous new home. It was funny. Made me laugh.

She's so cute, little black button eyes. Fits in the palm of my hand. She's around the size of a silver dollar. I have one of those. My granddaddy gave it to me when I was ten.

Pulled it out of the pocket of those old saggy brown pants he always liked to wear. They were his favorites. Hard to get them off him to put in the wash. Loved those pants, he did.

His "lucky silver dollar" he called it. Gave it to me for helpin him roll his cigarettes. His hands were gettin too shaky to do it, sprayin tobacco all over the table. Gave me his lucky silver dollar. Said I earned it. Hell, I would have done it for free. I liked rollin his cigarettes. He had this fancy-smancy cigarette-rollin machine. It was really fun. Made me feel like I had a job. A real job in a cigarette factory, cause I had to roll a lot. It was an all-day proposition, cause my granddaddy liked to smoke. When I think of my granddaddy, I always picture him with a cigarette hanging outta the side of his mouth, either that, or droopin from his fingers. His fingers that look like they been rollin around in iodine.

I loved that cigarette machine. Asked if I could have it when he died. Don't know why everybody got so mad. I mean sheesh, they'd asked me if there was anything of his I wanted. No figurin out grown-ups sometimes.

It was fun rollin cigarettes, peaceful. Made me feel good in my belly to help him, do somethin for him. It's not easy. Hard work. Get a crick in your neck, and your eyes get strained from concentratin so hard. Cause making good cigarettes is hard to do. There's a trick to it. Gotta get it right. Can't just slap the papers, the tobacco in any ol' way. You gotta do it right. Special. Like the cigarette papers, you gotta take 'em out gentle, so you don't crinkle them. Hold 'em careful, between your thumb and forefinger. Don't get nervous and grip too tight, cause you got it, even though it might seem that you don't. So light, those cigarette papers, so delicate you can barely feel 'em. Then you place 'em in the curvin cigarette-shaped indentations. Lay them down like little blankets. Next you get the tobacco can, open it up, smell deep. Not that it helps makes better cigarettes, it's just part of the ritual. It's that first deep breath, as all the tobacco smell *wooshes* out. Smells so good. By the end of the day, it gives you a headache, but that first smell . . . Well, let me put it this way, it just wouldn't feel the same if you didn't.

Now, you take out the tobacco, gotta hold it gentle so you don't squish it, pack it in. If you pack it in too tight, you can't smoke 'em, cause it's impossible to suck the air through. Gotta pack it just right, not too fat, not too thin. Just right, that's the way you gotta do it. Nice and even. Then you crank the handle, roll 'em out. *Pshoo, pshoo, pshoo, pshoo* . . . Out come four cigarettes. And they look good. Real good. Just like store bought.

Yep, that's how I ended up with Granddaddy's lucky silver dollar. Would have spent it by now, probably would have spent it. Have been plenty tempted, cause it's good, worth money. I mean, you'd think, it being metal and all, not like your everyday one-dollar paper bill, you'd think maybe it's not good. Maybe you can't spend it. But you can. It's good. Was plannin on spendin it. Was havin fun plannin on what kind of candy to buy. Didn't want to do it lickety-split. Was havin fun going to the liquor store, rattlin my silver dollar around in my pocket, trying to decide if this was the day I was going to blow it. Was tryin to decide when my granddaddy up and died. Just like that. Surprised the hell outta everyone. He was havin stomach pains. Stomach pains creepin up on him, catchin him by surprise, doublin him over, stealin his breath.

"Nothin," he used to say, breath wheezin outta him like an old accordion. "Nothing a shot a whiskey can't cure." And he'd take that shot of whiskey. Have me run get it for him. And his face, it would screw up real bad when he swallowed, sweat poppin out on his forehead. Take that shot of whiskey, suckin in between his teeth, like it was burnin bad as it went down.

Yep, that was my grandpa. Here one day, gone the next. Dead as a doornail. Cancer, they said, cancer everywhere. Eatin up his stomach, his liver, his lungs. Cancer all over the damn place.

Wonder what it looked like in there, all that cancer. Wonder if that's why he was gettin so skinny? Did it make holes in him? Like little train tunnels, or worm tracks? Can you see it, the cancer? What's it look like? And that's another thing I don't get. If the cancer was eatin him, then wouldn't the cancer be gettin fat? And since the cancer was inside him, wouldn't he have stayed the same weight? Why was he losin weight all the time? I wanted to ask my science teacher Mr. Stanley, but I was worried he'd think I was macabre. Another spellin word. Macabre. Nice to get a chance to use it. Although honestly, I'd rather not be using it in context to my granddaddy, cause I miss him.

Anyway, he died, and well, here's another thing I haven't told anybody about. Don't want them to make the connection, but I feel awful bad, and I worry about it a lot. See, I help my granddaddy. He gives me his lucky silver dollar. I take it. Keep it, see, cause I don't realize how important it is. I keep it, and he dies.

Lucky silver dollar scares me and fascinates me all at the same time. Like a moth. You know how they always circle around hot light bulbs, dippin in, out, swoopin, singein their wings, and yet keep comin back. Keep comin back until it does them in. That's me and the lucky silver dollar. Scares the hell outta me, but I can't stop lookin at it, touchin it. Terrified I'm gonna lose it, accidentally spend it, and then boom, I'm up there in heaven with my grand-daddy. That's me, like a goddamned moth, circlin around the lucky silver dollar.

So I save my lucky silver dollar, don't spend it. Keep it safe.

Anyway, that's neither here nor there. I was tryin to describe my turtle. As I told you before, she's around the size of a silver dollar, but she's much fatter, be more like if you stacked up three or four dollars on top of each other. That's how tall she is. And she's cute, so cute. I've decided to call her Boxcar Julie. Boxcar for short, cause when she comes out of her shell, it's like she's a little boxcar chuggin along. Little tiny legs, chuggin along. Chug . . . chug . . . chug . . . So determined. Hard little shell on her back. Very handy thing, carryin her safety with her wherever she goes. Cause, I don't know if you're aware of this, but that shell keeps her safe. It's real hard, hard like a rock, or a super thick toenail. Like maybe a camel's toenail.

Boxcar's shell is tough. Camel tough. And all she has to do when she feels danger, or a predator, like a lion or somethin, all she has to do is *zoomp*. Tuck everything up into her shell. Tuck it all up in one second flat. *Zoomp*.

Everything tucked up, safe and sound. Nothin, nobody, diddly-squat can harm her. When she's tucked up like that you could probably drive a cement truck over her and she'd just be sittin in there laughin. Not that I'd ever do a thing like that. Never. But I bet Billy Robinson would. Do it just for fun.

I sure love her. Boxcar Julie. She's so cute. Maybe I'll take her to school in my pocket. She's so tiny, no one would even notice her crawlin around. Be like havin a little friend in my pocket. Cause I know she likes me. She knows I'm her friend. Knows I'll always take care of her, and make sure she has food and water and plenty of conversation.

Stupid ol' stinko keeps callin. Callin and callin, phone ringin off the hook. Kind of obnoxious if you want to know the truth. Kinda scary. Wish he'd stop. Wish both of them would. Buddy and Hazen. Stop buggin me. Big fat losers. Buddy tryin to sneak into my bedroom when my mom's asleep. Well, I've had it. I'm hurtin all over, cause seriously, it hurts real bad, when I pee, when I pooh, hurts real bad, burns like fire. Gotta suck my breath in just like my granddaddy when he was drinkin whiskey. So I'm gonna tell Buddy if he tries to lay a hand on me I'll scream the house down. That's what I'm gonna tell him, and I mean it too. I'll do it. Now normally, that wouldn't deter him, cause my mom can sleep through anything. But that on top of the school counselor wantin to have daily chat sessions with me, the two of those things put together, I think that might do the trick.

Damned phone. Wish it would stop ringin. It's hurtin Boxcar's ears. She doesn't like it.

She's so cute. You just wouldn't believe it. She's so cute

when she walks, tiny stout legs, chuggin along like a little choo-choo train. Maybe I should call her Choo-choo. That's a good name. Wonder if it would confuse her if I switched her name on her? Nah, better stick to Boxcar.

Wish I had a little house I could carry on my back, tuck myself up when I didn't feel safe. Wish I had a little house to carry around on my back. Dumb phone.

Oh . . . Ah . . . There it is . . . Stopped ringin.

Mrs. Moore, the librarian, says I can be her helper in the library at lunchtime.

I'm really excited about it. Love books, readin, the smell of them, the feel. You feel so safe, cozy, a good book in your hand. Especially hard covers. There's somethin so solid, so satisfyin about the weight of them, like the promise of a good meal. Feels kind of like that. Like you know you don't have to panic, know you're goin to be fed, know it's gonna taste good. It's a deep kind of contentment. I especially like the ones where the bindins are just a little worn. Frayed. I like it, cause it makes me think about how many times these books had to be read, enjoyed, to get that worn out. Sometimes makes my mind right dizzy just to think about it. Specially the really, really old ones, where the pages are all yellowin and soft around the edges, held together with old scotch tape. Real old tape, discolored, gone brown like the color of sugar candy from age. Old, old books, probably from the fifties or somethin. And I feel like I gotta read them real quick, like time is runnin out, cause they might just disappear, vanish, right before my very eyes before I get a chance to devour them. Those ones I treat extra special. Carry them one at a time, use both hands, walk careful.

Love workin at the library. Puttin things in alphabetical order. Everything in its place. Love the library. Love Mrs. Moore. She smells nice, all homey like. And she smiles at me. A soft gentle smile, like she really likes me. Kinda like she's the mother chick and I'm the baby chick, except instead of teachin me which bugs taste the best, she teaches me about books and authors and I don't have to go outside with the other kids and see Ol' Sicko waitin in his car. I love Mrs. Moore.

⦁—⦁

Can't sleep, can't eat, Gemma on the brain. Wasted lunch hours spent at the school, combing the playground for her, but he can't find her, she's not there, or if she is, she's not coming out. Staying holed up inside, playing shy. That's what he thought at first. But it's been three days now. Three days of waiting, watching. Three days of nothing. And he doesn't know, maybe she's sick, hurt. Worried. Calls her house five, ten times a day, but no one answers. Calls until six. After that, he can't call. Doesn't want to talk to her mom. Not yet. Not just yet. Not ready for that one yet. But tomorrow's Friday. It's Friday. And he's got this feeling, like time is running out. Got this feeling, like a big, angry rottweiler is ripping hunks outta his gut. Like if he doesn't move quick God is gonna give up on him. Not going to waste his time on him. A wuss with no balls. Gotta act quick, decisive. Gotta do something strong. Getting sweaty. Getting sweaty. Time is running out.

⦁—⦁

José talked to me today! Said "hi." Just like that, all shy like. Kinda surprised me, caught me off guard. But I covered it well, said "hi" back, smiled all friendly and encouragin like. He didn't say anything else, cheeks just got red and he bent over his social studies book, like he was real interested in it all of a sudden. It was kinda cute. Made me hopeful. Think maybe we'll be friends after all.

And another good thing, Mr. Jamison kept his word about José. I've seen him out on the playground a couple of times since I talked to him. Out on the playground durin his lunch hour. Seen him through the library window. Makes me feel good to see Mr. Jamison out there. Cause that's the one thing I worried about, workin in the library, that there was no one outside to look out for José.

Think I'll be a witch for Halloween. Either that or a gypsy woman.

CHAPTER TWO

Mama and Buddy are fightin something fierce. Screamin, yellin, carryin on. Musta been out on another all-day drinkin binge, cause this is a doozy.

I'm hungry, but there's no way in hell I'm going out in that kitchen. Got my bedroom door locked, pushed the dresser up against it for good measure. I'm no fool.

Sure am hungry, though. Wish they'd finish, or go out or somethin, so I can go and make myself some dinner.

· ➤ ·

Ten o'clock, and they're still at it. Seems to be windin down though. She's not screamin anymore, not throwin things. Cryin now. That's what she always does at the end of their fights. Great noisy heavin sobs. That's what she does, mucus-filled sloppy-drunk slobbery sobs. Hope the neighbors can't hear.

Hungry. Really hungry.

Oh shoot. Now they're doin it. I'm never gonna get my dinner. My belly's hurtin. All squeezed up and angry with me. Maybe I should go to Burger King. Only three blocks away. Shouldn't go out at night. Not by myself. Not a very safe neighborhood. Okay in the day if you know where to go, but at night, woohoo. Only three blocks away, though. Could run. Could bring Boxcar Julie, then it wouldn't be so scary. Wrap her in some toilet paper so she won't get cold. She'd probably like to see it. Bet she's never been to Burger King before.

I'll wait five minutes and see. Maybe they'll move into the bedroom.

· ◆ ·

He waits. He is patient. Drove the last block with his headlights switched off, rolled up outside of her house soft and silent like a Batmobile. He sits in his car, engine off. Sits in the darkness, half slid down. Sits low, waits, watches, willing her to come out. Elton John's "Tiny Dancer" running through his brain. Humming it out soft, pads of his thumbs beating out the rhythm on his steering wheel. And he's got an excitement in his belly. Like right before a big date. "Come out, baby . . ." he whispers. "Come on . . ."

And she comes. Like he's got a direct line to her brain, she comes. Not out the front door though. She comes out a window, her bedroom window maybe. One leg first, then the other, crouching for a moment on the window sill, then swinging her body out, over, hanging on the ledge, dropping to the ground. Old hat, like she's done this a million times before. And he's glad to see her, but he's pissed too. "Who's she sneaking off to fuck?" he thinks, slinking further down, heart racing, slinks further, not sure what he's gonna do. And he can hear her footsteps coming, closer and closer. And to tell the truth he's not sure really what happened next. How it all happened. He's there, bent at the waist, head lying on the seat of his car listening to her shoes reach the pavement, and the next thing he knows he's outta the car, his coat somehow found its way off his

body and over her head, and she is kicking and screaming and scratching, and he doesn't know what to do next,
but she's making a hell of a lot of noise, so somehow he
gets the trunk open, gets her inside, slams the lid down fast.
Accidentally bangs her on the head with it. Doesn't mean
to, but she's moving so fast, clambering up on her hands
and knees. Had to slam it down fast, hell, with all the
noise she's making. Slams it down fast. Hops in the car and
drives away. Drives away, heart banging like a red brick in
a dryer.

"Now what?" he thinks. "Now what?" But he doesn't
know, so he just keeps driving, her making little scrabbling
whimpering noises, scuffling around in his trunk.

. ➤ .

Julie fell outta my pocket. She must of fallen out when ol'
fuckface here threw me into the trunk, cause I can't find
her anywhere. Must have fallen out then. Stupid ol' asshole!
Knew it was him. Knew it was him even though I couldn't
see a damned thing, that stupid stinky coat over my head.
Stupid dickface. I knew it! I shouldn't have come out! What
am I gonna do now? What's Julie gonna do? What does she
know about city livin? I never should have taken her with
me. Stupid! Dumb! She didn't need to see Burger King. And
now what? Now what Missus Smarty-pants? What's she
gonna do, crawlin around the streets at night? Who's gonna
feed her? Take care of her? Keep her safe? And I made that
nice home for her and everything! What if a car runs over
her, or a cat eats her? What if Billy Robinson finds her in
the mornin on his way to school? That would be bad. That
would be really bad . . . I'm not cryin cause I'm scared. I'm

not. I'm not scared at all, and that's a fact. I'm not really cryin, it's just . . . it's hard to breathe in here. Dark. Darkest dark. Like I'm drownin in black ink. That's all. It might seem like I'm cryin, but I'm not. I'm not scared . . . I'm just . . . It's just that . . . I'm worried about Boxcar, is all. That's what I'm cryin about. That's why I'm cryin, I'm worried about her . . . I hope he doesn't kill me . . . Stupid jerk . . . Hope he just does me and lets me go . . . Hope that's all he wants. Shoulda answered that phone . . .

- ◆ -

Better now. Stopped cryin. Stopped cryin now. Kinda embarrassin, I let myself go like that, get outta control. Don't usually do that. Not a crybaby. Better now. I've got a plan. A good one! See, I'm bein real quiet now so he'll think somethin happened to me, that I'm dead, asphyxiated from lack of air in this stupid stinky trunk. I'm bein quiet now, not movin, barely breathin. He'll think I'm dead or asleep or somethin. So when he comes to the trunk he'll be off his guard. When he comes to the back, opens the trunk, at first, I'm gonna lie real still, pretend to be asleep. I'm good at that, had lots of practice with Buddy. Sometimes it works, sometimes it doesn't. Sometimes, he just wants the pussy, and it don't matter if I'm asleep or not. Enough of Buddy. This is what I'm gonna do. Hazen opens the trunk. I pretend I'm asleep. Pretend I'm asleep to catch him off guard! Then, when he's least expectin it, I'll jump out of the trunk, quick as a wink, and run! Run fast! Get away! I'm a good runner, see. One of the fastest in my class! I'll get away, see! I'll run like the wind! I'll get away from him. Far, far away!

- ◆ -

He ran her down three times, three times before she finally stopped running.

Ran her down, hit the ground hard, him on top of her, falling on her body. Falling on her soft, fragile body. Her sweet, tender body. Falling on her, pinning her down with all of his man weight. Pinning her down. Her wanting it so bad that she's panting like a cat in heat. Cute, how she kept trying to get away. Wouldn't stop running, even though she knew, had to have known, he was going to run her down. Made him feel powerful. Made him need to fuck her. Morning sun just rising, not there yet, but almost. Everything painted in gray. Gray, charcoal, black silhouettes. Everything gray but her, one vivid splotch of color. Cold, could see puffs of steam escaping from her mouth as she gasped for air, chest heaving up and down. Had to have her. Dust, grit, grinding into her hair. Had to take her out on that abandoned road, her fighting and cussing. Her screams breaking that waiting, still, silence of the wilderness. So beautifully isolated. Her cries echoing, reverberating off the rocks, the trees. Bouncing, ricocheting off of them like some kind of wild mating cry, some kind of beautiful love song on a National Geographic show. Primitive, beautiful. Did her again and again until she stopped fighting him. Stopped biting and screaming. Just quiet sobs of relief and acquiescence. Beautiful. He'd done it right.

·—•—·

I hate him. I really hate him. I'd kill him if I could. If I knew how to drive, I'd steal the car, grab it when he wasn't lookin, drive over him. No problem. Drive right over his big, fat, stupid head! Squash his brains out, squirt them out like strands of spaghetti, that's what I'd do. That's what I'd do if I had a car. Kill him. The stupid, snot-eating prick. Hate him.

— ◆ —

I'm so happy, I can't even tell you, I'm so damned happy! Guess what? Guess what? You aren't even going to believe it . . . I FOUND BOXCAR! Yep, it's true!

What happened is, I heard this noise, this little scrabblin noise. He was at a stoplight or a stop sign or somethin. Not important, the thing is, the car wasn't movin, and that's how I heard it. It was just a brief stop, engine idlin, me in the trunk, and I heard this *scrabble . . . scrabble . . . scrabble* noise. A faint little noise, like fingernails dancin across the kitchen counter.

The car started goin again, and I couldn't hear nothin, thought maybe that scrabblin noise was a figment of my imagination . . .

But then! *scrabble . . . scrabble . . . scrabble* . . . I heard it again. And it wasn't until the second time I heard it that I recognize the sound, and my heart leapt, it jumped, cause I knew it was Boxcar Julie! And I tell you, I became like a madman, a person possessed. I was scrabblin too now, keeping my body still so I wouldn't accidentally squish her. I became like a crazy woman, feelin around, hands pattin, searchin every last corner. And when my fingers found her, I started cryin. Cryin like a baby, I was so happy. And I kissed her and kissed her, so happy that she was safe. So happy.

— ◆ —

I forgot somethin, you know, earlier. I was so happy to see Boxcar, couldn't see her actually, but to feel her, not to be alone in this dumb old trunk. Was so happy, but I just wasn't thinkin straight. Worried now. Scared for her. See, I don't have her food. Her special turtle food. I don't have water in this trunk. Don't have her full spectrum light to keep her warm. Am holdin her inside my shirt, up against my tummy. Tryin to keep her warm that way. Feels funny when she crawls along on it. Makes me giggle. Tickles.

I like havin her here, but I'm worried. Gonna get away first chance I get. Was bad enough when it was just me, but now I got her to think of. She counts on me.

Gotta get away. Gonna have to be tricky. Gonna have to do some hard thinkin. Real hard thinkin, come up with a plan.

I tell her, "Don't worry, I'm gonna get us out of this, don't you worry." I'm not sure what I'm gonna do, but I tell her this to keep her calm, so she won't panic. And I think it makes her feel better. But I gotta come up with somethin fast. I mean, this is inhuman. She's been in this trunk for a whole day and a half. No food, no water, no sunshine.

Worried, so worried. Old dickface isn't gonna like her. Gotta keep it a secret. "Gotta keep it a secret," I tell Boxcar that. Took my sock off, got it ready, gonna wrap her in it when the car stops. Gonna have to move fast, wrap her in it to keep her warm. Put her in my pocket. I'll be quick. I'll be quick so he won't know.

This situation is bad. Real bad. I feel sad for her, I really do. Cause I don't know what her future's gonna be. I'm sad, but even though, I gotta say . . . I know it's selfish, but I gotta say, it sure is nice to have a friend. Someone to share the road with. To talk to, cause, you know, it's pretty damned lonely back here in this stupid trunk.

- ➤ -

He's let me up front. He's let me ride up front with him. Here's my opportunity. My chance. Don't wanna blow it. Gotta be careful. Gotta be fast, decisive. Heart poundin, throat jammed shut. Eyes lookin. Lookin for a good spot. Don't have my seat belt on. Ready to move, move quick. Mouth dry. Actin normal. "Nice day." That kind of thing, mind jumpin, spinnin, checkin out options. Gonna do this, gonna do this thing. Don't wanna let Boxcar down.

- ➤ -

Unfortunately, he has to ride with her in the trunk again. Trussed up like a little piglet. Can't share the road, the scenery, conversations. Can't feel her pussy to help pass the time, alleviate the boredom of the road. Can't do that. She won't behave. Kept leaping outta the car at every stop, every light. Had to tussle her to the ground. Damned inconvenient. Draws unnecessary attention.

So, no more front seat driving for her. Her own fault. Into the trunk with her.

But even that wasn't good enough. Screamed and yelled, banged her feet on the lid of the trunk, making the car bounce slightly. Had to have music on. Music blaring loud to cover up her noise, the banging in the trunk.

So that's why he ties her up. Ties and gags her. Not cause he's an animal. Please. It would be much nicer riding with her up front.

He ties her up cause it is a necessity. It is a must-do, for both of their safety.

• ▬ •

He's tied me. Tied me good. Can't move, can't speak. He's got his stupid, stinkin underwear in my mouth. Ripped them up with his huntin knife. Cut 'em up real slow like, never takin his eyes off of me. Made me nervous. Like maybe he was thinkin about usin his knife on me. And the idea, the thought of that, made me get real quiet. Didn't move. Didn't do anything. I'm not even gonna say what he did first in his cut-up underpants, it's too disgustin. And then he made me open my mouth. I did what he said, holdin my body real still, keepin my eye on the knife.

Him laughin and laughin. Callin me "sweetheart." Tellin me this way I'll behave. Won't be makin a big noisy ruckus no more. This way I won't forget him.

Tells me I'll be missin him while I'm in the trunk, but at least I get to taste him. "Isn't that love?" he says in a sweetie-sweet voice. Says I'll get to taste him. That I'm the lucky one, I'll get to taste him the whole livelong day. And I would have argued, but he had the knife, so I didn't do anything. And he tied his underwear around my head. Tied it real tight. Jammin it way back in my mouth like it's reins, like I'm a horse. Tied it tight, so my face is stretched out like this. Like I'm at the dentist and he needs to get a good look at all my teeth. Got some of my hair caught up in the knot. "Umm . . . yummy," he says. "Taste good?" he says. And he pulled the back of the knot so my head would nod up and down. Made him laugh all over again.

He took off all my clothes, tryin to act all matter of fact. Stripped me stark naked. Even my underwear. Made me stand in the middle of the room. Belly feelin like I'd swallowed a whole bottle of Clorox bleach. Cause Boxcar made a tiny bump noise when my shirt hit the ground. And I'm prayin she didn't hurt her head. Prayin to the Almighty that she'll keep her wits about her, won't panic, won't crawl out.

And him, tryin to act all casual, sat down on the sofa, started pretendin to read the newspaper. But he didn't fool me. Not one bit, I could see his thing stickin up in his pants like a rollin pin. And I knew what was comin next.

So now, here I am, naked as a jaybird. Trapped in this stupid trunk. And I gotta tell you it's cold. Not that I'm complainin or anything, I mean I'm grateful, downright grateful that he didn't leave my clothes at the motel. He's got them up front with him. So Boxcar's okay, cause it's warm up there. There's heat up there, with him, with my clothes. So she's okay. Okay for now. Just as long as she stays in my clothes. But other than that, things are bad. Pretty bad I have to say. Can't try to get away. Tied up. And even if I wasn't, I'm sure as hell not going to try to run away without my clothes on.

Hate this gag. Hate it. All slobbery and gross. Hate it. Hurts. My mouth, jaw sore, tired. And I have to focus. Focus real hard as the taste of him goes down, think of other things so I won't throw up. Cause it would be dangerous. Real dangerous. There is nowhere for the throw-up to go. Can't go out, the underwear is in the way. Would have to go back down. Wonder if it would kill me? Choke me? Wonder if you can drown on throw-up. So I try not to think of it. That's the best way. Can't cry. Feel sorry for myself. Figured that out right quick. Started to, when he first tossed me back here, but that was dumb. Real dumb. Cause everything clogs up, hard to suck air in, chokin on snot, tears, and cum. Had to calm myself down. Think of other things. Glad Boxcar stayed in my pocket. As far as I know, she's still tucked up in there, wrapped in my sock. Ridin up front with him. I try to send nice thoughts to her. Peaceful thoughts. Hope she doesn't worry about me. Think I'm mad at her cause I'm not playin with her, talkin to her, puttin her on my belly. I try to send her thoughts, let her know that I would play with her if I could but I can't. Hope she's not worried.

I send her imagination places that we're going to visit when we get out of this mess. Really beautiful ones. One of my favorites it a beautiful meadow, all serene, and green. And I'm lyin on my back, hidden by the tall grasses, lyin on my back, face up to the sky, her on my belly. And the wind blows slightly, gently, soothes my face, my warm skin. My eyes are shut, but I know the sun is shinin, can feel the heat of it on my face. And it feels so good.

I create these images and send them to her. Travel in our minds. Helps me not panic. Freak out. Cause I gotta tell you. If I let my mind go, even touch for a moment on this trunk, the hours I spend in here, the darkness, the closeness. If I let my mind go to it, to the smell of it . . . Forget it. It's curtains. Don't let my mind go there. Have to be strict.

It's hardest when he first puts me in. That's the hardest, when you know the trunk's gonna close. Isn't shut yet, but you know it's gonna. Know you're gonna be trapped.

That's the worst. That's when the panic closes in, squeezin the life right outta your throat. That's the hardest time to keep it together. Have to fight it real hard, cause it wants to suck me under like a tidal wave. "Be strong," I tell myself. "Don't panic, don't cry out." I pretend I'm in the war, and it is a test. And the safety of my country hangs in the balance. Or I pretend I'm in a movie. And I'm the heroine and it's just make-believe and at any moment the director's gonna yell, "Cut!" And then he'll come up to me, and kiss me on both cheeks, sayin, "Beautiful, darlin, beautiful. I knew you had it in you."

That's the crucial time, when the trunk's about to slam shut. That's the time I have to start weavin, weavin fast before the darkness closes in on me. Create beautiful places, best if they're out in nature. Create beautiful places in my mind. And it's amazin, cause if you focus hard enough, you actually feel like you're there. Really, really there. It's really wonderful and useful too.

Maybe that's what I'll do when I grow up. Teach people how to do this. I could call it "Gemma Travel." And I'd only charge rich people. I'd teach kids and poor people for free. Maybe that would be a good thing, cause I could help people and support myself too.

And the cool thing is, it doesn't just work with location. I do it with food too. Create anything I want to eat. Anything. Macaroni, spaghetti, big fat ol' burger with everything on it, cheese, bacon, extra ketchup. And then I eat it. Eat it real slow. Can taste it, smell it. I kid you not. I can create chocolate milk shakes, hot fudge banana splits, Milk Duds. Anything, just gotta concentrate real hard. And you know, I gotta tell you, it comes in handy, cause sometimes he forgets to feed me, and me and Boxcar get real hungry.

Actually, she isn't eatin so well. I'm worried about her. I tried to give her some of my hamburger last night, but she wouldn't even come out of her shell. Left it in my shoe with her just in case she wanted to nibble on it in the night. But I don't think she ate much.

- ◆ -

Wonder if my mom misses me? If she's noticed I'm gone? Wonder if she notices Boxcar is gone too? That we're both missin. Is she lookin for me? Has she told the police? Are they lookin for me too?

Wonder if Buddy's gonna tell her what he was doin to me? Wonder what she'll say? If she'll be mad at me? Want me to stay gone? Hope he doesn't tell her. Hope he keeps his stupid mouth shut. Wonder if he'll stick around, stay with her, now that I'm not there for his own personal entertainment? Wonder if Buddy's told her about Hazen? That maybe it was Hazen that took me.

I wonder if it's sunny? If the skies are blue? Or maybe there's a storm rollin in. A fierce thunderstorm. With rain and lightnin. I love storms. Makes me feel all wild, excited. Like a daredevil. No fear. I'd run out, barefoot, no coat, no umbrella. I say that like I got an umbrella. I don't, but if I did, I wouldn't bring it outside. Not in the fierce, beautiful ragin storms. I'd only use it on the dainty drizzle days. And it would be red. A beautiful, pomegranate red. And I'd be all elegant, like those prize show horses you see on TV. You know, the ones with pretty ribbons and braids in their hair. Be all graceful and refined. I'd walk like they do, pickin my feet up like I was a fine lady. And I'd twirl the handle, not much, just a little so the umbrella would spin, like those fancy ladies in those old-time musicals. That's what I'd do.

But in a dare-you-dance storm, in a wild, midnight, ragin storm . . . No umbrella for me. I'd just run out and dance. Dance with the gods. Dare them to take me, make me fly, fly away, on one of their magnificent thunderbolts. I wonder if a storm's rollin in.

Miss the sky. Miss breathin in, long and deep. Miss that. In this trunk before it's light. Only let out when it's night again. Won't even let me out to pee. Gave me a dumb ol' mayonnaise jar. Now how am I gonna use it with my stupid hands tied? It's hard to do, I'm tellin you. Real hard. Slops on me and everything smells of pee. I hate this trunk. Stupid, stinky, ol' dickface.

Wonder if it's Halloween yet? Wonder if it was fun? Probably gonna be too old next year. Depends if I grow. People tend to give you dirty looks if you trick-or-treat when you're too old. I'm lucky I'm short. Wasn't sure if I could go this year, was touch and go. Drank a lot of coffee, and it did the job, was gonna be able to squeak one last year out of trick-or-treatin. One last year of free loot.

Stupid dickface. Ruinin my last chance at Halloween. Stupid pig. Hate him. Really hate him.

Wish I could see the sky.

- ◆ -

She'd snuggled up next to him, crying out in her sleep.

Bad dream, another bad dream. And he comforted her. Stroked her, as her body trembled from her night terror.

He held her, his little Gemma, comforted her. Let her know she was safe in his arms.

· ━ ·

Saw my mama on the TV, cryin. Buddy was holdin her hand, lookin all sincere. Stupid jerk. His fault I'm in this mess. His fault, shoppin me out.

Wonder if he told them? Wonder if he told them what he knew? About Hazen and all. Wonder if he told them?

Probably not. Probably just interested in his own skin. Two-faced jerk. Standin there lookin *so* concerned.

Saw my mama cryin on the TV And the announcer's talkin about, sayin somethin about "an epidemic," somethin . . . somethin . . . "teenage runaways." Not sure quite, was the tail end of his sentence. Wanted to watch, but Hazen flipped the channel. Flipped it fast, ears all red.

One, two, three channels. Turned it off, paced the room a bit, and then *Bam*, no more TV, no more room, didn't even get dinner. Just threw me in the trunk again and off we drove.

Had to camp out that night, camp out in the woods. Kept me in the trunk. Gave me his jacket though. That was nice. Gave me his jacket to keep warm.

Camped out in the woods, coyotes howlin, circlin. Safe in the trunk, knew that, but still I was scared. Scared somehow they'd find a way to eat me and I'd never get home. Just end up, a pile of old bones. Gnawed clean, all the flesh ripped from them. An unrecognizable pile of bones. And my mama, Mrs. Moore, Mrs. Watson, the kids at school, none of them would ever know what happened to me,

Gemma. I'd just be these old bones rattlin around until those too got chewed up and gone.

And I got sad thinkin about this. Got sad. Got a powerful wave of homesickness. Wanted my mama, my home, my bed. Wanted it so bad.

· ◂ ·

Gotta keep on driving, keep on moving. Cause when he slows down, when he doesn't keep himself, his mind, busy. Allows himself to think. Sometimes, when he doesn't control it, isn't prepared for it, a wave of panic sweeps over him. A wave of panic that has him slamming on the brakes and running into the nearest bathroom at hand, be it at a rest stop, a gas station, a bush if he has to. Cause when these waves hit, he gets the runs. Gets them bad. Bends him over for a good ten, fifteen minutes. And as he's crapping, running through his head, like a fucking mantra, "How did this happen?" "In too deep now." "No turning back." In these moments, it seems like, all this just happened to him, like a runaway train. God just threw this at him. As a test maybe, who the hell knows. No road map, no preparation.

Scares him sometimes, that he doesn't recognize his life. Like he's gonna wake up any moment now, and be back to the old Hazen. The old Hazen Wood. The one before Gemma.

Always got that feeling now. Always got the feeling, that from here on out, the map of his life is going to be divided. Divided in two. Look back and see that distinct crossroads, see it as clear as the thumb on his hand, see where he veered off, or on, course. Always, these thoughts are careening through his brain, joining the chorus, the full orchestra symphony that has consumed his body. Dancing about, tangoing with, the violence his bowels are inflicting on him.

Motel after motel. It doesn't matter. Traveling the country. Never stopping anywhere too long. Never staying in one place long enough for anyone to get familiar. Ask questions. Dusty motels, full of grit and disappointment. And there's something about it, the dirt and the seediness that excites him and depresses him all at the same time. Like a drug. She's like a drug. A bad habit. Sunk him into the depths, made him into one of those desperate junkies, living for the next fix, the next stop, so he can feel her body under him again.

· ➤ ·

I used to wonder, wanted to sneak out, hop in the trunk of my mama's car. Thought it would be fun, kinda cool to ride around in one. Like in a spy movie.

That was before I knew that people actually did. I thought it was just a fun, fanciful thought. A "what if?" thought, like what if magical carpets really could fly. That kind of thought.

Had no idea. Will never look at cars, car trunks the same way.

Wonder how many other girls are stashed away in trunks. Trapped in smelly trunks, tryin to get away.

Doesn't have to be this way. There's more room in this trunk than you'd imagine. I mean, it wouldn't be so bad, ridin around in a trunk, if I didn't have to. If he wasn't makin me.

If I was doin the plannin . . . If I was the one stealin a

kid, and I was gonna have them ridin in a trunk for a long period of time, I'd make it all cozy for them. Like a little fort. Nice soft pillows to lean against, a little blanket for when it gets chilly. Snacks. A "little bitty readin light." You know, the kind in the fancy catalogues, where the woman clips it to the top of her book and she can read while her husband sleeps beside her with a smile on his face.

I'd get one of those lights and a ton of books. All kinds of books, magic books, adventure, learnin books, history. A ton of books, so all this time, ridin down the road, I could be learnin too.

◦—◦—◦

Boxcar isn't feelin' well. Wouldn't come outta her shell. Didn't wanna swim. Put water in the sink like I always do. Nice and lukewarm, comfy-like. Just like I always do.

Every night I do this. Wait till he's asleep. Creep outta bed, quiet, so quiet, like a ghost, like the fog. Wait till he's snorin, then out I get, silent, so silent. I get Boxcar outta my pocket and off we go to the bathroom. Shut the bathroom door, slow. Slow and easy, knob twisted open so the latch won't snick. And when the door is shut, then, nice and easy, nice and slow, I turn the knob in my hand. Hold my breath for this part. This is the tricky part. Turn the knob just so, and the latch slides quietly into place.

Then I turn on the water. Just a thin stream, so the faucet won't make noise. Turn it on gentle, like I'm a heart surgeon. Turn it on, push the plug down, let the water gather in the sink. And Boxcar likes it. Usually takes a long, long drink. Swims a little. Little circles round and round. And I talk to her, quiet whispers. I talk to her, keepin one ear open in case he wakes up. Notices I'm not in bed with him. Cause he doesn't like it. Gets real mad if he wakes up and I'm not there.

I talk to Boxcar. She is my best friend in the whole wide world. I miss her durin the day. Miss her so bad, now that she rides up front with my clothes. And we're quiet in the bathroom, Boxcar and me. I whisper, quiet whispers. Quiet as a dandelion puff. I tell her everything. All about Buddy and my mom. All about José and Mrs. Moore. About Hazen and the things he does to me. And she listens. Listens and looks at me. Looks at me with these sad, sad eyes. Cocks her head like she's sayin, "Yeah . . . yeah . . . I know how you feel . . . I hate him too . . . I'm so sorry . . ."

But she wouldn't come outta her shell today. Wouldn't come out. Didn't want to drink, didn't want to swim. I put her in the water, just a titch. Hoped that would cheer her up. Make her come out, swim a little. But she didn't. Just sorta turned upside down, all floppy like. Was worried she'd drown, swimmin like that. So I took her out right quick. Dried her off. Tucked her back in my sock.

Worried about her. So worried. Think maybe she's depressed. Tired of life on the road. Tired of ridin up front with ol' stinko. Don't blame her. Probably had much more fun in the trunk with me.

—◆—

Tied her hands a little too tight. Was in a hurry, slept in, was almost light outside. Did a sloppy job of it. Hurrying, trying to get her into the trunk before the town woke up. Tied them just a bit too tight. Were all blue and purple when they stopped for the night. Had to rub them for a good hour to get the circulation going.

A near thing. Could have lost her hands. Told her too. "You gotta behave," he said. "Gotta stop fighting me for your own good. You could have lost your hands. Could have lost your goddamned hands with this foolishness." Smacked her around a bit to get her to focus. "Could have lost your hands. Would have been a freak. A freak with no hands . . . How would you have liked that? A freak with no hands, just cause of your stubbornness. Just cause you think you're too good, too fucking goddamned special to ride up front with me."

And she could have. That's a fact. A fact he drilled into her, fucking her that night. Could have lost her hands like in World War One. In World War One, soldiers were losing their limbs left, center, and right. Get wounded, lose consciousness, and collapse. Would have to get limbs amputated, cut right off, because they'd fallen, passed out, with a leg, an arm twisted up under them. Unconscious, didn't, couldn't move. Had to have body parts cut off with no painkiller, just an old rag to chew on. Lopped off with an ax, a machete, a knife, whatever the hell was handy. Lost circulation, got gangrene, had to be cut off. And that's the truth. That's the goddamned truth of the matter.

Have to come up with another solution. Another option to their traveling dilemma. Will sleep on it. It'll come to him. He is patient. He will pray tonight and God will tell him. God will tell him what to do.

— ◆ —

"Get your hunting knife." God told him. And so he did. Got his hunting knife out. Had to do it. Couldn't be helped.

Gotta think of it like a choke chain, a training device, a temporary measure, until she learns, accepts the order of things. "And woman shall submit to man, as man shall submit to Jesus." It's right there in the scripture, right there in the blessed Holy Bible. "Woman shall submit to man," or something like that, can't remember the exact phrasing. But it's there in black and white. Look it up later, maybe tonight. Read it to her. Help her understand her duty. He's not being tough on her, just teaching her, training her. And that's why he's taken to holding his hunting knife on her. For her own good. To teach her obedience. Holds the handle against the small of her back, the tip of the blade caressing the soft, sweet flesh just under the ribs. His arm around her waist, look like two friendly people on a little outing.

The knife, their secret. Their sweet, private secret, his knife, his cock.

And sometimes, he nips her slightly. Nips her with it. A love nip. Just to let her know, just to remind her of his love. And he likes it. The knife thing, the way it makes him feel. Her breathing, all shallow, swallowing hard, eyes big. Walking all careful, no sudden movements, doesn't want to get nipped. Behaving so well.

And he tells her, reminds her as they drive, how it was her own choice. She'd promised, given her word, that she'd behave. And did she? No. Made a scene at that Texaco station outside of Portland. After he had been nice enough to let her out of the trunk. Let her out of the trunk and ride up front. Ride up front like a big girl. She'd given her word. Her word of honor. And what did she do? Broke it. Plain and simple. Made a big stinky scene at that Texaco station. Had to forcibly haul her into the car, leave without paying. Had to do that just to keep her safe. Keep her with him. And he reminds her of this every time he takes the knife out. Cause that incident scared the hell outta him. Too close, too close for comfort. Don't need to be drawing attention to themselves. That's the last thing in the world they need.

So now. He does that thing with the knife as a matter of course. Just till he gets her trained.

Got it down to a science. Holds it, lying flat under her baggy sweatshirt. The one he'd bought for her in Tacoma. Holds it under that. The cool metal up against the heat of her skin. So she knows, can feel, that he is the man now. And it feels good. She knows that he'd just as soon gut her as make love to her. Gut her like a week-old fawn. Fast and easy, his blade piercing, slicing into the young flesh of her belly. Her sweet soft belly that takes him in so tenderly. Just as soon kill her, as lose her. And he tells her. Tells her that so she'll know of his love. And she listens. She listens to her man. She behaves now. Is very docile now. His sweet, beloved Gemma.

— ◆ —

I hold very still now. I don't move now. I try not to let him know I'm afraid.

He cuts me. He likes to cut me. But I'm not afraid. My heart pounds, pounds hard, and it forms a stairway. The thumpin of it. It's like it forms a stairway and I follow it up, serene, peaceful. It's like I become my own angel watchin me. Watchin me behave so good. I become my own angel, keepin me safe.

I float up above me, so that even when he cuts me, even that, it's like I don't really feel it. Just heat, just sharp, hot, heat that calls me back, slams me back into my body. Slams me back, but only for a second, and then I drift up. Drift up my staircase again to safety.

— ◆ ·

He likes to brush her hair. Long, smooth strokes. Likes to brush her long, blond hair. Has her sit in her baby doll pajamas. Her pink, see-through, baby doll pajamas. Size petite. Picked them up at the same sex shop he got her vibrator at. Her very first vibrator, a gold, sleek one. Likes to use it on her sometimes. Sits on a chair administering it, her sprawled on the bed, he likes to watch it go in and out, slide in and out. Likes that.

Not tonight though. Not tonight. Tonight he's doing the hair-brushing ritual. Wanted to try out his new prop. And it's working. Working good. Got her to hold a fuzzy white teddy bear he'd picked up at the gas station, with a red ribbon around its neck and a red heart with "I love you" written in white. And she's holding it. His very own Lolita.

What a night, what a beautiful night. Very difficult to get to a hundred strokes, a hundred strokes of the hairbrush. A difficult task, he's set out for himself, a near impossible task. Gets so hard he has to squeeze his eyes shut so he won't stain her lovely pink nightie with his seed. "Not yet," he says. "Not yet." Wants to draw it out. Has to think disgusting thoughts, old wrinkled women's vaginas, shit like that. Has to think shit like that to keep from cuming.

Just keep counting. Fifty-eight . . . Fifty-nine . . . Keep breathing. Remove from his body. Sixty . . . Sixty-one . . . Sixty-two . . . And he's brushing and brushing. But it's getting hard. Old ladies' wrinkled bits just aren't working. And there she is, so beautiful. Such a good girl, sitting in front of the mirror. Lollypop face, legs slightly spread, just the way he placed them. Just the way he placed them so he can get a glimpse, just a tiny glimpse of her naked little twat. Her sweet-smelling child's twat he had soaked and scrubbed and washed clean in her nightly bath. Washed clean and pink. Then dusted lightly with a sprinkling of Johnson's baby powder. Keep counting, keep brushing. "Sixty-seven . . . Sixty-eight . . ." Keep brushing with his fine sterling silver hairbrush. The one he'd bought on impulse, had to, cause she's so special. So special with her long blond hair, corn silk soft. And her lips, slightly swollen from sucking . . . Damn! Keep counting, keep counting. "Seventy-four . . . Seventy-five . . ."

She squirms. Just a little, shifts on her seat. Like maybe she's sore from last night, sore from him. Just a few inches of movement, and he can't wait. He just can't wait.

"How the hell am I . . ." he says. He tries to keep his voice level, keep the excitement out of his voice. A simple matter of disobedience and punishment. "You tell me . . . How the fuck am I going to brush your hair, if you keep on fucking squirming?"

And he is hard now. Hard as a fucking teak coffee table.

But she doesn't answer, never does now, just loses her color and looks down at her hands.

And he was gonna make her walk over to the bed, lie down across it, paddle her behind there. But he can't wait, the whore got him too hot now. He yanks her out of the chair and swipes at her butt a few times. She doesn't dance outta the way like she used to. Just stands there, mute, head down, staring at the floor, trying to ruin his fun. But it's not gonna happen, no way, this is just too sweet. Doesn't even need to smack her hard, just enough to get her tushy nice and rosy and then, he bends her over, pushes it in. Takes her from behind, bent over the vanity. And he watches in the mirror, watches his big ol' powerful steam engine slam into her, leaving a little streak of blood in its wake. And it is good. It is so good with that teddy bear clutched in her hand.

- ✦ -

He stopped holdin his knife on me. Just wears it on his belt in its leather holdin container. His leather knife pouch with a snap around the handle for easy access. Comes out real fast and smooth. That snap just pops open. Showed me back at that Motel Six. How fast he could get at it. Fast.

So I don't do nothin. Just smile and act nice. Don't do nothin. Just act perfect and fine. I don't run away. I don't fight him. Don't do that no more. Cause if I'm even thinkin about it, somehow he knows, and he gives me the backhand across my face and shakes his belt at me to remind me what's hangin on it, how fast he can get at it. And I smarten up right fast. I'm not a fool. Although I don't know what's so funny about it. Hate the way he always laughs at me after he shakes his belt. Laughs and pinches my cheeks like he thinks I'm cute, funny. Hate it when he does that. It's so condescending.

That was a spellin word. It was one of my spellin words right before I was taken. Mrs. Watson always gave me a couple of real hard ones. Gave them to me special cause I'm such a good speller. She'd give out all the spellin words to everybody, write them out up on the blackboard. And then she'd say, "And these two are for Gemma." And she'd write out two real tough ones. And everyone would say they were really glad they weren't me, and I'd groan a little and pretend like I didn't like it, but I did. I'd always groan real soft so Mrs. Watson wouldn't hear, cause I wouldn't want her to get the wrong idea, stop doin it. Just a little groan, so the kids wouldn't think I thought I was great or anything. But to tell you the truth, it makes me feel good. Like I'm smart, like I'm special. I like it a lot. And I always study real hard, so I get one hundred percent. One hundred percent!

Building a future for myself. A foundation. That's what I'm doing. Want to go to college. Got big plans.

Little worried, though. Don't know how long Hazen's gonna keep me. Scared I'm gettin stupid. Scared I'm gonna get behind the class. Gonna come back and be the dunce. Have to sit in Billy Robinson's group. Hope Hazen gets tired of me. Lets me go soon. He's bein a little nicer. Lets me ride up front. Still does me at night, but he's put his knife away, that's somethin. Maybe if I'm really good. If I explain how important school is to me. If I tell him Mrs. Moore really needs my help in the library, that she's probably getting overwhelmed with returned books that need to be put back in their place. If I tell him that, maybe he'll take me back home. Let me go.

— ◆ —

Worried about Boxcar. Real worried. Think she's powerful sick. Hasn't wanted to swim, eat, or drink for three days now. Don't know what to do. Am goin outta my skull with worry. She's just sleepin, sleepin all the time. I tried to shake her, not hard, just a gentle shake to see if I could wake her up. Tipped her slightly to the side, tryin to see in her shell, see how she was doin. One of her arms, one of her legs, and part of her head fell out. Not out on the floor, just flopped out a bit. Like her muscles were just tired of holding them in.

And she's startin to smell a bit too. Think maybe she has the flu. Has diarrhea, can't hold it. Too sick. Like maybe she's got diarrhea. Diarrhea squirtin out. Too sick to do it outta her little shell house. Just doin it inside. Poor little Boxcar. She's kinda stinky, but I don't tell her. Don't want to hurt her feelings. She can't help it if she's sick. I just tell her, "I'm sorry you're not feelin well." "Wish I could get you to a doctor." That kind of thing.

Worried about her. So worried. Fightin back, always fightin back the tears. Tryin to be strong. Don't want her to know how worried I am. Don't want her to worry. Want her to use all her strength for gettin well. Gettin healthy. Don't tell her my worries now. About Hazen and my mom, and school and all. Don't want her to worry.

— ◆ —

Did her good last night. Real good. Think maybe he made her cum, cause she was sobbing and shuddering something fierce. Her whole body was convulsing. Moved to tears she was. Good little lay. Not fighting him quite so much now. Getting more used to the fact that he is the man. Getting more adjusted. Doing quite well, his Gemma.

In Bellingham. Flirting with the idea of crossing the Canadian border. The great Northwest. Hazen Wood and the Great Canadian Rockies. See the Royal Canadian Mounted Police. Loved them when he was a boy. Visited Victoria with his grandmother. Was seven. Greatest trip of his life. Got to pet one of those great big horses on the nose. Was so soft. The rest of the horse was rough, the hairs short and prickly. But the nose, soft, so soft. It snorted when he was petting it. Shook its head, rattling its reins. Made Hazen jump, and his grandmother and the Mountie had laughed. He laughed too, and then petted it again, its breath warm, fragrant, sweet. Smelled of hay, and grain, and horse. And his grandmother took a picture.

Always wanted to be a Mountie. Maybe he'd join. Nothing stopping him. Get himself a red buttoned-up uniform, great brass buttons, a big stick. Get himself a fucking big Canadian stallion. Join the R.C.M.P.

"What do you think, Gemma? Think I'd make a good Royal Canadian Mounted Police?" He asks her, smile on his face. Likes it, likes the dichotomy of it. Would be fun. Representing justice, the law. He'd be damned good at it, that's for sure.

But she doesn't answer. Rarely does. Just looks out the

side window, face pale, shut. Hair, falling forward around her face, closing her off from him.

"What do you think, Gemma? Shall we go to Canada?"

There is a pause, an intake of breath, and then she answers. Answers in that soft, shy voice of hers. A hesitant skip in it.

"No, I . . . I don . . . don't wanna . . . go to Canada . . ."

Ah, he's got her talking. "Why not?" he says all jovial. "Aren't you curious?"

"No," she says. That's all. Not a brilliant conversationalist, his Gemma.

"Well, I want to see it. I'm the man. I make the decisions. Cause what you want, to be honest, darlin', what you want doesn't matter one iota to me."

And he swings the car onto Route 5 towards the Canadian border.

"What about me?" she says, so softly he can barely hear her. "What are you going to tell them about me? What if they want a passport? I don't have a passport."

"A what?" he says, but he heard her. Forgot about passports. Wonder how other people did it. Other people in his situation. They always seem to end up hiding in Canada. Canada or Mexico. Everybody he's ever heard about. On the news and whatnot. They got across.

But then again, she's got a point, they might want a passport, might ask some questions. Things are supposed to be tougher now. Harder since 9/11. What if they ask him a lot of questions? What if they want to talk to her? Probably okay, but sometimes, she's unpredictable. Wouldn't be good. What to do?

His mind flipping through options like a fliporama book.

The ones with no words, where you flip the pages and it looks like a little, short, silent movie playing out. Flipping through all possible scenarios in his mind, all possible conclusions that could occur.

"Okay . . . ," he says, turning the car around. "Okay," he says, like he's making a generous concession. "You don't want to go to Canada, we won't go to Canada."

She snorts through her nose, a small, suppressed, noise. But he decides not to take umbrage, pretends not to hear. Cause actually, he's glad she thought of that. Don't know what he was thinking.

- ◆ -

Hazen almost took me to Canada. Scared the hell outta me. I pretended to be all calm, but really, honestly, I didn't know what to do. He almost got us there, to the Canadian border, almost did, but luckily I was smart. Luckily I remembered about passports. Remembered Mrs. Bird talkin about them in social studies. How she needed her passport when she went on her honeymoon to France.

Now I don't know if Canada needs them, passports, but I pretended you did. It was lucky I remembered that. Cause if we went to Canada, and he became a police, I'd never stand a chance of gettin home. I'd be stuck with him forever. Who'd believe me over a police officer? So, that was a close call.

- ◆ -

He keeps buggin me about Disneyland. Quizzin me on Disneyland. Don't know why. Told him once today, if I told him a million times, I've never been.

But he won't let it go. Gotta talk about it all afternoon, all evenin, about how great it is and how much I'd enjoy it.

Well, I know that. I mean, DUH! Who wouldn't like it? Yeah, DUH! I know I've never been. What's it to you? Insensitive jerk.

And I don't know why he keeps mouthin off about my mama. He doesn't understand, my mama loved me. She just didn't have time, is all. She was just real busy. And Disneyland's expensive. Damned expensive. Not everyone can afford just to "Go to Disneyland." Stupid asshole. Would punch him on the nose if I could. Punch him on the nose, shut him up.

But he's got the knife, so I just sit, nice and sweet. I just sit, think my thoughts, watch the sky, tune him out. Make him like a slow fade on the radio dial. His mouth is movin "Blah . . . blah . . . blah . . ." But I hear nothin.

• ➤ •

Can't get their conversation out of his head. Never been to Disneyland. Never been. Hell, she hadn't lived more than five hours away. Six, tops. And she'd never been. Fucked his belly up to think about it. Poor kid.

She'd love it. That's for sure. If ever a place had Gemma written all over it, Disneyland was it.

He thought about it and thought about it. All through their evening bath, the nightly romp. Watched the evening news carefully that night, ABC, CBS, CNN, NBC.

Watched all the news, local and national. Flipping the channels carefully, scanning. Watched until the early hours of the morning. No mention of Gemma, nothing, nada, zip. It was like she never existed. It was like God was handing her over now, saying, "You've done good, Hazen, showed me you're worthy. You've done good. She's all yours. Yours to do what you want with."

And a good thing too. A damned good thing. From the bits and pieces he'd picked up from the TV over the last few weeks, she'd had a bad situation, a real bad situation at home. Neighbors talking, "Probably a runaway." "Mother in and out of rehab." Not to mention that lowlife Buddy. Accosting her, raping her at every chance he got. Selling her to every asshole that crossed his path.

Christ, Gemma should be thanking her lucky stars. Thanking sweet Jesus that he'd picked her up. Saved her, rescued her from that hellhole.

And now she was his. All his. Totally his. His girl. His baby doll. And he was gonna take her to goddamned Disneyland. "I'm gonna do it." He finds himself saying. "I'm gonna do it." Saying it out loud. Hearing the words fill up that old, rancid motel room. Swelling up his heart, blood pumping. Filling his body with that adrenaline rush, like when you first step into the boxing ring. That testosterone high. "I'm gonna do it!" he yells, pumping his fists in the air.

"Gemma! Gemma!" he says, shaking her awake. Waking his sweet baby up. Her, all tousled and sleepy eyed. "Gemma!" he says. Happy, so happy. Cause this thing he's gonna do, it'll do the trick. When she sees the risks he's willing to take, to show her a good time. When she sees that, she's gonna wrap her arms around his neck, she's gonna tell him for sure, cause she's gonna realize just how much she loves him. How much he loves her, cause what he's planning to do, it's dangerous. Damned dangerous.

"Baby, wake up. I'm taking you to Disneyland. I'm taking you to fucking Disneyland!"

And he watches as she wakes, the confusion, the sleep, the delight, all battle with each other. And she leaps out of bed, dancing around in her little bare feet, arms hugging herself in excitement.

"Really? Really? Disneyland? Disneyland?!" And she's excited. So excited. They both are. And he swings her around the room. Just like one of those old-fashioned love stories. And life is good. Real good and getting better.

And he can't wait. Can't wait until morning. Too revved up. Got a long way to go. Two state lines to cross. They get in the car. Shivering in the night air. Brought the blanket from the motel. Wrapped her up in it. Let her stay in her baby dolls. No need to get changed. Let her crawl into the back seat to sleep.

Driving to California. The sunshine state. Driving to California, night sky, stars, moon still out. Headlights sweeping, arcing across his car, his face, his baby tucked away, wrapped up and sleeping in the back seat. Just like in one of those old time movies. And he feels good. Damned good. Driving to California, taking Gemma to Disneyland. Gonna show his baby a good time.

- ◆ -

"We're goin to Disneyland," I tell Boxcar. "Disneyland!" I've always wanted to go. Heard so much about it. Disneyland. Can hardly wait. So excited. Wish the car had wings. Wish the car had friggin wings like "Chitty Chitty Bang Bang." Wish it could fly. Wish I had a magic ring that I could just turn three times and we'd just be there. Wish that. So excited.

Hazen's takin me to Disneyland!

I'm bein good. Real good. Don't want him to change his mind. Turn the car around. Am doin whatever he wants. Whatever. He's gettin no guff from me. None whatsoever. Don't want him to change his mind.

And he's happy. So happy. Not half so bad when he's happy. And he's tellin me all about it. All kinds of things. How much I'm gonna like it. How it's the greatest place on earth. How much fun it is, how excitin, how expensive . . .

I'm so excited I can hardly take it. Feel like I gotta pee every five minutes. But Hazen doesn't mind, throws his head back and laughs. Doesn't mind that we keep havin to stop at rest stops.

I'm so excited!

— ◆ ·

Pulling his car, his locomotion, his charcoal gray Dodge Intrepid right up to the front door of the Disneyland hotel. Not a Motel Six. Not even a Best Western. Uh huh. When Hazen Wood does something, he does it right. Does it with style. Nothing but the best. Nothing but the best for his baby.

Pulls up to the front. Right up to the goddamned front door.

It's a hot, humid day. A sweaty, sticky day. A great day for cotton candy.

Cotton candy and Gemma. A beautiful day.

Valets in white uniform with gold trim leap out, off the curb to open his car door. Cause they know, they can feel that he's the man. And he looks over at Gemma, and her mouth is hanging open. Just hanging like a trap door someone forgot to close.

"Here we are," he says, striding up to the red carpeted walkway. Striding up, gesturing expansively. "Here we are. Just for you baby—Disneyland!" And she scampers after him, timid as a mouse, smiles up at him. A "You did it!" kind of smile. An "Oh my God, I'm so lucky to be with you!" kind of smile. Like she just can't believe her good fortune. Like dreams really do come true.

And then, sweet Jesus, without him even asking, she takes his hand. Slips hers in his, first time ever, takes his hand cause she wants to. Takes his hand, eyes big, face shy. Half hiding, peeking out from behind him. And they walk like that, hand in hand into the hotel lounge.

・━・

The hotel room is fantastic. Seventeenth floor. Can see out over the whole universe. It's fantastic! Huge king-sized bed. All pale and pastels, mirrors everywhere, sliding mirrors on the closet doors, in the elevators, in the bathroom. Free coffee, a coffee machine.

"Can we go? Can we go?" Gemma dancing around, eyes sparkling, beautiful, so beautiful. Mine, he thinks. Mine. And it is so satisfying, looking at her. Knowing that she belongs to him.

"Come here," he says. And she comes. So obedient now. So good. Well trained. "Give me your undies." She hesitates, a flicker of something, but then she slips them down, out from under her skirt and hands them to him. Looking away, eyes on his knees, but she gives them to him. And he pats her on the head. "Good girl," he says, and he is proud of her. How good she is. Come a long way, his Gemma. "It's the way of things." He says, teaching her now. Teaching her the rituals of Disneyland. "You aren't supposed to wear underwear at Disneyland. Nobody does." She glances up at him quick, eyes searching his, but he doesn't let on. Keeps his expression straight. And her eyes slide away again.

"Can we go now?" she asks, voice shy, tentative.

"Not yet. Things we have to do, chores that must be done, preparations that must be made before we can go. You want this to be perfect don't you?" And she nods slowly, face wary.

• ➤ •

He's done her two times, sweet and gentle. Two times tender and slow. Filled her up once, twice.

The Disneyland hotel. Expensive as hell, but worth it. So worth it. Being with her. Taking his time, her chomping at the bit. Wanting to go. Wanting to see Mickey Mouse and Dumbo.

But she's gotta wait, gotta be patient, gotta be good. Gotta let him catch his breath, do her again, one last time. Gotta act like she wants it. Really wants it, and then he'll take her, catch the tram. Take her to see Peter Pan's Magic Adventure.

• ➤ •

Kept her underwear, wouldn't let her wear them. The two of them, walking around Disneyland, hand in hand. And every now and then he likes to squat down, pretend to tie her shoe, take a peek up, take a look at the goods. And even though she doesn't want to, let him tie her shoe again, she does. Because he holds all the power. She knows if she causes a scene, if anyone looks at them sideways . . . Boom! No more Disneyland.

So she lets him check her out. Face blushing. He loves that. Loves when she blushes, so childlike, so innocent. Cheeks flushed, eyes averted. Lets him check her out. Peek. Sneak a feel.

Pirates of the Caribbean. What a high that is! Dark, all dark, fireflies and crickets. The slap of water against the side of the boat. Gemma and Hazen, snuggled up in the back row like two lovers, have the back row of the boat all to themselves. Slides his hand up under her skirt, fondling her. Quick, surreptitious feels. Her body stiff beside him. Not saying a word. Because she's good now, his Gemma. Doesn't say anything. Lets him touch her up because she likes it. It gets her hot too. Sexy little whore. Knows how crazy she makes him. Little lollipop slut. Longs for it. He makes her beg for it. And she does, she does. Begs him for it, just like he taught her.

She's well trained, his Gemma. A well-trained little slut.

— ◆ —

I wish he would stop. Wish he wouldn't do that. So scared someone's gonna see. Throw me in jail. Wish he would stop. Don't like it. Ruinin the fun. Wish he wasn't here. Big meaty hands on me. Sweaty, greasy hands. Glazed eyes, doin his heavy breathin, "I'm gonna fuck you" breath. Wish he would stop. Just wanted to be normal. Just to be normal for one day.

I wish he would stop. Just for one day. I wish he would stop.

- ◆ -

What a day. What a glorious day. Gemma, what a spark plug. She seems to love roller coasters. A little daredevil. Had never been on one. Never, in her whole life, and yet here she is laughing. Head thrown back, skinny arms thrust in the air.

"I can fly!" she's screaming. "I can fly!"

Sunshine. Laughing. Happy, so happy. And it's like time holds still and all of life is encapsulated in this one moment. The entire point for his existence is wrapped up in her sweet face. And he can't help himself, throws caution to the wind, and kisses her, tongue forcing its way, deep, deep into her mouth, Kisses her long and deep, even though she's fighting him, even though they're in public, even though they're trying to pretend, be sneaky. Can't help it, even though they are on the Matterhorn and it's broad daylight. Can't help it, needs to take her, claim her.

Doesn't want to stop, but she pulls away, clouds filling her eyes, laughter gone.

"What?" he says, but it's too late. Gone too far. Too obvious, too public.

Can't do nothing but watch as she wrenches herself away, arms snapping across her skinny flat chest like a door slamming shut. Yanks away, sitting stiff, squashed up against her side of the ride.

"What?" he says, but he already knows.

"What?" he says voice more belligerent than he feels inside. And he grabs her arm and pulls her around. "Look at me when I talk to you!"

And her head snaps around, her eyes dark with loathing. And the intensity of her stare makes the hair stand up on the back of his arms, his neck. And his stomach feels like he'd just eaten a bowl of cold lard. And he regrets turning her around. Cause he knows, he can see it, just for a flash, before the veil drops down across her eyes, he can see the magnitude of her hatred.

· ◆ ·

Bad day, getting worse. Hustling her out of the park, and she's resisting, carrying on, doesn't want to leave. Forgetting all the lessons she's learned as of late. Behaving badly. Hanging on to lampposts, bushes, trees. Grabbing hold of anything, screaming. Calling stuff out. Bad stuff. Stuff that could really cause problems. She's screaming out freaky, scary stuff. It's like she just doesn't care. Is pissing on, trying to destroy all the great life he's created for her. And she's smiling. The little bitch is smiling and laughing and crying and screaming. Tearing up the place. And he's trying to get her under control. Trying to shut her up. But people are looking, turning away, listening. And security comes. Spit-and-polish California kids.

"Excuse me, sir . . . We're going to have to ask you to leave."

And he tells them they're leaving. Apologizes for her behavior.

"She suffers from severe Tourette's syndrome, poor thing. Acts out. Medications worn off. Was going so well . . . poor dear . . . Wanted so badly to see Disneyland . . . If you could just help me, help me contain her." He pries her hand off a tree, trying to act light, so light. Trying to keep the sweat from showing. "I'm scared she's going to hurt herself. Poor baby." Keeping his voice calm. "Just not herself in times like this. If you could just give me a hand?" Gripping her tight, hanging on to her, don't let her escape. She's wiry, wiggling hard, trying to break free. "Whoopsy daisy . . ." A laugh here, a little laugh. "Too much child for one man to handle . . . She's just tired . . . The poor thing."

And they help him. So helpful, these pasty-faced milk-sops. They help him hold down, pin down her arms, legs, bundle her out, carry her out like a rolled-up carpet.

They help him, eyes averted. Embarrassed for him, the trials of his life. The things he has to put up with. They buy his story, hook, line, and sinker. Buy his story in their pansy little "security" suits. Stupid little twerps.

Help get her all the way to the room. Her fighting, screaming, cursing, biting. Little spitfire.

And she's saying things that have his belly run cold. But they don't hear. It's like they have inner tubes stuffed in their ears. They only hear him. Hazen Wood. They only hear what he tells them. It's like he's Svengali. They believe what he feeds to them. Spoon-feeds to them. Their portion of Pablum.

They put her on the bed. Hazen sits on her. She's tearing at her face now. Raking huge claw marks across it.

"Is there any thing else, sir?" they say, embarrassed at her passion. "Anything else?"

"No. Thank you. Thank you for your kindness. Thank you so much."

And they are straightening out their uniforms, filing

out of the room, trying to catch their breath. Cause even though there were three of them, counting Hazen, four. Even though there were four of them, Gemma gave them a run for their money.

The door clicks shut behind them. And it's like, with the door shutting, all the air, all the fight, leaves her body. Just wooshes out, like a balloon deflating.

But he doesn't care, doesn't care if she's sorry. He waits. Waits until he can hear them get in the elevator, hear the elevator door ping shut.

Then he beats the crap out of her. Thoroughly and systematically. From top to bottom and back up to the top again. Beats, pummels, whips every inch of her body, using his fists, elbows, knees, feet. Releases his belt from his pants, uses that, both ends, buckle and leather. Covers every inch of her body, so she'll know, remember, never, ever to do that again.

· ‑•‑ ·

Covering a lot of miles these days. The incident at Disneyland appeared to have tipped the authorities off. A few mentions on TV. Not a nightly thing, but enough to be worrisome. Posters. Gotta be careful now. Gotta be more careful. Somebody said something. Some nosy little busybody. So they drive now, not much else to do. Just drive, and drive some more. Gas, so expensive. Goddamned Disneyland took a hunk outta his VISA. Everything getting maxed out. Over the limit. Just a matter of time before it all explodes, implodes, whatever.

Don't think. Keep driving.

Can't stop, rest, settle. Her face is looking too bad.

Bruises are taking a long time to heal. Buckle took a few hunks outta her face. Can't stop. People would ask questions. Looks bad.

Didn't realize. Didn't mean to mess her up so bad. She asked for it, but still. Hard on Hazen's belly to look at her. Makes it hard to do her. Her lying there like a limp rag doll.

And another thing. The little freak was carrying a dead turtle in her pocket. A dead, stinking, rancid, rotting turtle in her pocket. How messed up is that?

The damned thing fell out of her pocket.

"What the hell is this?" Couldn't believe his eyes.

"Wh . . . what?" she stammered. What? I . . . I don't . . . know what . . . you're . . . ?" Trying to cover, the little shit, always trying to cover.

"Why are you . . ." He enunciated clearly, so there could be no mistake, no miscommunication, as to what he was referring to. ". . . carrying . . . a dead turtle . . . in your pocket?"

"She's not dead." Gemma was speaking fast, overlapping, cutting him off.

"The turtle's dead."

"She's NOT dead. She's sleeping! She's SLEEPING! She's JUST SLEEPING!" The kid was yelling and crying all mixed up. All hysterical.

But fact is fact. There's no two ways about it. Not doing her any favors playing make-believe.

"It's dead. The fucking thing's dead. Jesus Christ! You blind or something?"

He whacked her across the face to knock some sense into her. "This turtle's DEAD!" And the ludicrousness of the situation had him busting out laughing. Couldn't believe she'd been carting this dead turtle around for God knows how long. Very unsanitary. Stinks to high heaven. Little freak.

And then, to top it off, when he disposed of it, did her a favor, flushed the damn thing down the toilet, she acted like it was her grandmother, for Christsake. Plunged her arm down into the toilet. Into the goddamned toilet. The thing's gone. Flushed. Outta here. And the little nutcase was on her fucking hands and knees, scrabbling around in the toilet.

Carried on, weeping and wailing well into the night. Wouldn't talk to him all the next day. The silent treatment. She's giving *him* the silent treatment. Jesus Christ, he did her a favor. It's not like he killed it. The thing's eyeballs were half rotted out of its head. It was dead. The stupid thing was dead.

· ▬◄ ·

Don't worry. I've figured it out. Boxcar wasn't dead. Only pretendin cause she was scared of Hazen. Saw what he'd done to me. Was scared of him, so she played dead. She's a good actor, so he believed her, didn't hurt her. Flushed her down the toilet.

At first I was real upset about this. Cryin and cryin. Weird thing is, I felt worse about this than when my grand-daddy died. And I loved my granddaddy.

It has me a little worried. Like maybe I'm a bad person that I cried way more when Boxcar got flushed down the toilet than when my granddaddy died. I mean, she just got flushed. He died. Dead. Never to come back. I was sad when my granddaddy died. I cried a bit, but only maybe an hour, an hour and a half tops, when you added all the different times together. So what's that say about me?

In my defense, however, I did think Hazen was killin her. I mean, my granddaddy died in his bed, I didn't see nothin.

I mean, to be honest, when Hazen flushed her, I thought he was murderin her. It was like he was the Nazi, and I was the mother, and I was bein forced to watch the destruction of my child. Of course I was gonna flip out. Who wouldn't?

But after a little while, I figured it out.

Boxcar was pretendin. Hazen flushed her. She got a fun ride, like the roller coaster at Disneyland. "Wheeee!" Down the drains, the pipes, the plumbin. Twistin, turnin this way and that. And, now this is the excitin part . . . Where do the plumbin pipes lead? Well, they have to lead somewhere. So if you think about that for a moment, you deduce, you figure out, there is only one possible solution . . .

They lead to rivers! And the rivers lead to lakes. And lakes are the very best place *in the whole world* for turtles to live. The very best!

And so now, think of it, Boxcar is livin in a beautiful lake, has probably met a handsome turtle husband, gotten married, and has lots of happy little baby Boxcars runnin around. And her nice thoughtful husband helps her find worms and flies and other tasty tidbits. Shows her the ways of the lake, builds her a cozy home.

Boxcar's fine.

Actually, if I'd thought of it, I probably would have flushed her myself.

- ◆ -

I got away. Walked out. Just walked right out, calm as you please.

He'd gone next door to get coffee. Denny's. Hadn't tied me up. Hadn't taken my clothes. Went to get himself coffee. And I upped and walked out. Just walked right outta the room. Didn't look left, didn't look right. Didn't want to attract attention to myself, which might seem crazy, cause there's no one else in the room. But that's how I felt, like someone was watchin me, like I had to be careful, very careful, move slow, not attract any undue attention. Moved slow, walked out the door like I had a right to.

Just walked my body out of that door. Down the stairs. Not too fast, not too slow. Blood rushin in my ears, like an ol' washin machine. Glance down, my hands are shakin. My heart, like the stereo, with everything but the bass turned off. It's just boomin away. Throbbin so hard it's makin the front of my blouse jump like this—*Boomp . . . Boomp . . .* —with each beat.

Walked down the steps to the first floor, cement steps. Enclosed. So scared I'd meet up with him, comin up, carryin his coffee.

Walkin careful, breathin soft. No sudden movements, ready to run. Ears on hi-fi stereo sound. Listenin, strainin for his slag-stepped feet.

Walked out. Out of the room, down the steps, and around the front of the buildin. And once I got to the front, I began to run. I ran and ran and ran. Heart poundin, shoulders scrunched down like it was rainin and I was a cat not wantin to get wet. Don't know why I was runnin that way. But I was. Runnin all weird like I didn't have a right to. Like I half expected a big fist to grab ahold of, haul me back to him by the scruff of my neck. Runnin like I had an invisible bungee cord attached around my neck, and I don't see it, don't know it's there, but he does. And he's sittin there laughin, takin his time, drinkin his coffee. Just laughin and waitin for the bungee cord to snap me back, yank me off my feet, slam me back, fling me back, so I am lyin, cowerin like an emptied-out rug at his feet.

· ◂ ·

Caught her. Caught the little bitch. Drove the streets of Denver for four days. Four wasted days looking for her. Found her in an alley eating pizza out of a dumpster. Eating garbage. Eating it! Almost didn't recognize the little slut, almost drove past. Her hair, one big massive tangle, face grimy, clothes torn, filthy. Almost didn't recognize her. She's the one who gave it away. If she hadn't gotten the trapped-in-the-headlights expression, if she hadn't tried to hide, bury herself in the garbage, he would have driven right by. That's how dirty she was.

But she tried to hide, and that's how he found her. That's how he caught the little slut. More trouble than she's worth. Had to get in the stinking dumpster, drag her out. Drag the bitch out. Her acting like a wild animal. Weird animal sounds, primitive noises, coming out of her. Clawing, scratching, biting.

Got her back in the trunk. Being none too gentle. Roughed her up a bit. More trouble than she's worth. Slammed the trunk door down on her. Stupid little slut.

Not about to let her up front. Can't trust her. Besides she's too disgustingly filthy.

. ▬ .

She's quiet now. His Gemma. She's peaceful now.

Had to clean her extra hard. Had to scrub her skin raw. Had to use Clorox, Comet, and a scrub brush. Had to clean her good. Get the germs off. Took two hours to comb her hair out.

But she's good now. Not fighting him anymore. Probably relieved he found her. Probably was scared on the streets, poor tyke. Probably glad, grateful to be back in his arms, safe with her Hazen again. Probably understands now, how hard it is to survive on one's own. Survive on the streets. Probably had some scary experiences. Doesn't want to talk about it. Just shakes her head, eyes fill up. Doesn't say anything, but Hazen knows it wasn't good. Knows she's not gonna try that anytime soon.

Took her to bed. Wasn't planning on it. Was still a little shaken, a little mad about her latest escapade. But she seemed to need it, want it, four days without. Gave it to her everywhere, then pulled out, shot it all over her face. Her eyes squeezed shut tight like she's taking holy communion.

Likes seeing it like that, glistening, streaked across her face. And he rubs it in. Massages it in, small circular movements, like he's an esthetician at some fancy beauty salon. Like he's giving her the treat of some priceless face cream. Actually, it's probably damned good for the complexion, full of protein.

Yeah, they stayed up late. Did her well into the morning.

Felt the need to be thorough. Just in case. Just in case the little slut sold out while she was away. Probably didn't. But just in case, just to make sure. Needed to mark his territory, so to speak. Felt good. And honestly, she seemed to enjoy it too. Didn't fight him one bit.

CHAPTER THREE

On the road. Not talking much. Gemma quiet. So quiet. Think Denver messed her head up. It's like she's surrounded in gray fog. All the sunshine gone from her face.

Hazen doesn't know what to do. Trying to make plans, but it's damned near impossible. Wants to show her a good time, but his Visa's not working anymore. Guy at the Chevron station cut it up. Pompous little prick. "I'm sorry, sir . . ." So smug. "I'm afraid I'm going to have to insist on cash." Like he's got a whole hell of a lot of that floating around.

Used up all the cash in his bank account, debit card's just for decoration now. So it's down to American Express, which he'd rather not use cause they charge an enormous interest rate. And they want you to pay the damned thing off every month.

Gotta stop moving. Gotta get a job. Used Gemma's finger, she didn't want to play, no matter, he used her finger, eyes shut. Pointed it at the map. Finger landed on Chicago. So Chicago it is. Not much further. Day or two drive. Not much further. Get a job. Settle.

·—·

Got an apartment. A brownstone. By the tracks. Noisy as hell, like a goddamned earthquake when the trains whiz by. Can't be helped. Best he could get, given his limited financial situation. Pay by the week.

Purchases a lock to put on the outside of the door. A double bolt lock to keep her safe. Has her stay in the trunk while he buys and installs it. Gotta keep her safe. Chicago is a dangerous place. Not a good place to get lost in. A person could disappear in Chicago, never be seen again. And he tells her that, over and over. Instills it into her brain. The Mafia runs Chicago. The sex trade. They have little girls like you for lunch. It's a city of whacked-out perverts. Can't be too careful.

Tells her over and over, but installs the lock too. Just to make sure. Just to be safe. Just in case she flips, isn't herself one day. Just as a safeguard, a safety precaution.

- ← -

She was crying again. Not cause he was doing her or anything. Just crying for no reason. And when he'd ask her what was the matter, she'd just rock back and forth, clutching her knees, face streaked, eyes swollen. Back and forth, like those scenes in the movies of crazy people.

He tried to get her to stop. Tried holding her, comforting her, yelling. Nothing worked. Didn't know what else to do. So he left. Door double-locked from the outside. Always double-locked from the outside, just in case. Doesn't want a repeat of Denver.

Denver, that's when he figured out that they needed to settle, couldn't keep traveling around, trying to keep ahead of the lost child posters that seemed to be popping up everywhere.

Needed to settle, put down roots. Needed a safe place for her. Impossible to keep track of her twenty-four, seven. Besides, he needed a job, spent too much trying to show her a good time. And what'd she do? How did she show her gratitude? Ran away. Gave him grief. Messed his head up royally.

And now she's crying.

It's not his fault. He did what he had to do. That's what a man does. Takes care of things. Killed him to do it, but he did it. He cut her hair. Her beautiful long hair. He had to cut it, dye it brown, so people wouldn't look twice.

Didn't mean to cut it so short. But she just wasn't cooperating. Wouldn't hold still. Virtually impossible to unwrap her scrawny little arms from around her head. And she was crying. "Don't do it. Please don't do it. I'll be good. I won't be bad anymore." Sobbing and sobbing, wrenching her head from side to side so he couldn't get the scissors near her cause he scared he'd poke out her eye. Finally he had to sit on her. Had no choice. Had to sit on her. Pin her down.

Legs gripped around her. And even then, she was so stubborn. She kept wrestling her arms out from under him, grabbing what hair was left, tight little fists, trying to clutch it to her head, even though half of it was already gone.

And now she's crying again. And Christ, it's not about her hair, that was two days ago. She just started crying, and he hadn't done anything. Anything at all, it's like something in her snapped. Ever since Denver, it's like something in her just snapped. And it's freaking him out. Cause she's just not acting normal.

Walking the block, round and round. No coat, ten below

freezing with the wind chill factor. Blowing off the lake. Ten below in the beautiful metropolis of Chicago and he's trying to cool off. But his face is on fire, and the contrast of the hot and cold tears up his eyes as his lungs try to suck in air.

Five times round the same block. Same stupid block and then it comes to him and he knows what to do. And that's when the cold slams into him. Into his bones, cause his head's stopped spinning, because he has a plan.

The store doesn't have fresh ground beef, only frozen. Corner store. Small, dark, cramped. Aisles piled high with tired, dusty cans. Boxes, labels faded, like they've given up hope of ever going home.

He finds the tomato sauce. Two cans should do it. Onion, spaghetti noodles, salt, pepper. Finds what he needs. Pays. The cold in deep now, has him on the balls of his toes, bouncing slightly. Not much heat in the store. The Chinese man, his wife behind the counter, they both have coats on.

"Cold day," says the Chinese man. And Hazen doesn't know if this Chink is laughing at him or not. Laughing at him because he forgot his coat. His face doesn't seem to be, but you never know with these sly bastards.

The wife doesn't look up from her newspaper. Doesn't bother, just sits there on her wood box in her parka.

Back outside. Cold. So cold. Back to the apartment. Runs up the stairs, four flights. Hard to get the keys out, turn them in the locks. Hands, fingers numb. Can't hear her. Can't hear her crying from out here.

Opens the door. Cautiously, slowly, like it's not really his to open. Doesn't hear anything. Opens it further. And he sees her. Sees Gemma, lying on the floor, curled up on her side in a fetal position. Face pale, eyes shut, swollen. Her breath rapid, a shallow pant, like a cat in labor. Her body, shuddering, convulsing maybe every six or seventh breath. Hand curled up by her face like she wants to suck it. And he wonders. Did she suck her thumb when she was little? He wonders this. Her teeth stick out just slightly. Just ever so slightly when she smiles. And he wants to ask her. But he doesn't. Maybe she's sleeping. Probably isn't the best time. Will ask her later, when they're happy. After, when he's made her some homemade spaghetti with real sauce, meat sauce, not from a jar. He'll ask her then, when they are eating and happy.

· ➤ ·

The spaghetti doesn't do it. She just keeps pushing it around on her plate.

"You gotta eat," he says. "You gotta eat . . . It's good. Homemade."

And she pretends, but he can tell she's not eating.

"You're getting skinny," he says. "You're getting too skinny . . . You gotta eat proper so you can grow up and get big and strong and healthy."

And she looks at him. Looks at him out of the side of her eyes. Eyes screwed up slightly like she's trying to look mean. And she says, real dismissive, like she can't even be bothered. "I'm not a five-year-old."

"You're acting like it," he says, more of a thought really. Christ, he could barely hear it himself, and he's the one who said it. But she hears it. With those bat radar ears of hers. And the next thing he knows, she's slamming her fist down into her plate of spaghetti. Chair falling backwards, crashing to the floor.

"I'm not a five year old!" she yells. "I'm not a sissy, god-damned five-year-old!" Her face mean, so mean, all screwed up and venomous. But she's crying too. Trying to punch the tears away with her fists.

And he's never seen her like this. First the crying jag, and now this. Doesn't know what the hell to do.

He pretends she didn't say anything, just keeps trying to eat his spaghetti. But she flies at him. Right over the table. Sends his plate of spaghetti crashing into the wall. Flies at him, claws outstretched, like an electrocuted cat. Slashing at him, taking chunks of flesh out of his face, arms, neck, before he wrestles her to the ground. Wrestles her to the ground, smacked her a few times across the face to calm her down. Fucking little ungrateful bitch. Smacks her a few times, kicks her in the stomach for good measure, and then leaves her lying there on the floor. Lying there in the spa-ghetti and her own vomit. Stupid bitch. Goes and takes a shower. Leaves her there, looking like shit. Hates that brown hair on her. Short ugly brown hair's made her all spiteful. Made her all spiteful like a mean alley cat.

- ◆ -

He dreamt about her, the old Gemma. Smiling, running towards him, arms outstretched. She had her long, blond hair back. And she was beautiful, so beautiful, wearing this little white halter top, jean shorts, bare feet. Her colt legs kissed by the sun. "I love you, Hazen. I love you," she says. And he swings her round and around. And then she's kneeling before him and she is taking him in her mouth, and it feels so good.

And when he wakes up, it's like the dream was real, and he reaches for her, but she's not there. And he remembers yesterday, her acting so crazy. "Poor little kid," he says. And he gets up and goes into the other room and she's still lying there on the floor. Lying where he left her, curled up in a little ball on her side. She is shivering in her sleep, arms wrapped around tight. "Oh Gemma . . ." he says. And he feels kind of like her father, her so young and all. "Oh Gemma . . ."

He picks her up, and she nestles in, snuggles in to him in her sleep. And he carries her to the bathroom. She wakes up on the way. In the hallway. He can tell, cause her body stiffens. But she doesn't fight him, and that is good.

He runs the bath, takes off her clothes, smooths the hair out of her face. "Poor baby . . ." he says. And she doesn't say anything. He washes her clean. All pink and shiny. Washes his little girl. She doesn't look at him, just looks down at her limp Raggedy-Ann hands, cause she knows she was bad. "It's okay . . ." he says soothingly. "Daddy forgives you . . ." he says. She doesn't say anything. And he feels a surge of excitement. "Daddy forgives you . . ." he says, heat racing to his cock. "Daddy forgives you . . . Give Daddy a kiss." She hesitates, but she does it. A shy closed-mouth kiss. But he's the boss, grabs the back of her head with his hand, takes her mouth. Deep. A deep, satisfying kiss. "Oh, you're good. You're good to your daddy." And he takes her out of the tub, he dries her off, powders her, takes his baby to bed and he fucks her. Gives it to his baby, again and again. Can't get enough. Makes her call him "Daddy." And she doesn't want to, but she does, cause she knows he is the king. So she does. And it is good. He goes at it until it starts to get light and she is asleep and exhausted. And even then he can't sleep. So excited by this new thing. So damned excited. Making new plans as he strokes her limp and passive body, licking, lapping up, the traces, the salt, the tired tears of her acquiescence from her face.

- ➤ -

He wakes up to the sound of her vomiting in the bathroom. "Gemma?" he says. But she doesn't answer, crouched over the toilet, clutching the toilet bowl like a life preserver. "Gemma? You okay?" But she doesn't answer, she's too busy barfing.

She's there for a long time. There until there is nothing left to barf, just dry, rasping heaves of air. Air and snot.

When she finally comes to bed, she is shaky and pale and sweaty and smells of vomit.

"Are you okay?" he says. But she just turns her back to him. Lies curled up on her side, eyes shut.

"Are you okay?" But he is talking to nothing, cause she's shut him out.

- ➤ -

She's better in the afternoon. Subdued. Stopped throwing up, which is good. And Hazen, he takes care of her. Makes her Lipton's tea, and she drinks it, all shaky and pale. And because she's been sick, he does her gentle, no games, role play. He makes sweet gentle love. Soft and slow, so as not to disturb her belly. He does her nice, cause he's not an animal. He knows how to take care of his woman.

And they have a nice day. A nice, peaceful afternoon. Spend it in bed, she's not fighting, or crying or trying to run away. She lies there with him like she's supposed to. Lies there and lets him touch her. Lets him touch her any way, anywhere he wants. Doesn't fight him, doesn't slap his hand away, no biting. They have a wonderful day. She's coming around. She's finally growing up, and realizing just how much she loves him. And Hazen is happy. So damned happy.

•—•

This flu of hers is not going away. Not getting better. Won't eat. Can't eat. Just keeps throwing up. Throwing up over and over again.

"Tomorrow," he prays, praying all the time. "Tomorrow, she'll be better."

But she's not.

•—•

Gets a job. A temp job at a dog-grooming salon. Shampooing dogs. Clipping their toenails. The things he does for her. And he has to laugh here, cause she has no idea. How could she? She's just a kid, for Christsake.

Hasn't eaten properly for two weeks. Getting so skinny, throwing up all the time. Barely talks. Just lies on the bed facing the wall.

He tries not to think about it. Gets too sweaty, plunges his whole body into hot and cold shakes. All the "what if's?" "What if the doctors can't fix her?" "What if he doesn't get her to one in time?" Gotta work hard. Can't fuck up. Gotta get some money cause doctors cost money. Lots of money.

Maybe she'll get better before he gets his first check, cause they could really use the money. Food and shit like that. Could really use the money.

- ◆ -

Says he's gonna take me to a doctor. Can tell he's scared. I'm not. Not scared of dyin. Seems like it might not be so bad, just a lettin go, like the rope swing, at the community pool back home. Swingin out, far over the blue sparklin water, hangin on with all your might, and then when you can't hang on any longer, rope ridin too rough on your hands, and you feel like it's just gonna yank your arms right outta their sockets, so you just let go, you release the rope. You're scared, but you do it. And it's beautiful, it's like you tumble, in slow motion, to the cool, refreshin embrace of the water. I think that's what death is like, a stoppin of the struggle. Might not be so bad.

And I'm tired. So tired. Everything, such an effort.

He's worried I'm dyin. "Don't die on me . . ." he says. "Don't die on me."

But I gotta say, if this is what dyin is like, it's not so bad. Other than the constant throwin up, which I could do without. Other than that, it's not so bad. I guess you just get tireder and tireder until one day, you just fall asleep for good.

Wouldn't mind. It's not like life is such great hot shit.

Gonna take me to a doctor. So he says. Gonna take me to a doctor. The doctor's gonna help me.

- ◆ -

"I told them," he says. "I told them your name was Angel Drummond. Drummond was my grandmother's maiden name. You would have liked her. Mabel Drummond. Used to make me Baked Alaska for dessert. That's how much she loved me. Took her all day. Making the angel food cake, hollowing it out. Letting me eat the leftover insides. My Grandmother was an angel. A saint. That's how I came up with your name." His palms are sweating, skidding all around the steering wheel. "Are you listening to me, baby?"

But she's just sitting, side of her forehead resting on the window, like her head weighs too much. Legs tucked up on the seat, arms wrapped around her knees like loose, tired wrapping paper. And Hazen gets this feeling in his belly. This bad feeling and he wants to turn the car around and go back to their apartment. Take her back home. But she's been so sick.

"What's your name?" he says, watching the road, watching her. "What's your name?"

"Gemma," she says. "Gemma Sullivan." Voice dull, face expressionless.

And Hazen gets that feeling again. That bad feeling, like copper taste in his mouth.

"No! Your name, dammit! Your Angel-goddamned-Drummond name! Am I talking to a wall? Your new name! The name you gotta use or they won't see you."

"It's a stupid name." And her eyes slide over to him, slide over slow, like it's an effort. Slide over all slitty-eyed and sullen, lower lip plumping out.

"Still got a little fire in her," he thinks, "talking back. Still got a little fire, even though she's sick." And he loves it when she pouts like this, so cute, lower lip jutting out, just slightly.

Her lips are dry, cracked, from being so dehydrated, but it doesn't matter, still gets him good. That pout, even when he's mad at her. Can't help it. Has to pull the car over, into a parking lot. It's early so it's not too full. Pulls the car to a far corner where they won't be disturbed. And she's looking all nervous, skittish. Taking it back about his grandmother's name, but he makes her do it anyway. Broad daylight. Windows steaming up, rain beating down. Ten a.m. in the morning and Hazen Wood is getting himself sucked off in the Simpson Sears parking lot.

- ◆ -

"What's your name?" he says as he zips up.

"Angel," she says, but she pauses, is reluctant, isn't believable. So he smacks her a little. Not hard, just enough to wake her up.

"What's your name?"

"Angel." Eyes drooping, half shut, but she's trying, forcing herself to talk faster now, so that's good.

"Angel what?"

"What?" Panic, a little panic in her voice.

"Angel what?" Smacking her around a bit. Gotta be tough. This is too important. Gotta be tough. Beat some sense in her. "What's your last name? What's your last name, you dumb bitch?"

And she's crying, making a half-hearted attempt to try to get away, but he's got a good grip on her arm, and she's weak, she's pretty weak now.

"What's your last name?"

"I don't know. I . . . don't know. I . . . I can't . . . remember."

"Drummond," he says shaking her. Shaking the name in. Then he says the name slow, into her face. So close he can feel the words ricocheting off of her face and back to his. "An . . . gel . . . Drum . . . mond. Say it."

"Angel Drummond." Head drooping like a broken buttercup stem.

"Again."

"Angel Drummond."

"Faster."

"Angel Drummond."

"Good. Ten times in a row, fast."

"Angel Drummond . . . Angel Drummond . . . Angel Drummond . . . Angel Drummond . . . Angel Drummond . . . Angel Drummond . . . Angel Drummond . . . Angel Drummond . . ." She's tired, but she'll say it. By God she'll say it, over and over until he says it's enough. "Angel Drummond . . . Angel Drum—"

"Okay. That's good. You can stop now. That's good. That's very good, honey." And he strokes her hair to show her how pleased he is. "Strap in." And she listens. She listens good. She pulls the seat belt around her and straps in.

"What's your name?" he says as they pull out of the parking lot.

"Angel Drummond," she says, no hesitation. And he feels better. His belly feels better. Just needed a blow job. Just needed to let off steam.

He watches her walk into the building. Office number, instructions, written down carefully. Watches her enter the three-story brick building, her shoulders scrunched, head tucked down against the rain. Looks cold, wishes he had more money, would buy her a coat. A winter coat. Wrap her up snug. Thinks about that. Helps pass the time. That's what he'll do. Buy her a coat with his next check. Thinks about that. Tries to. Belly racing. Wants to run into the building after her, drag her out. Doesn't want her talking to strangers.

"I got you a woman doctor," he'd said. "Got you a woman. Thought you'd be more comfortable. Wouldn't want some pervert touching you up, checking you out."

His belly is racing. Goddamned racing. Breathe. Take a breath. Think about the winter coat. The nice warm winter coat he's gonna buy her. Maybe a sheepskin coat. A genuine sheepskin coat. Those are supposed to be warm as shit. Yeah, that's what he'll do. Buy her one of those. Will look good with her hair when she grows it back in.

But that's it, that's all there is to the coat distraction. Mind keeps going back to Gemma inside. She'll remember her name. He made sure of that. She'll be careful, knows what she's allowed to say. Just have the doctor check her out, give her some medicine, and that will be that.

"I mean, what the hell was I supposed to do?"

It's getting cold in the car. Body's shaking a bit. Shivering like a sissy. But he doesn't turn the heat on, doesn't want to attract attention, doesn't have the money to waste on gas. Keep moving. Keep talking. "It's not like she can run away, Hazen ol' boy. She can't leave the building without you seeing her. She knows you're in the parking lot. She knows you'll just find her again. So just calm down. Calm down, ol' man . . . Besides, she's too sick. Too sick to run."

Stays there in that car, in the parking lot for what seems like forever. Got out twice. Was going to go to the phone booth on the corner. Call. See what was the holdup. But every time he got halfway there, he'd get worried. Wouldn't be able to see the door from the phone booth. Might miss her. Every time he'd get worried, get back in the car.

And now, staring so hard at that doorway, his eyes are hurting. Staring, willing her to come out. Sweaty, so sweaty.

And then she comes out. Sweet Jesus, she comes out. And his heart leaps, and he's able to breathe again. Didn't realize he'd been holding his breath, didn't realize until he saw her skinny hunched-up body, just how much he'd been missing her. Worrying that something had gone wrong. Worrying that maybe she'd found a way to run away again.

He jumps out of the car. Helps her in. Kissing her, little kisses all over her head. Strapping her in. Happy, so happy.

"What'd the doctor say?" he says, wiping the fog off the window, slopping it off with his hand. "What'd the doctor say?" And he'd started backing out, but he stops, cause she's acting weird. Puts on the brakes, stomach dropping like an outta control elevator. "What did she say?" Gemma is looking small. So small. Tiny. Scared. "Gemma?" he says it softly, so as not to scare her. "Gemma honey, are you all right? Did she give you medicine? What did . . ." He's looking at her, looking for clues. "What did the doctor say? Gemma?" She's crying now, so he's prepared for the worst.

"I'm sorry . . ." she's saying. "I'm sorry Hazen . . . I'm sorry . . ."

"It's okay, sweetie . . ." And he's holding her, comforting her in his arms. "Tell me, baby . . . What's wrong? What did the doctor say?"

"I . . . I have to come back . . . This afternoon . . ." She's crying so hard.

"It's okay, I'll bring you back. It's okay."

"Two o'clock . . ."

"It's okay, we'll do that. Don't worry. We'll do that. Two o'clock. We'll get you some lunch and then we'll come back. How's that sound? Sound good?" And she nods, head buried in his chest, and he comforts her, soothes her, his frightened sparrow. Soothes her, cause he's her man. A good man. "Did the doctor tell you what you had?" Inhaling her, her scent. Lips in her hair. "What was wrong, baby? You can tell me."

"She . . ."

"Uh huh. I'm listening."

"She says I'm . . . She says . . . The doctor . . ." Her voice box, not cooperating with her mouth. But he's patient. Hazen's patient. Just waits for her to find the words.

"She says, the doctor . . . She says I'm pr . . . pregnant."

"What? What did you say?"

"That I'm . . . I'm pregnant . . ."

And he needs to see her face. See what this is about. Takes her chin in his hand, tilts her head up, out from his chest, forces her to look at him. Cause this is serious. Serious, important stuff. He needs to know.

"Are you joking?" Searching her face. "Is this a joke?"

"No . . ." Voice small, eyes sideways. And she's shaking, trembling all over.

"You mean to tell me you're pregnant? That's . . . that's

impossible. You don't have your period yet . . . Are you bull-shitting me? Don't bullshit me!"

"No, I'm not, honest. That's . . . that's what she says." And she's crying, panicky. And he's not trying to be harsh or anything, but he's gotta know.

"But you're twelve. You're only twelve. You don't even have any boobs, for Christsake!" And it's not like he's say-ing this as a criticism or anything, it's just that the whole thing is just too weird to comprehend.

"She says that I am, that I'm pregnant. That it can hap-pen sometimes, even at my age. She says that I am. And she says . . . she says that I have to come back for an ultra . . . an ultrasound to make sure that . . ." Crying, choking on her words. "To . . . to . . . make sure that . . . that everything's okay." Crying hard, so hard. "I'm sorry . . . I'm sorry . . ."

"You're pregnant."

"Uh . . . huh . . . uh . . . huh . . ." Her head, bobbing up and down like one of those wooden dolls with the round wobbling heads. The kind where you flick it with your fin-ger and the head nods forever.

"You're actually pregnant."

And he just can't believe it. Feels like his chest is gonna explode. That he's gonna be a father. That Gemma's gonna have his baby. What a day. And he was so worried. So wor-ried for nothing. What a day!

And he's laughing. Laughing out loud. Of course. She was pregnant. That's why she was so sick. Laughing out loud. Still laughing when they pull up to Denny's.

"You can have anything. Anything you want. Eat the whole damned menu—it's on me."

"We're celebrating," he tells the waitress. Orders Gemma

a full fried chicken dinner, a glass of milk, cause she's gonna be a mother. But she's not hungry, just pushes her food around, pretending to chew. "I'm sorry..." she whispers. Cause she just doesn't get it.

"Don't be sorry. I'm happy, Gemma. I'm happy. I wanted to have babies with you. Granted, I thought it would be a few years down the road. But God, Gemma, God works in mysterious ways. And who am I to question God? God led me to you. Told me. He told me to take you. And now, God, in his gracious wisdom, has decided we are ready. He has decided we are ready to take that next step. To have a family, to have a baby." And Hazen finds himself kneeling down. Right there in Denny's restaurant, he finds himself kneeling down on that grease-smeared floor, "Gemma...will you marry me? Will you do me the honor of being my wife?"

"Get up," she's saying. "Get up." And she starts crying all over again. And Hazen, he realizes he did it all wrong. Should have done it romantic. Flowers and violins and shit like that. Girls like that kind of stuff. So he gets up. Gets up and eats his eggs and bacon.

On the way back to the doctor's, she's shaking, trembling all over. "Don't worry, Gemma," he says. "It's okay, baby, it's the way of things." Soothing her, stroking her wrist. "Don't be scared. It's gonna be wonderful." He smiles at her. "You'll see, Gemma. You'll see. I'm gonna be the best daddy in the whole wide world," he says, covering her hand with his. Romantic, so romantic, him and his Gemma, starting a family, his baby growing in her.

He drives along, eyes on the road, watching the traffic. Driving careful. Going slow. Gotta keep her safe, Gemma and his baby. "Don't worry, it's gonna be beautiful, you'll see."

But his reassurances don't seem to be helping, cause Gemma, she's tense. So tense. All knotted up. Face small. Like a little scared fox. A cornered fox. Ankles crossed, held. Hands, white knuckled gripping. Like she's terrified and trying to be good.

"What's your name?" he says when they get there. Says it in a jokey sort of voice, just to remind her. Jokey, so she'll know he's a nice guy. Know he's not going to hit her or anything. Just to remind her, so she won't forget. Mess up when everything is going so good.

"Angel Drummond," she says, eyes big, dark in her face. Face so white, like she's gonna faint or something.

"That's my girl." And he ruffles her hair. Winks at her, trying to cheer her up. "Go knock 'em dead." And she starts out the door. Poor little kid. So scared. She starts out the door, when he remembers the money, that he forgot to give her some money for the doctor. So he tries to grab her, just catch hold of her arm, not hard, gentle like, not like he was gonna hurt her or anything. But it startles her or something, cause she levitates a good foot of the ground and cries out like someone has stabbed her.

And he's trying to calm her down, trying to explain, but the weird thing is, instead of getting closer, it's like he's being propelled backward, yanked backwards. Somehow, his car door has burst open and his body is slamming into the pavement. Body pulsating, jerking. It's discombobulating, and then he hears the noise, the loud explosion. Hears the noise, feels the heat. Like someone has slit his stomach open with a red-hot poker. And Gemma, it's like her voice is faint, far off in the distance. And she's screaming, screaming, tearing her hair out, trying to get to him, but there's a woman. Some stupid busybody woman has grabbed ahold of her, is gripping her tight. Where the hell did she come from? And Gemma, screaming, wanting to be with him, but this bitch is holding her.

And there is all this yelling and bodies and jostling.

"Gemma . . ." he says, and he tries to get up, get to her. Tries to help her, tries to save her from this bitch that's holding her. Holding her back. "Gemma . . ." he says. And there is that noise again, more pain, unbearable. And it's like Gemma, it's like she's a rag doll on a spin cycle, all her colors, her features blurring, running together. "Gemma . . ." he says. He can't see her now, he can still hear her, faint, so faint, like a carousel in the far-off distance. They rode a carousel once. And he bought her lilac-colored cotton candy. It was sunny, windy, storm clouds on the horizon. Such a beautiful day. Wind kicking up swirls of dust. Little miniature dust tornadoes that got grit in the eyes and the mouth. "Don't cry," he says. And it's funny, his voice sounds far away. "Don't cry."

CHAPTER FOUR

It's over. They caught him. The police. It's over.

Let me talk to my mama on the phone. The police officer. Let me talk to her.

I was fine when they dialed. All calmed down, except for the shakin, cause that part won't seem to go away. I was fine until I heard her voice.

"Gemma?" she said, her voice all full of worry. "Gemma, honey, are you all right?"

"Yeah, Mama," I said, but then I started bawlin like a baby. Big noisy sobs. Couldn't stop. Wanted to talk to my mama, so much I wanted to say, but words just couldn't make it past all the cryin that was floodin out.

And she's sayin, "Are you okay? Honey, speak to me." But I can't.

I'm noddin, but she can't see that. I'm noddin my head up and down like crazy, but that does her no good. And she's cryin too now. And the police officer, Mrs. Cindy, she takes the phone, and she's smilin and her eyes are fillin up too, I didn't know police officers cried. But there she is, eyes fillin up. Luckily, just her eyes, just a titch, luckily. So she's able to answer all my mama's questions.

I listen from where I'm sittin, to the tinny buzz that's my mama's voice respondin to what Mrs. Cindy's sayin. Listen to Mrs. Cindy answerin. I listen, blanket wrapped around my shoulders, my body, like an Indian child. I listen, bundled up warm, snatchy hiccup breath still rattlin through me. Can't stop shakin. Just can't stop shakin. Even my teeth, clatterin away, like I'm cold, like I'm sittin in a bathtub full of ice cubes. But I'm not. I'm warm. Got a blanket and everything. Got an Oh Henry bar. Got away. Got nothin to shake about. But here I am, shakin like my body's a maraca.

Mrs. Cindy, the policewoman who doesn't look like one. No uniform, just regular clothes, but she says she is. We're at the police station and she's been rummagin through stuff on the desk, and nobody's been lookin at her funny, so I figure she must be tellin the truth. And I'm watchin her talk, watchin her mouth move, and it's kinda weird, I never met her before, never knew her, and yet she's the one who kept me safe when Hazen was tryin to grab me, make me go back in his car. And now she's talkin to my mom. "Uh huh." she says. "That's right." And then Mrs. Cindy says, "Okay." And she bends down to hold the phone to my ear.

"Your mother wants to tell you something," she says.

And I try to calm my tremblin down so I can hear good. I try to hold my hiccuppy breath. And I hear my mama say, "I love you, pumpkin . . ." And she hasn't called me pumpkin since I was three and a half, so of course I start cryin all over again. But I manage to get out "I love you too." And that's good. Cause I was happy, real happy to hear my mama's voice. And she's flyin out tonight. She's flyin out tonight, so I'll get to see her tomorrow.

- ◆ -

Floating in and out of consciousness. Tubes attached, electrodes, monitors attached, spitting out data. Beeping noises, the "blip" of the heart, still beating. White walls, ugly curtains, metal rungs, sliding open, shut. Irritating noise. Pain, too much pain. Sink back, he sinks back into dreams of Gemma.

- ◆ -

All kinds of questions. Lots of questions. Most of them don't seem to have much to do with anything. Police officers askin questions. Social workers askin questions. A new doctor, a police doctor askin questions. Collectin "DNA," which basically meant I had to get naked again, let them poke and prod me, scrape my tongue, the inside of my mouth with a long, single-ended Q-tip. She collects samples from other areas too. Embarrassin areas, prefer not to talk about them. Felt like I was in science class, but instead of doin the learnin I was the amoeba under the microscope. Bein looked at, them runnin a little rake, a comblike thing through any area that had hair . . . and I mean any. Takin pictures . . . not pictures of my privates, she didn't do that, thank God. Just wanted to take pictures of my bruises and whatnot, that's all, thank God. Don't think I could have taken that.

Then they took me to a lady who talked in this mamsey-pamsey fairyland voice. Just like that stupid voice the actress who played Glinda the Good Witch of the North used in "The Wizard of Oz." Hated the way she talked, all phony and sugar and spice. All la-dee-dah. Stupid, sappy voice, careenin around like she's been tipplin at the booze, waftin her arms about, like she's conductin an invisible orchestra. Ruined Glinda for me. Seriously.

That's the thing about books bein made into movies.

They take the best books, the most wonderful magical books and ruin them. "The Wizard of Oz" is a prime example. A great book. But the *movie*? Blech! "Willie Wonka and the Chocolate Factory"? Great book, sucko movie. Haven't seen the new one, but I bet it sucks too.

And this woman, this Ms. Lind-somethin, dressed in her earth tones, is drivin me nuts. Drivin me nuts, and I gotta see her tomorrow, and the next day too. I don't know if I can take it. I really don't. I don't know what planet she was born on. I mean, I know she's tryin to be compassionate and all. But please. I am twelve years old. I do not want to play make-believe with a doll. I do not want to paint stupid pictures.

"Oh . . . you've drawn a tree . . . Ah ha . . . And why is it, do you suppose, that your tree has no roots? Do you feel the lack of family roots, uh . . . support . . . perhaps?"

"No." I'm trying to be patient. "I didn't have time to draw roots. You said 'time's up.' Otherwise I would have drawn roots. Leaves too. I ran outta time." A perfectly good answer. But that's not good enough. Oh no. There's some deep dark reason I didn't draw roots. So I don't know why she's botherin askin me any questions, because. please, she's already decided what it is she wants me to say, and what she will and won't write down on her pad of paper.

I can tell. When I say somethin she doesn't like, doesn't agree with, her eyes narrow, and she sniffs. Sniffs, pauses, and then asks me the same dumb question phrased a different way. I mean, how stupid does she think I am? I know what she's doin.

Why doesn't she just ask me the things she wants to know? Not that I'd answer, but why doesn't she just come out and say it? Why's she gotta tiptoe, try to be sneaky, try to be all sweetie-sweetie? She's not a nice person. I can tell, she's all wrapped in how "good" she is, how "wonder-ful." Has nothin to do with me. I can tell. Has nothin to do with me, has everything to do with winnin. Winnin what? I can't tell you. But that's what I think. This woman wants to win come hell or high water, and death to anyone who gets in her way.

And you know what? There's nothin wrong with that. I can respect that. Just be up front about it. Don't pretend you're somethin you're not.

I don't know. Maybe I get so mad at her, cause if I'd been meaner to Hazen right off the bat, if I'd told him I thought he stunk, that he was a jerk. If I'd told him I couldn't stand his guts, maybe he never would have stolen me. Thought he was in love with me. If I'd been honest about who I was, what I did or didn't want, maybe he wouldn't be in the hos-pital right now, fightin for his life.

Fightin for his life, just got a wave of grief. I don't know why. It's not like I liked him. I don't know, it's so confusin. Everything's all mixed up. Feel sorry for him. Feel sorry. Didn't know he was gonna get shot. Shot twice. Didn't know they were gonna do that. Hadn't thought it through. Was just thinkin about me, savin my skin. Hadn't thought about his.

Feel bad. He took me to Disneyland, wanted to marry me. Let me wear his coat sometimes when I was cold. He tried to show me a good time. Feel kinda bad. He couldn't help it that he fell in love with me, needed to steal me. Couldn't help it.

Feelins.

Feel like a bad person. Like I led him on. Should have told him right from the start how I felt, even though I was scared.

And I definitely shouldn't have brought him back to the doctor's office. I knew they were gonna be waitin. They'd told me that.

"Act normal." The police said on the phone. "Don't let on. Don't tell him anything." "You're just coming back here for an ultrasound. That's all. That's all you gotta think about. That's all you gotta keep in your head. You're coming back for an ultrasound."

And that's all I did. That's all I told him. Didn't tell him about the rest. Didn't tell him the doctor had figured out somethin was wrong, got it outta me. That she'd talked to police for a long time on the phone. Didn't tell him they needed me to bring him back, that they needed time to set it up. The net to catch him, needed to secure the area. Didn't tell him that. Didn't tell him that they needed to catch him with me. "It's the best way," that's what they said to me. "Need to do it clean, need to do it safe."

Didn't know they were gonna shoot him. They hadn't told me that. Might not have gone through with it. Him, so happy about the baby. Wantin to marry me and all.

Just thought they were gonna catch him, is all. Let me go home. Didn't know they were gonna shoot him.

- ◆ -

My mama wasn't able to get on a flight last night, all booked up. But she's gonna be here today. Today or tomorrow.

Said a strange thing, though, right before she hung up. Her voice, all quiet, muffled. Wasn't really sure if she said it. Sounded like her hand was cupped around the mouth-piece, like someone was in the room and she didn't want them to hear. Said somethin like "Don't tell 'em about Buddy..." all fast and breathy. Said somethin like that, I think...

Not really sure if that's what she said. Not to tell them about Buddy. But if she did, what did she mean by that? Does she know about Buddy? Buddy and me? Does she know what he did? Shoppin me out? Fiddlin with me? Doin me at night? Does she know all of that?

What did she mean? "Don't tell 'em about Buddy..." What did she mean by that?

I already told them somethin. I already did. I thought it was all right to tell them. They got me away from Hazen. I didn't mean to, they were just askin me questions and questions and one thing led to another, and they wanted to know how I met Hazen... And, well, I told them. I mean it's the truth. Buddy set it up. That's the truth. I didn't tell them about Buddy doin me too. Didn't tell them that. They asked me. They guessed at it. But I wouldn't tell them nothin about that. Just shook my head. Didn't let no words come out. I know I'm not supposed to tell about that.

But the thing is... What did Mama mean? "Don't tell 'em about Buddy..." Does she know? Does she know what Buddy was doin to me? Is she all right with that?

My belly, my heart's in an uproar. Ever since my mama's call. Head hurtin. Watchin my words. Not sure what I can say, what I can't. Insides twisted. Careful, so careful. Who's the bad guys? Whose side am I on? Who's on mine?

Scared, so scared. Don't know when my mama's comin in. Don't know what she's gonna say. Don't know. But I'm thinking ... I've been thinkin on it, and I'm thinkin I heard her wrong. That happens sometimes. I think I'm hearin one thing, and really that's not what the person's sayin at all.

I'll be careful just in case, with my words. I'll wait till my mama comes, make sure, make sure I heard her wrong.

— ◆ —

My mama came, smellin of Jack Daniels, face powder, and lipstick.

Walked in the door, short skirt and high heels. She looked fine. Hair swept up, caught in a clasp at the nape of her neck. Signed me outta the foster home. Temporary care. Glad to leave. Too many messed-up kids in there. And some of them, you know their mamas are never gonna come. You know they're in there for good. Downright depressin place.

My mama came, signed me out. Felt proud, walkin down the hallway with her, holdin her hand. Walked past Eunice, this big black girl. Big, stuck-up, fat girl. Bossy as all get up. Stupid too. Bet she can't even read. Walked past her, and it felt good, cause last night, when we were all supposed to be sleepin. We were supposed to be quiet, no talkin. Last night, she said I was makin my mama up. Can you believe that? Said I was makin her up.

"Probably has no mama," she'd said. "Little Miss Priss is probably jus' makin her up." And all her suck-up buddies were just laughin away. Reminded me of Billy Robinson. A female version of him. I would have fought her, but I'm no fool. Just her, I would have fought, but there were too many of them. So I did nothin. Just ignored them. Nothin more than pesky little mosquitoes. Just rolled over, went to sleep.

But I had the last laugh. Yes, I did. My mama picked me up this mornin, 11:45 a.m. My mama signed me out. Didn't see no mom for Eunice. Didn't see no mom signin *her* out.

Felt good. Saw the look on her face when we walked past, the look of jealousy and longin. Like she wished she had a mama who flew halfway across the United States of America just to get her girl outta foster care. Saw the look on her face, and I was glad. Felt like a mean person, feelin so glad, but that's the way it is. I liked it.

•—•

Stayin at a Howard Johnson. A smokin room. Funny, I was missin my mom, but I forgot how much she smoked. That's one thing I forgot about. Hazen didn't. That was one good thing. He didn't smoke.

Don't like cigarette smoke. Clogs up my throat, stings my eyes.

But my mama, she's suckin away on those cigarettes like there's no tomorrow, huge billowin clouds of smoke. The whole room is full. It's like a gray haze, gotta squint to see through it.

And she's walkin, pacin. Not bein so cozy now that we're outta the foster home. Away from curious eyes.

Don't know what I was thinkin. Am kinda wishin we'd stayed at McLaren's Hall for a bit longer, cause it seems like the huggin that was goin on there is all the huggin I'm gonna get.

And she's lookin at me sly, out the side of her eyes, and she's drawin in, takin a huge drag off her cigarette. And then she says, blowin out, head tilted to the ceilin, eyes still on me, she says, "Did you think on what I said?"

And I know what she's talkin about. My belly can feel it. But I'm still hopin I was wrong, so I say "What? What was that?" But I know. I know.

"Buddy," she says, and she's not even pretendin to look at the ceilin anymore. She's lookin at me. Directly at me.

And the way that she says it, the way she's lookin at me, I know. It's like I knew before, but I didn't really. But now, there's no gettin away from it. And my belly wrenches sideways, my mouth dries up and my brain, my brain is scramblin around on the floor on all fours. Sayin "Oh my God. She's known, she's known what Buddy was up to all this time."

And it's this weird thing, it's like those scary sci-fi movies where people shape-shift. Like you think it's your mother, but it's not. It's really a werewolf, or an alien instead.

It's like that. A shape-shift, like somebody else morphed into her body. And my whole past, my whole last five years, ever since I was seven, ever since he moved in and started touchin me, it's all zoomin past, like a train in a tunnel. And I want to ask, I want to know, I want to say, "You knew? When? What? For how long? How long did you know?"

But I don't say anything. I just sit there on the bed, in Howard Johnson, lookin at my hands. Scared to look up. Scared what I'll see. I just sit there, feelin like I've just swallowed a truck full of cement.

—◆—

Still throwin up all the time. And everybody's askin me, the doctor, the social worker, Mrs. Cindy, even my mom's askin me what I'm gonna do about the baby? That I have to make a decision. But I don't know. Christ, I'm only a kid myself. I don't know.

Some people are talkin to me about abortion. Sayin that's the answer. Sayin it might be dangerous to have a baby at my age. That I have my whole life ahead of me. A whole life to have babies. That I should get an education, go to college, build a life for me, a future. And I'd like to do that. Go to college, build a future . . .

But I don't know. I saw President Bush on TV once with his friend Jerry Falderal, or somethin like that, and they said, I remember it clearly, they said somethin about, rape not being a good reason to have an abortion.

Somethin like, Murder is murder, and abortion is murder.

And I can't get their words outta my head. I don't wanna be no murderer, so I don't know, I think I gotta keep this baby. Gotta keep Hazen's baby in my belly whether I want to or not. Gotta keep it, even though it's makin me barf all day long. Gotta keep this little baby.

They did an ultrasound. They actually did one, so that made me feel better, like I wasn't lyin to Hazen about that. They did do one and there is a baby in there, so that was all true. That part of it. I really am pregnant.

I'm kinda scared, about being a mother and all. Don't know how I'm gonna afford it, take care of it. Kinda scared, I mean, I did my best, the best that I could with Boxcar Julie, and look what happened to her. Flushed down the toilet, maybe dead. Couldn't take care of a damned turtle, how the hell am I gonna take care of a baby? And that's the other thing. I wanted Boxcar. Paid good money for her. I wanted Boxcar. And it's not that I'm tryin to be mean or anything, it's not that I'm tryin to hurt the baby's feelins, but the truth of the matter is, no matter which way I turn it. Round and around in my brain. No matter which way I turn it . . . I don't want to have a baby. Not now. Especially Hazen Wood's baby.

But that's the thing, that's what I keep comin back to. Our president's words. And he feels that abortion is murder. Doesn't matter what the circumstances. He feels that abortion is murder. Feels so strongly about it that he's tryin to make it outlawed. That if you had an abortion, you'd be a criminal, have to go to jail. That's what he wants. And he's the president. The president of this country. And you don't get to be president by bein a dummy, you gotta know somethin, you gotta be smart. Otherwise, nobody would have elected you. You gotta know somethin.

Our president says murder is murder, and that's what I'd be doin if I had an abortion. I'd be committin murder. So, that's the way it is, I guess. Probably gonna have to keep this baby. Scared outta my skull, but I don't wanna be no murderer.

—◆—

Mrs. Cindy, the police officer, actually, she's a detective. That's her official title. I didn't know it before, that there were different ranks of police officers. And that a detective is better than a police officer, and a sergeant is better than a detective. Well, not better, just higher up, like the boss of, or somethin. Anyway, she's a detective. She detects things, solves mysteries, murders, things like that. And that's why she doesn't get a uniform. Detectives don't get to wear them. She used to when she was a police officer, but not anymore. I think I'd rather be a police officer, the uniforms look fancy, and you get to have all that stuff hangin around your belt. Much cooler than a suit.

I gotta say, I feel bad, lyin to her, cause I kinda like her, have a soft spot for her on account of her savin me from Hazen, and the bullets and all. Not only that, but she knows about the whole Hazen situation, knows I had sex with him, broke the law, him being a grown-up and all. She knows about that, and she hasn't thrown me in jail.

Now I don't know if she hasn't just cause she's bein nice, feels sorry for me. Or maybe the law about that kind of thing is different here in Chicago. Hazen did say that in Chicago, men like to have little girls like me for lunch, so maybe it's different here, the sex with grown-ups? I don't know. But I can tell you one thing, I'm grateful not to be in no jail. Just wish I didn't have to lie to her about Buddy and all. Don't like bein a liar. Makes my belly hurt every time the subject comes up. Feel bad about it, but my mama was quite clear. Talked about Buddy well into the night.

Didn't go into any specifics about anything to do with me and Buddy, still can't figure out if she knows, not sure. She doesn't talk about that, brushes past it, glosses over it. Like we're whitewashin the fence. Arms makin huge sweepin movements as if she's got a paintbrush in them, wipin, paintin him white.

Doesn't want to talk about, go into, ask any questions about that.

Kinda weird, everyone askin me questions about Buddy all day long, and my mama askin none. And when I got up my courage, figured, what the hell, felt like I just had to know, when I got up my courage, to try to bring it up, she just got this closed-shut look. All shuttered, like the storm windows you see on pictures of houses up in Massachusetts and Maine. All slammed shut, bolted, and locked. So I let it go. Didn't talk.

Later, lyin in bed, starin at the ceilin. All the lights off, room dark, curtains drawn to block out the flash of "Ed's Diner." Can still see a bit of the glow from the pink and green neon tubes that write the name in cursive. Can still see a bit where Mama didn't draw the curtains tightly enough together. Can see Mama's silhouette, the shape of her face, her nose.

Neither one of us sleepin. Minds spinnin.

And I feel so lonely, like I've lost my mother, and I want to crawl into her arms, like I did when I was a baby, and have her rock me, and sing to me and smooth back my hair. And tears slide down my face, but she doesn't know. I can cry silent now. That's one skill I learned while I was away. Can cry silent now, keep my body still. Can cry so nobody can tell unless they are lookin right directly at me.

Lonely, so lonely.

And she doesn't know that I'm cryin. She doesn't know that. She's just thinkin about her life, runnin through her life. Starts talkin up into the darkness, fillin the room with words. Talkin about what a good man Buddy is. How he helps with the finances. How she doesn't know what she'd do without him. How he's kind to her, buys her things, pretty things. How he doesn't beat her. Doesn't beat her like my daddy used to do. Apparently my Dad used to beat the crap outta her. I didn't know this, but that's why they got divorced. Used to beat her on a nightly basis. "And you don't want that for me, do you, honey?" she asks, a pleadin quality to her voice.

And I say, "No . . ." cause I don't know what else to say. I say, "No . . ." cause I want her to be happy. Really I do.

And she rolls over and gives me a hug. Wraps her arms around me like I want her to. And she whispers "Thanks, baby . . ." And I breathe her in deep. She kisses me on the forehead, and I want to cling, I want to cling like a man drownin, but I can tell that she doesn't want me to, so I let go.

"Night . . ." she says, and she rolls over to her side, facin away from me, and falls off to sleep.

And I listen to her breathe in and out. A steady rhythm, in and out. I listen to my mother breathe, and I know what I gotta do.

So I lie in the mornin to Mrs. Cindy, about Buddy, and all the things he's done to me. I play stupid to her questions, my belly all messed up, like it's been suckin on lemons.

My mother waitin outside the room, ear to the wall.

I lie to Mrs. Cindy. See the disappointment on her face. Her disappointment in me. Like she knows that I'm lyin, right to her face. She knows.

Feel bad, like I'm disrespectin her. Don't know if it's right, don't know if I'm bein "good" or "bad." Don't know nothin, except it's what I have to do, need to do. Don't want my mama back to gettin beaten up every night. Had enough of that myself. Don't want it for her.

I lie, do what I need to do, keep her safe. Keep my mama safe. Outta harm's way.

- ● -

They're back. The bull-dyke detective and her pussy-whipped partner. He remembers her. She was the one who was holding Gemma back from him while they were blasting the crap outta him. Detective Salyn, that's her name. Gotta remember it for when he gets out, cause that bitch is dead meat.

Her partner? Hazen doesn't remember him from the parking lot. Doesn't know if he was there. But one thing for sure, the dipshit sure loves coming here. Strutting in, filling up the hospital room with his so-called maleness. Blond, muscle-bound prick. He knows the type. Hazen Wood knows the type. Knows never to trust them. That's what he knows. Chisel-jawed, weight-lifting, steroid-popping perverts. There's a reason why this sort feels the need to spend so much time on their body. Only one reason, and Hazen is wise to his ways. Not gonna turn his back on that one, not gonna bend over when he's in the vicinity. Incompetent, self-righteous faggot.

And they're quizzing him, advising him, reading him his Miranda rights, like he's the criminal.

He tells them about Buddy. They got the wrong man. Arrested the wrong man. But do they acknowledge that they have screwed up royally?

No. The shits. Stuck him in some kind of hospital prison. Guards all over the place. What's the point of sticking him in with a bunch of psychotic criminals and guards? First of all, he hasn't done anything that any red-blooded male wouldn't do if he was in Hazen Wood's shoes.

Secondly, guards? Like he's gonna be able to run anytime soon. He was blasted full of holes last time he checked, courtesy of the inept, incompetent Chicago police. Knew he should have gone to Canada. Those Mounties, now they would have treated him with respect.

Incompetent assholes. Don't listen to him, don't pay attention. He told them about Buddy. Told them that he and Gemma were just friends. Told them they bloody well better let him outta this hospital prison or there's no telling what he'll do.

Gonna sue them first off. Gonna sue them for all they're worth, filling him with damned bullet holes. Think they're the judge, jury, and executioner all rolled in one.

Told them the situation with Gemma, that she'd told him about Buddy raping her. Asked him to save her, take her away. "What's a man to do? She was in a bad situation. A very bad situation, and to be brutally honest, that mother of hers . . ."

He told them they were questioning, they were after the wrong man. He's the hero in this scenario. Hazen Wood, the goddamned hero.

But the bull dyke doesn't hear him. It's like his words are just bouncing off of her. Just looks at him like she thinks he's dog shit under her shoe.

The other one, the faggot, seems to listen better. Might be a faggot, but seems to understand the way of men. That he had to, was trying to, protect the kid.

Wore him out. All their questions. Nurse had to tell

them to leave. Tight-lipped little automaton, but at least she could see that he was being overworked, overstressed, needed to rest. Sleep.

- ◆ -

After seein the stupid shrink, Ms. Lindstrom, who keeps on sayin, "But what I don't understand is why you didn't run away? There you were, out in public places, why didn't you just walk up to someone and ask for help?"

And I've tried to explain, really I've tried, I've tried to be patient, but my God is she stupid. I mean, Jesus Christ. I've told her about how he locked me in the trunk, me tryin and tryin to get away, make noise, bangin my feet on the trunk door, cryin out until my voice was raw and ragged. Told her how, when he finally let me out, let me sit in the car, how *every* time the car would slow down, I'd jump out, run. *Told* her and *told* her. And people *saw* me, *grown-ups* saw me, *heard* me, and *nobody*, not one person, helped.

And I *did* run away. I got away in Denver. He just found me again. I mean Jesus Christ. There's only so much you can do, he was *holdin a fuckin knife* on me! What was I supposed to do? You know? There is, I'm *sorry* to say, only so much you can do. Only so many times you can try to run away. He's just gonna catch you. And when he catches you, it just gets worse, way worse, the beatins. And nobody, *nobody* will help you. Cause the simple fact of it is, people don't care. People just don't care. Turn away. "Not my problem," they say. Turn away. It's like you've turned invisible. Like at Disneyland. How many people helped me? Not one *single* person.

And I tell her all this, how I tried, how it just didn't work, but she just plays stupid, acts like she hasn't *even* heard what I've *just* said. Asks me, real patient like, if maybe I *liked* Hazen, *liked* bein with him, *liked* the excitement of bein on the road. Bein a runaway.

I mean, come *on*, am I crazy? No. I did not *like* bein with Hazen. I did not *like* bein on the road. I tried to get away. But after a while ... it's like, what's the point? Nobody cares whether you live or die, so what's the point of fightin? What's it gonna get you? I'll *tell* you what it'll get you. It'll get you a broken jaw or worse, that's what it'll get you. You fight back, and you get slammed in the face, slammed in the trunk, get a damned knife in your ribs, that's what it will get you. Stupid, judging, ignorant bitch!

She didn't seem to want to talk much after that. Got kind of quiet, offended, sniffed a lot. Wrote notes.

Then, after havin that little chat with Ms. Lindstrom, Mrs. Cindy wanted to talk to me again. And I don't know what that's about, kinda nervous. Don't know if she's found me out. Not havin what I would call a good day.

Anyway, Mrs. Cindy came by Ms. Lindstrom's office, picked me up. Actually, her real name, her full name, is Detective Cindy Salyn. When I found out that she was called Detective Salyn, I was embarrassed, didn't want her to think I was tryin to be rude, overly familar, callin her by her first name. Didn't mean no disrespect. Just didn't know. So first thing, right off the bat, our very next conversation, I snuck it in. "Good morning, Detective Salyn." I said. And then later, I slipped it in again, but this time, she stopped the conversation said, "Really, Gemma, call me Cindy. Cindy's fine." Said it like she meant it, patted my hand, so I call her Cindy. Mrs. Cindy. I put the Mrs. there cause it sounds more polite.

Actually, it's not my fault I didn't know the Detective Salyn name, cause when she was holdin me, when I was shakin so bad, after they'd first caught Hazen, and he was bleedin on the ground. That's when she told me her name, not her fancy name, just her regular one. Her walkin-around one.

She'd told me, holdin me tight, that I was safe. Over and over she said it, like a lucky charm. "You're safe. You're safe now," she'd said. "My name's Cindy," she'd said. "You're safe with me. I'll keep you safe . . ." And me, panickin, like a trapped rabbit. "It's okay . . ." Arms wrapped around me tight. "It's okay . . . I'll keep you safe."

Anyway, she wants to talk to me. And I worry that I'm in trouble. That the laws are the same in Chicago as California after all.

"What?" I say as we are walkin to her car. "Did I do something wrong?'

"No, sweetie," she says. "Just want to talk to you a bit, outside of the police station. Thought we could pick up some McDonald's, take it to the park, have a picnic. Would you like that?" And she smiles at me, holdin open the front door of her car.

I get into what looks from the outside like an every-day normal-lookin car. But things aren't always what they seem. And the minute I get in, I know it. This is a police car pretendin to be a regular one, and I can tell the difference. For one thing, there's a lot of noise comin out of her glove compartment, and it sounds like some kinda fancy callin radio walkie-talkie that crackles and snaps like super loud chewin gum, like my granddaddy chewin on his Wrigley's watchin his boxin. He could snap it good, but he wouldn't teach me. Said it was "a bad habit," "impossible to break," "and once you started, God help you, but you just couldn't, weren't able to chew gum silently ever again." "No," he'd said. Sittin back in his Barker lounger. "I'd rather go to hell and back than teach a granddaughter of mine to snap her gum. Make you look cheap," he'd said. And that was the end of that. Wouldn't teach me. No way, no how.

Mrs. Cindy shut the door solid behind me. Walked around the front of the car. Someone's talkin out of the glove compartment now, a gravelly voice, forcin its way through all that static. Snappin out messages in some kind of code or somethin. Another voice, comin over, respondin. And I'd really be enjoyin this, bein up front, in a secret police car but my mouth, my heart is too nervous.

"Why's your glove compartment makin all that noise?" I say when she gets in. And now I'm noticin this thing, I don't know what it is really, looks like a police light, but why isn't it attached? Why is it sittin on the floor?

"Oh sorry," she says, and she reaches over me and shuts off the noise. "I forget it's on. So used to it." And she tells me it's a police radio. How it helps her communicate with the other police, with the dispatcher at the police station, things like that. And I say, "Oh."

So, I'm sittin in a police car. Doesn't look like one, but it's a police car all the same. And she's lettin me to ride up front with her. And I know what that means. Seen enough police shows on TV to know that the police make the bad guys sit in the back. So that means she trusts me. Doesn't think I'm bad. Isn't gonna throw me into jail. Don't think so anyway. Lettin me ride up front like a pal.

Must trust me, cause, as I mentioned before, she's got all kinds of fancy secret police equipment up front, the police radio, the police light, and probably other stuff too, stuff I can't even imagine. This car is probably crammed to the gills with super fancy special police type things and if she thought I was dangerous, she wouldn't let me near it.

She trusts me. She's tellin me about her secret police radio, she's lettin me ride up front. Guess she doesn't know that I lied about Buddy, didn't tell the truth.

"Strap in," she says. And I put my seat belt on, careful not to touch anything, bump anything. Try to let her know with my actions, that even though I lied about Buddy, I lied because I had to. Try to let her know, keep my hands on my thighs, palms down. Try to show her I'm good, I'm trustworthy, that in all other things I'll tell her the truth. And we pull out of the parkin lot.

We go to McDonald's. I get a Big Mac, french fries, and a chocolate shake. And she says, "Ummm . . . That sounds good." And she gets the same thing. Pays for it.

I'm kinda embarrassed cause I have no money, but she waves me off, and we take our food and cross the street to the park.

It's nice. A crisp, sunny day. Cold out. Can see our breath. Our burgers steamin, sendin trails of good, juicy smells up to my nose, get my taste buds ready for that first bite.

And it tastes good out here. Tastes all warm and toasty good. Somethin about fresh, hot hamburgers warmin my hands, my belly. Somethin about being outside, in a park, free. Eatin those hamburgers, that just seems to fill me up. Like God is eatin hamburgers with us. Feels sorta like that. Not talkin, just eatin, side by side.

— • —

Drivin back in the car, Mrs. Cindy starts talkin, soft, patient. "I know about Buddy," she says, lookin forward. Lookin at the road. Doesn't say it mean. Doesn't say it angry. Just says it like a fact.

And my stomach drops, like I'm on a roller coaster blindfolded. So I didn't know, couldn't anticipate what was gonna happen, and we'd just swooped, dropped, hurtled down. Don't know how far, how long we're gonna drop. Don't know where we're gonna end up. I'm blindfolded, see. Fallin, blindfolded.

I keep my palms on my thighs. Sweaty palms. And I don't say anything. Try to keep my head forwards, glance out of the side of my eye, a quick glance. Try to read her face. I want to look, study it long, find out what she's feelin, if she's pissed off, mad at me. If she doesn't like me anymore. But I can't look long enough to figure it out. Too ashamed. Too embarrassed. Caught in a lie.

Think maybe she's takin me to the police station now. To book me, arrest me. I'm scared of jail. Maybe I should jump out at the next stoplight and run. Run fast. Get away. Don't want to go to the jail.

But then, if she was gonna throw me in jail, why'd she take me to McDonald's? Why's she lettin me ride up front?

Ride up front like a pal, like a friend, when she knows about Buddy. Knows that I lied to her.

And the streets are passin, a psychedelic blur. Colors, sounds, whooshin by, nothin clear, distinct.

"I'm sorry," I say, voice, like a feather, a goose down feather tumblin across the dashboard. "I'm sorry . . ."

But she doesn't yell, doesn't get mad, doesn't even look angry. Still lookin forward, she covers my hand with hers. "It's okay, Gemma," she says, voice kind, soft. "It's okay," givin my hand a gentle squeeze. "I understand. Really I do." And she glances over, smiles at me. A tender, understandin smile and then looks back to the road, to her drivin again.

— ● —

"Do you want to talk about it?" she asks, her car stopped now. Parked in the Howard Johnson parkin lot, engine still runnin, exhaust blowin a cloud of steam past my window.

And I do. I want to talk about it, pour it all out. But I shake my head no. Promised my mom. Gave her my word. It's warm in here, heat's on, but I'm shiverin.

"Well, you think on it," she says, gives me her card. "Here is my phone number, day or night, you need to talk, give me a call."

I take the card. It has her name on it. Detective Salyn, twenty-second precinct. Has her name typed out in dark letters, a titch of gold, a gold insignia or somethin in the right-hand corner. Two phone numbers in the bottom left-hand corner. I take her card, hold it in my hand, look down at it hard, cause I can't look at her. I look at it, face, ears, red.

"Thanks," I say.

There is a pause, nobody fills it.

"And thanks for the hamburger, and the fries, and the milkshake," I say.

And then, cause there doesn't seem to be anything else left to do, I get outta the disguised police car. Feel a little funny, like maybe people who see me, people who know about unmarked cars, people who can recognize them, maybe they see me gettin out, think I'm in trouble with the law. Maybe I am.

"Thanks," I say. I give my card a little wave at her, so she'll know, see that I have it. Didn't leave it on her seat. See that I have it, that I'm takin her offer seriously. Paste a little smile on my face. A polite one. Not a jaunty one, or a "pulled somethin over on you" one. Not a happy, happy smile, cause to tell you the truth, not feelin particularly happy. Just a "thank you for your time, see you again" smile. And then I shut the door careful. Want it to be secure, don't want it flyin open while she's drivin along. Want it shut safe and sound. But at the same time, gotta be careful, don't want her to think I'm mad that she brought up Buddy. Don't want her to think I'm slammin the car door, stompin off in a huff.

I close the car door carefully, firmly. Give her a wave over my shoulder, a half-turn wave as I head toward the door. A half turn, a "nothin happened here" wave, an everyday ordinary wave. Give her an "I'll see you soon" wave, and head for the lobby.

My mama's mad. Real mad. Been ragin ever since I got back. Circlin me like a lion tamer with a whip. Lashin me with her tongue. Eyes like fire, legs chewin up and spittin out every inch, every ounce of space in the room.

And I stand here, try to make myself small, try to make myself invisible.

Feel like I'm inside a big beach ball and someone is suckin all the air out, and it's closin in around me, and doesn't matter what I do, not gonna make no difference. They're gonna keep suckin, closin the trap, nothin I can do, nothin I can say.

My mama ragin and ragin.

I don't move, she's like a cobra. Don't want to move, attract its venom. Movement angers them, cobras. That's when they strike, cobras, mothers. Don't move, hold still.

I try to disappear into my shoes. Try to climb my stair-case, doesn't work, trapped in this no-air room.

My mama ragin at me, not believin me. My mama thinks I told. Told them about Buddy.

"I didn't," I say. "I didn't." But nothin I say, nothin I do, will convince her. And my protestations sound so weak, wishy-washy, so fake, that I almost don't believe them myself.

"Did I?" I find myself wonderin. Cause when you get right down to it, how else would they have found out, known, if not from me? But, I don't think I did. I don't re-member tellin them. Mama had told me not to. I'm almost positive I didn't. Did I?

Facts are facts. My mama knows, Mrs. Cindy says she knows, the police in Oakland know. Know enough anyway, cause they dragged Buddy out of work. Took Buddy out of work, middle of the day to go down to the Oakland Police Station for questionin.

"How could you?" she screams, her lipstick a scarlet slash against the livid white of her face. "You selfish bitch! You little whore!" Her saliva sprayin on me.

"The first decent man . . . The first decent man I've had in my whole life and you've gotta ruin it." Pacin, pacin back and forth. "Inconsiderate little bitch. Stuck-up little whore. Nothin's good enough for you, is it?" Turnin on me now. "Nothin's good enough for little Miss Priss!"

"That's odd," I think, which is a really weird thing to pop in my brain, cause I'm really scared, but here I am thinkin, "That's the same thing Eunice called me at the home. Little Miss Priss." But I don't tell my mama, she'll think I'm talking back. I don't tell her about that coincidence. I keep it to myself, cause I'm pretty damned sure she wouldn't be interested.

"Slut!" That's what my mama calls me. "Whore!" Words shootin out like bullets.

Says I just had to go and try to scare him away. Drive him away, with my lies and deceit.

"Just can't stand it, can you? Just can't stand to see your mama happy."

And I'm shakin my head, back and forth. Cryin, can't stop cryin. But it does no good, whatever I say, it does no good, she doesn't want to hear me.

·◄·

Feel like a damned invalid. Eating lukewarm pudding with a plastic spoon. Slopping it all over the place, hands shaking.

Can't stop his hands from shaking. Has a tremor, like his uncle Mike. Sad-assed Uncle Mike, shaking all over the place like he's hooked up to an electric socket. Parkinson's. Better not be getting Parkinson's. Wouldn't that just take the cake? Like he doesn't have enough shit going wrong. Gemma, setting him up like this. And after all he did for her. The little bitch. Just wait. Just wait till he gets out of here. Just wait. He'll clear it up. This whole misunderstanding. He'll clear it up, and then she'd better run. Run fast, cause he's going to get her. And get her good. Little, two-faced double-crossing slut.

And these nurses, what's up with that? Tight-assed nurses in their little uniforms, walking around with goddamned broomsticks up their butts. So smug. So superior. Like who bought the world and made them God? That's what he'd like to know.

Think he's a goddamned pincushion. Jabbing their needles into him left, center, and right. Sadistic bitches. Bet they enjoy it. Bet they get off on it. Hurting innocent victims. Made helpless, forced to lie back and be accosted cause they can't move. Can't move because of the ineptitude of Chicago's finest.

Can't move, can't even crap without assistance. "Excuse me, Miss, can I please have my bedpan?" Can't fucking move. Can't escape. Them, coming at him twenty-four, seven with their foot-long needles. Can't get away, attached to the bed by tubes, wires, and data-spitting monitoring machines.

Just wait till he gets her. Just wait till he gets that little two-faced slut.

- ◆ -

Kinda hard to cover up my eye. My eye that was swellin up.

Was worried they'd find out my mom did it, get mad at her, and then she'd get madder at me. But, didn't have to worry about that. My mom gettin madder at me, that is. Gettin madder wasn't on her mind apparently.

Took me to the police station for my appointment. All distant, removed. Face like ice.

Dropped me off outside of Mrs. Cindy's office.

"Good-bye, Gemma," she said. Kissed me on the forehead.

I remember thinkin it was weird at the time. Not "Good-bye." People say good-bye all the time, means nothin. "Good-bye." "See you later." "Adios." Means nothin.

But there was somethin about the way she said it, her tone of voice. All cold and weary, and sad.

"Good-bye, Gemma," she'd said. And that was it. Apparently, after I'd gone in to Mrs. Cindy's office, after the door had shut behind me. She walked out of the building, down the steps, got in her car, and drove away.

Wasn't there when I got out. Wasn't waitin in the chair like she was yesterday.

I waited for her. Waited for her for a long time. Waited until it got dark. Was scared to go to the bathroom. Just held it in. Held it in all day, in case I accidentally missed her, in case she decided to come back.

Finally, I had to leave the police station. Mrs. Cindy was finished at work. Came out of her office. Looked surprised to see me sittin there. "Gemma?" she said. "Is everything okay? Did you need to see me?"

"Oh . . . nah . . ." I said, tryin to be casual, my feet shiftin around on the floor. "I'm just waitin for my mom is all."

"Your mom?" I saw her shoot a glance at her watch, eyebrows up around her hairline. "You've been waiting here all this time?"

"Yeah . . . Well . . ." I kept my voice light, no problem here. "Sometimes she's a little late. I don't mind waitin. It's warm here, people are nice." I smiled to show her I'm not tired at all. Didn't let on my bladder was about ready to burst. "You go on home," I said, all reassurin. "I'll be fine."

Well. that didn't fly with her. Didn't want me stayin there by myself. Marched me back into her office, sat me down, made me call Howard Johnson's motel. Had to. Was outta time. Just was prayin my mom had calmed down by now. Wasn't mad at me anymore. Dialed the motel. Asked to speak to my mom.

"Hello," I'd said. "Could I please speak to Pamela Sullivan?"

"Who?" voice rough, scratchy. A smoker's voice.

"Pamela Sullivan, room two-eighteen?" Speakin careful, don't want to make a mistake, get the wrong room.

"Don't got no Pamela Sullivan here," said the voice.

"What?" I said, even though I could hear. My ears heard, the rest of me was racin to catch up.

"Checked out. Checked out this morning. Around ten-thirty, according to my books."

"Okay . . . Thank you," I said, and I hung up the phone. Had to shut my eyes. Didn't want to take in the room, Mrs. Cindy, the fact that my mama's gone and left me. Didn't want to take it in just yet.

"What was that?" I heard Mrs. Cindy say. I kept my eyes shut. Needed to, just a little bit longer.

"Is everything okay?" she asked.

"Yeah, fine," I said. "My mom just went out for a bit. Guess she forgot to pick me up. No problem. I'll just walk to the motel, no problem. She'll be back soon. She'll be back for me."

And my words are fine, but I guess my face is not, cause Mrs. Cindy doesn't buy my story. I guess my mom not pickin me up, on top of my new black eye, guess she didn't buy that story either, the walkin into the lamp story. Guess all of that made her suspicious. Cause she called the Howard Johnson motel back, got the real story. And bam—I'm back at the stupid ol' McLaren's Hall. The dumb ol' foster home for messed-up kids that nobody wants.

Back in stupid Eunice's dorm. And Eunice said, when she saw me, with a bitchy smirk on her fat ugly face, "Whassa matter? Yo' mama didn't want ya?"

And it's a little too close for comfort, and that's why, or maybe I was just mad. Fightin mad and needed to hit somebody. Don't know what it was really, but I lost it. Didn't care how many buddies she had. Didn't care how hard she could hit. I launched at her like a nuclear missile. Intent on damage. Intent on makin somebody, anybody, hurt as much as I was hurtin.

We got in trouble. Both of us. Not just me, which is surprisin. Cause honestly, after I cooled down, after I thought about it, it was pretty clear it was all my fault. I mean, she shouldn't have said that and all, but really, I overreacted.

Anyway, about my mama, apparently, she just upped and left. Walked out of the police building, got in her car, and drove away. Just drove away. Didn't look back. Drove to the airport, pedal to the metal, bought a ticket. Bought the first plane ticket back to Oakland. And that was that. Went back to Buddy.

"Good-bye, Gemma," she'd said. "Good-bye."

And when I called her collect from Ms. Finnegan's office, the lady in charge here. When I called Mama to ask her why? Tryin to keep the hurt outta my voice. Askin her "Why?" Why she upped and left me here in Chicago.

When I asked her she said, "Buddy needs me more than you."

That's what she said. That's what my mama told me and then she hung up. "Buddy needs me more than you." My own mother. Wouldn't take no more collect calls. Nothin.

"Buddy needs me more than you."

That night, I had a bad dream. A real bad dream. Woke up screamin, callin out, fightin. Sweatin all over. Sheets wet, soaked with sweat.

Back in the trunk. I was back in the trunk again. Couldn't breathe. Couldn't breathe

Woke up cryin, fist-in-the-gut sobbin.

And the weird thing is, when I woke up, Eunice was the one comfortin me, shakin me outta sleep, dryin my tears. It was Eunice, my claw marks fresh on her face, tellin the other girls to mind their own bee's wax. It was Eunice who held me, "Hush now . . . hush now . . ." It was Eunice who made them all stop starin, shut their eyes, and go back to sleep.

CHAPTER FIVE

You know, the thing is, I don't have it so bad. I mean, really, when you start to hear some of the stories flyin about here, I've been pretty lucky. Pretty blessed. I mean, at least I've got a mama. Because, well, you'd be surprised how many kids here don't.

Eunice, for example, her mama was a junkie, got shot dead. Don't know who did it. No daddy to speak of. Musta had one at some point or another. I mean, her mama couldn't have just got pregnant on her own, all by herself. So somebody's got to be her daddy, he's just never come forth to claim her is all. Never let her know who he is. Could be one of several people, but she doesn't know who. Knows he loves her, just doesn't know she's his is all. And that's what she's waitin for. Waitin for him to find out, realize he's got a daughter. Hear about her mama bein gone. Cause she knows when he hears about that, he's gonna come down to McLaren Hall right quick and sign her out. That's what she's waitin for.

And Kendra, she doesn't have either a mama or a daddy. Nothin. And nobody wants to adopt her. Just passin through, bouncin from one foster home to the next. Nobody wantin her. Not cute anymore. "Past the age." That's what they say, like you're a loaf of bread that's gone bad. Gone past its "sell by" date.

That's the way it is. You get past the cute stage, and that's it. Your chances of gettin out, gettin adopted are about zilch.

And then Jasmine, now she's pretty, cute as a button. Lots of people want to adopt her. Blond hair, blue eyes, like one of those fancy china dolls you see in the toy stores. Not only that, smart too. She's only four, but she can read good. I'm tellin the truth. Read books like "Go Dog Go," "Ten Apples Up on Top," things like that. And that's good for a little kid that's only four. Real good! I tell her, "You're smart as a whip. You're gonna do things with your life, girl. You're gonna go to college and win scholarships and be rich and famous. You just keep on readin. Keep your nose to the books. You forget about boys. Pay them no mind. You study. You make somethin of yourself. You make me proud." That's what I tell her, cause it's too late for me. Bein pregnant and all. Too late for me. But not for her. Lots of people would adopt her if they could. But they can't, see. Cause her mama won't sign the papers. Her mama's in prison for shootin her boyfriend, and she's hopin to get out someday for "good time." So that's why she won't sign the release papers. Doesn't want Jasmine goin to anybody else.

There's lots of stories here. Real hard, tough stories. Sad stories.

Makes me feel humble. Makes me feel lucky that I don't have it so bad. Got a mama who loves me. She's just mad is all. Is leavin me in here to teach me a lesson. Loves me. Know she does. Just wants to teach me a lesson. Will come around soon. Real soon, I hope, cause Christmas is comin.

Don't want to still be here at Christmas. Keepin my fingers crossed. Wishin on stars. Not just for me. Try not to be greedy. Alternate my wishes, one for me, one for Eunice, one for me, one for Kendra, one for me, one for Jasmine. That's what I do, spread out the wishes.

- ◆ -

His grandmother came to him last night while he was sleeping. There in the hospital. Sat down by his bed. Her voice, face, eyes, full of sorrow.

"What have you done, Hazen, my boy?" she said, over and over. "What have you done?" And there is something about it, the sight of her, memories of cookies baking and childhood, that just messes him up.

"I . . . I thought you had died, Grandma?" he said, but she didn't answer. Just looked at him with those dark sad eyes.

"What have you done?" Tears catching, running down the creases in her wrinkled old face. "What have you done?"

And he wakes up weeping. Weeping like he'd never wept before. Couldn't stop. Wept until his toes, his fingers, even the roots of his hair, every particle, every molecule of his body, was emptied into nothingness. The memory of his grandmother, her sad eyes, too much to bear.

Couldn't stop, until finally, exhaustion took over and dropped him back into sleep.

- ◆ -

Sittin with Eunice and the girls, when Jasmine comes runnin up to me. "Gemma! Gemma!" She's squealin, tuggin on my arm, jumpin up and down. "Gemma! Come quick! Ms. Finnegan wants to see you in her office! Ms. Finnegan wants to see you!" And her eyes are sparklin like a Christmas tree. All lit up.

Now normally, you get called down to Ms. Finnegan's office, maybe you get a little nervous, but I knew it couldn't be bad. Not with Jasmine jumpin up and down like she's got boingy springs on her feet.

"What is it?" I say, scramblin out from behind the table. "What is it?" And I'm excited too, even though I don't know what I'm so excited about!

And Jasmine, she pauses, proud to have all the big girls hangin on to her every word. Little chest all puffed out like a baby penguin. "Well . . ." she says, lookin around slowly, eyes big, enormous in her elfin face. "Well . . . somebody is . . ." Excited squeal, little hop. "Somebody . . . is here . . ." And then it all comes out in a rush, like she's been as patient as she could possibly be, but it's just too much excitement to keep welled up in her little body. And it all comes out in an excited rush, bubbles, tumbles out, words bouncin, leapin over one another, endin on such a high pitch that it's a miracle the windows don't shatter. "SOMEBODY'S HERE TO SIGN YOU OUT!"

And now everyone's excited now. Jumpin up and down, pattin me on the back, cryin, all talkin at once. "Oh! Lucky!" "You deserve it!" "I'm so jealous!" "Write! Don't forget to write!" "Bet it's your mama!" "Bet it's your mama, come to get you for Christmas!"

And we run out, me and Jasmine. My heart in my throat. Someone's come to get me out! "My mama!" I think, and my happiness leaps. My mama's forgiven me, and loves me, and wants me back!

I hurry, I get a plastic bag from the kitchen staff. "I'm goin home," I say. "I need a bag for my stuff."

"She's goin home!" squeals Jasmine, arms flappin like a bird tryin to take off.

And the cook, Martha, a big black lady with cornrows and a hairnet, gives me a bag, a floury hug. Tucks me in to her big, soft squishy breasts that smell like cookin and tired-out carin.

"That's good, sweetheart," she says, pattin my back. "You go on home." Calls all of us girls sweetheart, too many of us to keep straight.

"Have a Merry Christmas!" I say, sprintin out the big gray swingin doors, plastic bag billowin out behind me like a flag.

I gather my things, get all my belongins from my room. Don't have much. Takes all of two minutes to jam my stuff in the bag. And then we're back on the move, Jasmine and me, out the door, down the hall towards the office. Don't want to keep my mama waitin. Don't want her to change her mind about takin me back.

We come around the corner, my heart all full of hope and forgiveness and anxious love. Come around the corner, but my mama's not there. My mama's not there signin, fillin out the forms.

It's someone else.

At first I don't know who it is. Not used to seein her out of her work clothes.

At first I don't recognize Mrs. Cindy. Wearin blue jeans

and a cranberry-colored sweater. Not used to seein her like this, hair down, all soft, deep brown, shiny, like a coffee table that's been polished a lot.

"Where's my mama?" I say. And I guess she can see the jumble of emotions on my face, the confusion.

"You're coming home with me, Gemma," and she smiles kind of shy. Hesitant, like she's not sure of my reaction. She says, "You're coming home with me . . . That is, if you want to . . ."

And Jasmine, standin beside me, has gone all quiet. Slips her hand in mine. Lookin up at me, all worried, like maybe she screwed up.

"I'd have to remove myself from your case," Mrs. Cindy's sayin, "but I've talked to Bonnie. Detective Bonnie Sheffman. She's agreed to take over for me."

"Oh," says Ms. Finnegan, noddin her head at Mrs. Cindy. "She's good. Real good."

Then she turns to look at me, head still noddin, only slightly now, like a toy that hasn't quite wound down. "You'll be in good hands with her, Gemma," she says, like I should know what she's talkin about.

And Jasmine gives my hand a little tug. "Wha . . . who?" her voice, a tiny barely there whisper. "Is . . . not your . . . mom?"

"It's okay," I say. "It's okay, Jasmine . . . It's . . . it's Mrs. Cindy."

And I don't know, am not sure what this all means. If I like it or not. Hard to compute, sort out. But I nod my head, like everything's fine. Nod my head and put a smile on my face even though my belly's in a mishmash of feel-ins. "Great!" I say, as I look down at Jasmine's worried face and act all happy and excited. "This is GREAT!" and she looks better, relieved, like she can breathe again.

Mrs. Cindy smiles at me. "Oh, good," she says. "Then it's all settled." Pulls me in for a quick hug, then turns back to finish the forms.

"Are you sure you want to do this, Cindy?" Ms. Finnegan's sayin, in low undertones. Talkin quiet, thinkin I can't hear. But I can. Have good ears. Clever, smart ears. I can hear her all right.

"Twelve's a difficult age under any circumstance," she says. "And this one here . . ." Her voice drops even lower, have to strain my ears, so I can still hear. "She's had . . . more than her share of troubles . . ."

"I know," Mrs. Cindy says. "I'm her—" She corrects herself. "I *was* the investigating officer on her case. I am aware of—" but Mrs. Cindy doesn't get to finish. Ms. Finnegan is talkin again. Hushed, hurried whispers.

"It's just these kids . . . I mean, I know, my heart breaks for her, too." Takes a breath. "But Cindy, honey . . . you're only asking for trouble."

And I want to say somethin, argue back, tell her stop tryin to talk Mrs. Cindy out of it. If she wants to take me home with her for the holidays that's fine with me. Better than stayin in this stinkin ol' place.

But I can't, I'm not supposed to be listenin. So I just keep a smile on my face and pretend I'm playin a game with Jasmine.

"If you want company, adopt yourself a baby, or better yet, a dog. Less trouble, and you'll get more back. I'm telling you as a friend, don't do it. The repercussions for this type of abuse . . . Well, you of all people should know."

A look crosses Mrs. Cindy's face. It's quick. Irritation? Impatience maybe? Not sure what it was. Passes so fast.

"I know what I'm doing, Linda," she says, voice sure, steady, like it's the end of the conversation.

And I'm not sure what exactly they're talkin about. Know, however, that it's about me. That Mrs. Cindy wants to take me home for the holidays, and Ms. Finnegan doesn't think it's a good idea. Don't know why she'd be wantin to stand in my way. Was pretty sure she liked me. At least I thought that she did, before this

And what did Mrs. Cindy say about bein off my case? What's that mean?

Not sure what any of this means. How I feel. Don't know. Mixed, cause even if it's not my mom, even though she hasn't forgiven me yet, and it's Mrs. Cindy signin me out, although I'm not quite sure why. Even though all these things, I'm still in an odd way okay with it all. I'll be goin to someone's home for Christmas. That's good. To be goin to someone's home, even though I'm "past the age," and on top of that, I'm pregnant. Somebody's willin to take me in for the holidays. Wants me. And that makes me feel kinda okay, kinda good.

So even though it's not my mom signin me out to take me home, and it's kinda embarrassin that all the kids here are thinkin she is. When you think about it, compared to the trunk of a car, or spendin Christmas in this place . . . Or actually to be perfectly honest, Mrs. Cindy's is probably better than me goin to my mom's house too. Cause in the holidays, she's always drinkin like a fish, and with Buddy bein there and everything. And them thinkin I ratted on them, when you take into consideration all of these things . . . Mrs. Cindy's house . . . even though I don't know her that well . . . Mrs. Cindy's house is lookin pretty damned good.

· ━ ·

Able to walk. Get out of bed. Doubled over like an old man. Thirty-seven years old, hobbling around like he's ninety. Feet dragging, sucking breath in through clenched teeth. Doubled over, one hand, trying to hold his stomach together, the other clutching at the back of his ridiculous hospital gown. Always trying to gape open, show his ass to all and sundry. Who designed these things, anyway? That's what he'd like to know. Go out personally and gun the asshole down. Do the world a favor.

Impossible for anyone to get better wandering around in garb like this. Fucking, inhumane. And these slippers. These ludicrous regulation hospital slippers, dangerous is what they are, could break your neck in these things. Can't walk normally. Not that he can, but if he could. If he didn't have these damned bullet holes blasted though him. If he was healthy, he'd still be walking like an idiot. Asinine, poorly made, piss-stupid hospital slippers. Has to slide his feet, one foot in front of the other, carefully, inch by inch, shuffle along, so they won't fall off.

They say they're going to be transferring him soon, transferring him to the regular population as soon as he's on his feet. Well, fuck them. He's on his feet. He's on his goddamned feet. Let's go! Pompous incompetents. Think he's so scared? Think he's so fucking scared of jail? Hell no! Take him there! He's ready! Anything would be better than this idiotic place.

—◆—

I don't call her Mrs. Cindy anymore. She said it wasn't necessary.

I told her about respect and everything, and she said that's fine, respect is fine, but I don't have to call her Mrs. Cindy to show respect. Respect is shown by the way you treat people. The way you treat yourself. Can't properly respect someone else unless there is love and respect in your heart for yourself too. Said "Cindy is just fine. No need to be formal, we're friends." And I'm gonna to be stayin with them. So I said, "Okay, Cindy."

Felt good, smilin with someone. Drivin along in her regular car, not her camouflaged police one. Drivin along, like we're family. Like if someone was lookin in through the window, they'd think it was a mother and a daughter out on a drive. Maybe comin home from the grocery store, or from doin some last-minute Christmas shoppin.

And when I think that, about the last-minute Christmas shoppin, for the first time, I get a real excitement in my belly. Not cause we're shoppin, cause we're not. Not cause I expect any Christmas presents, cause I don't. I get this excitement in my belly, cause in thinkin it, kinda like Gemma travel, in thinkin it, it's like I almost believe it! That I really am her daughter! That we were Christmas shoppin! That I really do come from one of those happy, happy families that you see on TV, where the worst thing that happens is they lose their favorite family dog and then find it again.

And it's weird, it's like I get lost in the story of it. Don't even know that I'm bouncin on the seat, grinnin out the window, until Cindy says, "What are you thinking?"

"What?" I say, cause I heard her, but, you know, what I was thinkin is a little weird.

"You looked so happy."

And I kinda don't know what to do. Feel kinda embarrassed, don't know why, but I feel sorta like I forgot to get dressed and went out in public in my pj's or somethin.

Don't know what to do. She's smilin at me, might think I'm bein rude, her askin me a direct question, me not answerin it. Might decide to turn right back around, take me back to McLaren Hall.

"Um . . ." I say.

"You don't have to tell me if you don't want, if it's private. It's okay, won't hurt my feelings."

And then all of a sudden, I want to tell her. Feel stupid for not tellin her right off the bat. I mean, come on. I was thinkin about teachin Gemma travel, maybe makin it a profession, and here, the first person who asks me about it, I clam all up.

So I tell her. I don't tell her I was pretendin to be her daughter and we were comin home from Christmas shoppin. I don't tell her that. Number one, because I don't want her to think I was hintin, you know, about Christmas presents, cause I'm not. Hell, I know I'm lucky just to be goin home with her. Number two, if I tell her I was pretendin to be her daughter, she'd just think I was pathetic.

I do, however, tell her about "Gemma travel" and creatin places, makin food and eatin it. I tell her all about that. How

I learned it in the trunk. And as I'm tellin her, I find myself gettin excited about it, about my invention and I find myself sayin, "I'll teach it to you if you want?"

And then my ears hear her say, "Okay," my body feels all jangly. Not that I don't want to teach her, I'm happy to. I just get all nervous, my face feels like I just ate a red chili pepper by accident.

"Um . . . Okay . . . See, it's like this . . ." I'm tryin to be like a professional teacher, but the minute I start, I realize Gemma travel . . . is kind of a hard thing to explain. Don't want to come off as a weirdo. Sound goofy.

"Um . . . Let's see. What you gotta do . . . is, like, you pretend somethin . . . You start off with somethin easy . . . um . . . and then . . . you . . . um . . . you build it. See?"

"Hmm . . ." Cindy says. "Not quite," she nods, encouragin. "But keep going. I'll get it."

"Oh . . ." And as I'm thinkin back on what I just said, I can see how she didn't get it. I didn't explain it well. Didn't approach it in the right way. "Okay . . ." I say. "Just a minute, let me think . . ."

And then I come on the idea, just like, show her and talk her through it. And then I won't be lookin at her, gettin all nervous, I'll be showin her.

"All right," I say. "This is what you gotta do . . . First, you gotta shut your eyes."

I shut my eyes, and it's better already. "Now, you *might* be able to do it with your eyes open. I mean, you might, if you got good enough at it. Got to be an expert. I'm not at that stage yet. Well, maybe I am, haven't tried it actually . . . But for now, just shut your eyes . . . Wait!"

I open my eyes again.

"You're drivin, so, um . . . I don't think you should shut your eyes." I feel real dumb, cause, you know, I'm supposed to be the teacher, and with my stupid instructions, I could have gotten us in a car crash. "Shut your eyes . . ." How stupid is that?

I look at her. She doesn't look mad. Doesn't look like she thinks I'm the dumbest thing that ever set foot in her car. She's smilin at me.

I feel my face get hot all over again. "I mean, unless you want to shut your eyes. Then you're welcome to. It is easier with your eyes shut. But maybe cause you're drivin and all . . . um . . . maybe you should pull over to the side of the road."

And then I worry that maybe she thinks I'm bossin her, orderin her around. So I say, "Unless it's not convenient to pull over right now, and then probably the best thing to do is, I'll tell you, show you how to do it, and then you can practice when you get home. Yeah, that's probably the best. It would probably be kinda hard for you to do it properly, get the knack of it with me watchin you."

"Okay," she says. "That sounds like a good plan."

And when she says that, I feel so much better, cause she thinks I made a good plan. Gives me courage, like maybe I'm gonna be a good teacher after all.

"Okay," I say. "I'll shut my eyes so I can describe it better. There. Now, what you do is you imagine somethin, it can be anything, and you build on it. You start off small, specific. You gotta be specific or it won't work. If you're doin a place, doesn't matter if you've ever been there before, you gotta get specific about the details. Like say you're choosin a field ... I'll do that, it's one of my favorites. So ... You imagine you're lyin down."

"So you have to be lying down?"

"No ... I guess ... I guess I always did, on account of bein in the trunk. The more things you can use that are actually real, the better. It's like you steal little truths from your situation and you hang the place you're creatin on it, sorta like the truth is a coat hanger, and the image you're creatin is the dress. So, see, if I'm lyin in a trunk, then I imagine I'm lyin in a field. One less thing to create. Does that make sense?" I look at her to make sure.

"Uh huh," she nods and she seems to mean it.

"Okay, good." I shut my eyes again. So, you're imaginin you're lyin in a field. Now you have to choose how you're lyin. On your back? On your side? Are you facedown? Decide how you are lyin and then create the earth under you. Is it damp? Does it soak through your shorts, your T-shirt? Or is it dry and dusty, with the hum of summer insects? Does the grit fly up so you can taste it in your mouth? Is the ground soft? Lumpy? Is there one irritatin little rock that is diggin into your hip and you gotta pry it out with your fingers and toss it away? What kind of field is it? Mine was always grass, tall grass, swayin slightly, a gentle breeze, just rustlin the tops of them ... Tall grass ... No one can see me ... And I lie stretched out, flat out, arms, legs wide ... I take up space, cause it's okay. The grass is tall, nobody would be able to see me, even if they were walkin right close by. And I can hear the birds singin, callin to each other ... The sun is warm on my face, and the breeze ... it kisses me. And it is beautiful, so beautiful. I could lie here all day . . . Nowhere to go . . . No need. Just lie here soakin up the sun, the smell of the grass. Wide open field . . . Boxcar on my belly and . . ." Can't talk, voice stops, cause I get this sudden swell of sadness in my chest, thinkin about Boxcar, how her little feet used to tickle across my belly . . .

I open my eyes. Am back in her car, the rumble of it under my butt.

"And that's how you do it," I say. "That's how you do Gemma travel." I don't look at her though, just look at the gray glove compartment, hair tipped in my face . . .

"Wow," she says. "That's amazing. I'll have to try it when I get home."

I sneak a look at her, and she seems genuine, smiles at me like she means it. So that's good. Was worth it even though Boxcar snuck up on me. Am glad I told her the secrets of Gemma travel. Gave it to her for free, didn't charge her a single penny, cause she's my friend. Just told her.

But then I go overboard. Probably should have left it at showin her the field thing. But because it seemed like she understands about the field, I get all pumped up, start talkin about the rest, all the other things you can create. Tell her about big, pipin hot plates of spaghetti with tons of Parmesan cheese. Tell her about bacon cheeseburgers, makin candy, all kinds, Oh Henry bars, how I nibble the chocolate off the outside, then pry out the peanuts with my teeth, crunch 'em down good, gobble up the chewy caramel nougat roll in the very, very middle, lick my fingers, every single one, to get the last scraps of chocolate and stuff off. Tell her that you have to get that detailed, or your mind will figure out that you're lyin to it and give up on you. You gotta believe in it *that* much. Right down to the last drop.

I tell her about creatin forests with hollowed-out trees that I could hide in, ice cold creeks splashin and gurglin that I could dip my tired, hot feet in. I tell her everything I can think of. All of it, tumblin out of my mouth.

To be honest, I don't know if she quite gets it, understands it.

Think maybe I've overwhelmed her with too much information. Got her confused. Should have just stuck with showin her the field.

Probably shouldn't have waved my arms around so much either. I think maybe I got too revved up, too excited.

Don't know how good a teacher I am. Think maybe my technique needs to be practiced a bit. Got too shy at the beginnin. Didn't realize how hard it would be to describe, put into words. Don't know if I explained it right. Don't know if she could really do it yet. Gemma travel requires practice.

But I've told her, so that's a good thing. First person I've ever told. And it feels good. Good and sad all mixed up. Reminded me of being in the trunk. Good and sad, but mostly good. Glad I could give somethin back to Cindy, cause I really like her. And even though I'm not sure if she understands, I think she sort of does.

Says, "Wow, that sounds cool. You were clever to think it up." And I was clever. Real clever. Cindy says, "You figured out a way to save yourself. You have gumption and spirit." That's what she says. And I feel my face get all hot, but I'm happy too, because I do have those those qualities! And I did save myself! I hadn't really thought about it in those terms before. Feels good. And now we both think about it, that I saved myself, outsmarted Hazen. That I escaped. That I was clever, and had gumption and spirit. We both think about these things, drivin to her home, smiles on our faces.

- ■ -

I got my own room! My own room with a bathroom just for me! It's attached right to the room, don't have to go out into the hall. Just get off the bed, or up from the desk, open the door, and . . . there's the bathroom. My very own. I have my own bathtub, toilet, everything!

At first I thought it was the bathroom for the house, that everybody would have to walk through my bedroom to use the bathroom, brush their teeth. And that was fine. Felt lucky that I got to be the closest to it, in case I had to go in a hurry. But no. You aren't gonna believe it, but this house has *three bathrooms*! Three! One in my bedroom . . . I'm callin it my bedroom even though it's not really. It belongs to Cindy and Joseph. I'm just sayin it's mine while I'm here, cause it's more fun, makes me feel special, doesn't hurt anyone. I'm just pretendin. I know it's their guest room.

Anyway, back to the subject, there's one bathroom in "my bedroom," one in Cindy and Joseph's bedroom, *and* one downstairs off the hallway.

The one downstairs is a sweet little bathroom, tucked under the stairs. Doesn't have a tub or a shower, just a toilet and a sink and a real pretty mirror with gold all around the edges. And there's a tiny table near the toilet with magazines, a couple of books, and a vase of flowers on it.

The flowers aren't real. They look real, but they aren't. Crazy, huh? You'd never know just lookin at them. I found out by accident. See, I was sittin on the toilet, and I saw them, thought they were real pretty, so I leaned over to take a deep whiff, buried my face in them, and that's how I found out. The feel. They feel different than real flowers, and they don't have a smell. Just got a nose full of dust . . . Not a lot of dust, just a little, hardly any dust actually, no disrespect to Cindy's housecleanin. Actually, I probably didn't get any dust, just sneezed cause I've got a sensitive nose is all. No dust. This house is clean as a pin.

They both clean up, and me too. I'm helpin a lot. Tryin to be real helpful. Chase them outta the kitchen. Say, "I'll do the clean up. Don't you worry, go relax, watch TV, talk about your day."

I get them outta the kitchen.

I'm a big help. Want them to be glad they asked me to stay. To know I'm not gonna be any trouble, that Ms. Finnegan was wrong. Want them to know that I'm a good worker, a real good worker.

They leave kinda reluctantly. "It's okay, Gemma, you don't have to work so hard . . ." That kind of thing. But I chase them out, wave a dishtowel at them. "Shoo . . . shoo!" I say, make them laugh. And I tell them I like it, that it's peaceful to do dishes.

And you know what? It really is. I just told them that so they wouldn't feel guilty, but honestly, it *is* peaceful. Hot soapy water, makin dirty dishes clean. It's a good feelin. And another thing, it makes me feel good in my heart to do somethin for them. Them bein so nice, takin me in and all. And the way they joke and goof around and look at each other with such tenderness in their eyes.

Makes me feel good to be around them, them lovin

each other so much. Want to be around them all the time. Like they are the sun, and I'm a lonely bit of outer space debris, somethin no one has any use for, a broken window from a satellite or somethin. And I'm bumpin up against them, tryin to soak up, collect, store for safekeepin, a few rays, a few bright moments, a few memories to sustain me later. When I have to go back to McLaren Hall. Cause you know what? I've decided it's time to stop kiddin myself, my mama's not comin back. No way, no how, not a chance in hell. I mean, if she's was willin to just drive away, not come back, not take my phone calls, leave me in that foster home, especially at Christmas. If she's willin to do all that, then who am I kiddin? She's not comin to get me. She's given up on me. More trouble than I'm worth. And now especially, with the baby comin . . . Well, hell's bells, why would she want me? More trouble than I'm worth. Won't take my calls . . .

And I gotta say, when it first hit me, that my mama didn't want me, wasn't comin back never, it was like a fist to the face. Hit me hard. Unexpected. Eatin dinner with Cindy and Joseph, and we're talkin and the food's good, and then all of a sudden, *bam*!

I don't know what kicked it off. Maybe it was the skinny black-and-white stray yowlin outside. Skinny cat, mean eyed, all claws and sharp teeth. Doesn't want to be anybody's friend. Tried sneakin it some scraps, but it wouldn't come close enough to get them. And now, yowlin and yowlin. Joseph says it makes that noise cause it's in heat. Don't know how, pretty damned cold outside. But if Joseph says it's feelin hot, then it must be, cause I haven't been here that long, but you don't have to be Einstein to figure out pretty damn quick that with Cindy and Joseph, anything that's not the truth, is just not gonna fly. It's like they got truth radar or somethin.

Like yesterday. See, they got this bowl on the kitchen counter. Actually, they've got several. One has fruit in it, bananas, couple apples, couple oranges, and that's for everyone to eat. Don't have to ask. Just help yourself, feel like a snack, help yourself. They got another bowl, has onions, garlic, a couple of not very happy lookin potatoes. And then there this other bowl, has odds and ends, bobby pins, paper clips, rubber bands, and spare change. You know, quarters, nickels, and things.

So anyway, to make a short story shorter, I took some money, not much. Took some quarters, a few dimes. Was gonna say, I thought it was like the fruit, "help yourself," but my belly knew when I was takin it that I was doin wrong. Don't know why I did it. Didn't need the money. Nowhere to spend it. Didn't need it. Just took it. Wanted . . . I don't know what I wanted. Was scarin the hell outta me that I was takin the money, but once I started, it was kinda like a dare, once I started, I couldn't back down. Maybe I wanted to see if they'd notice, if they were payin attention, if they knew how bad I was.

First day they didn't notice anything, so I took a little more. Next day, nothin, so I took a little more, taken all the quarters now, so I started on the dimes. Had six dollars and eighty cents weighin me down, burnin a hole in my pocket, makin it impossible for me to meet their faces, talk in a comfortable way.

Six dollars and eighty cents I had, before they sat me down in the livin room and asked me about it. Their faces sad, serious. Asked me about the missin change. And me, embarrassed, runnin hot and cold like I got diarrhea. Sweatin, cursin my stupid self out. Expectin to get hit, kicked, screamed at, didn't know what. Definitely expectin to get sent back to McLaren.

But they didn't. Just looked so sad. Like their hearts were hurtin. Talked to me about truth and honor and trust. And I gotta say, I felt way worse than if I'd gotten a beatin. Way worse! And I can tell you this. I'd rather get a million beatins than risk disappointin them again.

So this is what I've decided, I'm not gonna steal.

I'd done it with Hazen, but he deserved it. Just a little bit here and there. Money, a sock, his toothpick, just little things, steal them and throw them away in the garbage. Watch him go crazy tryin to remember where he put the stuff. Drove him nuts, would go ballistic! Yeah, I'd steal things from him, wouldn't keep them. Although, that would have been fun. Couldn't risk him findin the things on me. Am not *that* dumb. Just little things. Made me feel good, powerful, like I was stealin somethin back. And he never knew. Never found out it was me disappearin those things.

Stole change from Buddy too, took it outta his slacks when I was doin the laundry. Didn't give it back either. Kept it, bought candy and stuff.

But takin from Joseph and Cindy, that was wrong. I'm not gonna steal from them ever again. I'd rather put out my eyes with burnin hot pokers. Seriously. They've been so good to me, and what do I do? How do I repay them? I steal their money. Makes me feel all sweaty and disappointed in myself just thinkin about it. I can't make it up. I did it, and it was wrong, but I can tell you this. I will *never* steal from them *ever* again!

So that's how I know that truth and honor and trust are so important to them. So if Joseph says the cat's yowlin cause it's warm, so be it.

Anyway, maybe it was the cat, the cries it was makin, that triggered it.

Or maybe, rememberin how I stole and then lied.

Or maybe it was just the sound of the neighbors' back door. Maybe it was that. The sound of that door slammin real hard, like someone's mad at you, don't want you comin in. Someone slammin the door in your face. That kind of slam. Sounded like that kind of slam. Maybe it was the noise of that?

Don't know what it was, but all at once, for no reason, I got this overwhelmin rush of homesickness. Made Cindy's baked cheese and tomato ziti clog up in my throat. Didn't make any sense. Am in the nicest home I've ever been in. With Cindy and Joseph who are so kind. And yet there I was, enjoyin myself, tasty food on my tongue one moment, all stopped up the next.

Had to leave the table. Tears comin fast and furious. Had to leave before they made their way to my face. Got to my bedroom before they fell. Stuffed the pillow over the top of my head so they couldn't hear me. Didn't want to disturb their dinner. Held the pillow down hard, cause noises are tryin to come out. Body doubled up in two, like I've swallowed a fistful of double-sided razor blades. Cause I'm thinkin about my mom. Her face, her smell, how she looks when she's happy. Images of my mom, rippin through me. Lovin her so much, and knowin she doesn't want me, could care less. Left me here in Chicago. Hurts. Hurts so bad. Pillow wrapped around, gripped tight with both fists, face, gapin mouth, like a beached fish trying to suck up air, everything that can express anything, slammed into the bed. Into the lilac-colored, spring-scented sheets. Slobber, mucus, snot. Can't help the sheets. It's like those documentaries you see on TV where the floods are just too big, and they destroy everything in their path. Homes, bridges, factories, schools. Everything, wiped out, destroyed, totaled.

And I know, in this moment, that my mama's never comin to get me. I know. And it hurts so damned bad. And I can't, no matter which way I turn it, I can't make it into somethin happy-ever-after. I can't. She's not comin back. She doesn't want me.

And I hear the door, and I'm embarrassed to be caught in this outta control, cryin so hard, position. But even embarrassment won't stop the flood, it's just tearin through me, outta control, tearin through me, destroyin things. And I think I'm gonna die, gonna be demolished by the force of it.

And just when I give up hope, and this is how I know there is a God, just when I feel the absolute bleakest, I feel a gentle hand come to rest on my back, and I'm breakin, I'm breakin into a million pieces, but I feel this hand, Cindy's hand, and it's like it's filled with light, it's calm and serene, like a cool breeze when you got a fever.

And it's guides the hurricane outta my body.

And I'm okay, and I survived, and I am in my borrowed room again.

And then, Cindy gathers me up, scoops me into her lap, like I am her baby. And she holds me. Rocks me gently, back and forth. And I cry for everything that has happened, and everything that won't. Face buried in the comfort of her bosom.

- ◆ -

I'm tryin to be real good. Felt kinda shy this mornin, about last night, cryin and all, disturbin their dinner. That on top of stealin and lyin about it the day before. Didn't mean to cause trouble, but I did, so that's that.

They aren't actin any different though, being friendly. And I'm still here. They didn't decide I was more trouble than I was worth, make me go back to McLaren Hall. And that's a hopeful somethin.

So, last night happened, but I want them to know that I'm not gonna be any more trouble. Am tryin to be a big help. Bein careful, thoughtful. Not gonna crimp their style, gonna make sure they got private time, alone time, not going to take it all with my "problems."

Want them to have a good Christmas too. Don't want it to just be me havin a good Christmas cause I have a home to go to. Want them to have a nice Christmas too.

- ◆ -

The priest left. Thank God! Been driving him fucking nuts. At first Hazen was happy to see him, thought it would be nice. Have someone to talk to. A man of the cloth. A man of God. Someone who would understand why Hazen had to do what he did. Understand the ways of God. The demands of Him.

But this nebbish? No idea! None whatsoever! Don't

know what God he thinks he's talking to, but it sure as hell isn't Hazen's!

Was starting to really get on his nerves. Yammering, yammering, yammering. On and on and on with his drivel. An endless droning on, talking about some wimpy, wipe-ass version of God, simpering on about "redemption" and "forgiveness."

Fuck that! This man doesn't know God! Doesn't know what he's talking about! Fucking forgiveness? Please! God doesn't believe in *forgiveness*. He believes in brimstone, fire, vengeance, and absolute, total destruction! Jesus Christ, hasn't the guy even read the fucking Bible? It's full of mayhem and murder, floods and plagues. He even has a few messed-up dudes killing their own families, children. He asks them to do this, to show their faith! And they do.

And what about hell? What about that? The little pansy couldn't explain that away, no matter how many flowery words he used! No way! No way to misconstrue that one. Forgiveness? Come on! God has you descending to the fiery pits of hell for all eternity, for some minor mistake or another!

Fuck forgiveness! That's not God's way! Screw forgiveness! He's gonna kill the little slut. Kill the little two-faced bitch that got him into this mess in the first place. Kill her nice and slow.

Her first, and then Buddy. Wipe Buddy out too. Then deal with the mother. Wipe them all out. Clean slate. Do the world a favor.

Little ass-wipe doesn't know what he's talking about. Fuck forgiveness!

They're moving him this afternoon. The doctor's given the okay. So they're moving him from the hospital ward to the jail ward, and then to make it even more cozy, they're slapping him on the bus tomorrow, early to take him to the courthouse to be arraigned. Six forty-five in the morning! It's inhumane. Bad enough that they're incarcerating him, slamming him in a county jail for nothing. Absolutely nothing. Following his dick, that's probably the worst "crime" he committed. And hell, if they're gonna start locking people up for that, for falling in love with the wrong person, for trying to do good and save some kid. If they're gonna lock people up for that, well, just forget about it!

They're moving him to jail, and he's trying to be cool, but his damned hands got the shakes.

At least in the hospital, he could pretend things were status quo. Nothing out of the ordinary here, all hospitals feel like jail. What's the diff? But now, they're moving him. Messing him up just to think about it. Got the runs again. Got them bad.

It's not that he's scared. It's not that Hazen Wood is fucking scared, he's not. It's just that this is county jail, and if things don't go well in court, we're talking about jail, not some nursery school. Those guys aren't just gonna want to be sitting around doing watercolors and knitting. There's gonna be some seriously messed up dudes in there, and they aren't exactly gonna want to sit around doing the "hokeypokey."

Not just that, the prison part, who cares, that's not what bugs him. It's the unfairness of it. What ever happened to justice? What ever happened to "innocent until proven guilty"? Innocent! So how can they just lock him up like that? Where was his trial? Why wasn't he invited?

"You have to be arraigned," his lawyer said. "Then you can have your trial." Arraigned! What the hell is that? And what does that have to do with anything? No jury, no trial, no proof of anything, and yet, they're moving him to jail on the hearsay of some messed-up, demented twelve-year-old. A maximum security, lockdown prison. And the inept, dweeby, ass-wipe of an attorney that the courts have assigned him is a joke. The imbecile couldn't find his way out of a paper bag, let alone figure out a plausible defense.

Always fiddling with his papers, avoiding Hazen's eye. It's like he's scared of him or something.

"And you're going to help me?" Hazen had said. "You're like a bad joke." And the guy didn't even have the balls to get offended.

"You're entitled to your opinion," he'd sniffed, acting like Hazen's slug scum. Like just sitting with him in the same room is like sitting in a room full of vomit. Superior little shit!

"You're entitled to your opinion . . ."

That was it! That was his mighty comeback!

The asshole has no balls. No pizzazz. And this is what's supposed to win him his freedom? This is what's supposed to win Hazen Wood his God-given right to freedom?

He's gonna kill that slut. Just wait. She's dead.

- ◄ -

Been havin bad stomach cramps, so I can't seem to work at full capacity.

Tryin to make up for the trouble I've caused them. Heard them arguin last night. Not loud and angry like my mama and Buddy. Just quiet, low voices, but it was an argument just the same. And I think it was about me. Think maybe that's what's causin my stomach to hurt so bad.

Am worried that maybe Ms. Finnegan was right. Maybe havin me here and all, is just too much of a strain on them. Too much of a burden.

Wish I hadn't stole that money. Maybe that's what they're arguin about. Maybe they're wishin they never took me. Regrettin it. Tryin to figure out a way to send me back. Maybe they're tired of gettin no sleep at night, me with my stupid nightmares. I'm tryin not to have them. Tryin so hard, to be quiet, to clean, do chores, show them how good I can be, that I'm not just all bad news.

Trouble is, I just get started, tryin to clean, and the cramps, they double me over. And it's bad. Hurts bad, like a side ache, when you're running too fast, too long. But not just in one spot, not just below my rib cage on the right-hand side or anything like that. This is a big side ache, but not on my side. It's in my belly, low in my belly. Hurts bad. Real bad. Doublin me over, snatchin my breath. Hittin me every few minutes. Real bad, like I accidentally swallowed several fistfuls of broken, dirty glass.

I cover it up, try to breathe through it, act all natural. Don't want them to think I'm one trouble after another.

Sure hope I don't have cancer like my granddaddy. He was always doubled over too. It was always grabbin his breath away. Sure hope that's not what's goin on. It's makin me sweat too, these pains, just like my granddaddy. He was always sweatin. Kinda scared about it. Hope it's not cancer inside of me, gobblin me up. Kinda scared.

- ◆ -

It got bad, real bad! The cramps. Ran to the bathroom, right in the middle of moppin the kitchen floor. Wanted to get it done before Cindy got home from work. Wanted to surprise her.

Couldn't get it done, though. Couldn't get through it. Cramps were just gettin worse and worse. Ran to the bathroom. Thought maybe I had food poisonin or somethin. That maybe I could poop it out. But instead of poop, blood came out. First a little, then lots. A sploosh of it. Blood and gunk out of where I pee. Fillin up the toilet with blood.

It was like somebody had exploded a bomb inside me. And at that point, I was pretty sure I had cancer and it was just gobblin up my flesh, devourin me whole, rippin out my guts, and spittin up blood.

I remember callin out. I remember that. Callin out for Cindy, even though she wasn't home, blood everywhere. I remember that, but that's all, don't remember anything else, guess I fainted. Don't know, all the blood freaked me out, I guess. Don't know what happened next, don't remember.

On the toilet one minute, in the hospital the next.

- ◆ -

I had a miscarriage. That's what they call it. That's the name for when you lose your baby. Lose it, cause God decided that it wasn't the right time, the right circumstances for that baby to be born. That God had made a mistake, givin that baby to me. Made a mistake, even though he's God. And when he realized what he'd done, he fixed it. Decided that it was best for me and the baby, if he gave the baby to another family to raise. A family who wanted, and needed it. A family that wouldn't be complete without it. That's what Cindy said. That's what we talked about in the car, on the way home from the hospital.

So that's good, that's better for the baby. Real glad about it. No question, real glad. Just the same, felt funny too, didn't want the baby to feel like . . . I don't know, hard to put into words.

I guess, what I'm tryin to say is, I didn't want it, the baby, to feel bad, like I'm so *happy* it's dead. Like I hated it or anything. Like I didn't want it to have a chance at life. Didn't want it to think that. I was just worried, is all. That's why I'm glad it's gone. I was real worried about bein a mother, is all.

When we got home from the hospital, I went into my bathroom to see the miscarriage. Cindy said I should just go to bed, that she'd clean it up, but, I don't know, I just had to see for myself. Make sure it happened. And I was lookin in the toilet, the water all red from all my blood. And that's was I saw it, this little bloody lump of something, around the size of half of my thumb, the top half. A little smaller, but around that size, and I scooped it out, held it in my hand. It didn't look like a baby, just a little splodge of bloody, mushy stuff. Might not have been my baby, but just in case, I didn't want it to get flushed down the toilet like it's a piece of pooh.

It was different with Boxcar, she was a turtle, it was a good thing, cause if she was alive, she got to live in a lake.

And if she was dead, which she probably was, then at least the other turtles would have found her body when it arrived at the lake and given her a nice burial. But it wouldn't be a good thing for a baby, to get flushed down the toilet. Didn't feel right. Not for a baby.

Didn't know what to do with it, didn't want to drop it back in the toilet just in case. So I just stood there lookin at it, holdin it in my hand.

And then Cindy comes in. "What's goin on?" she says, cleanin supplies clunkin around in a bucket in her hand.

And I show her. "Do you think it's my baby?" I say.

"I don't know, sweetie, it could be." She puts her arm around me. "Are you okay?"

I nod, but I'm feelin kinda funny. Kinda mixed, holdin a little splodge in my hand that could have been my baby. Not that I wanted a baby, but I feel weird anyway. "What should I do with it?" I ask.

"I don't know . . . What do you want to do?"

"Maybe . . ." Feel kinda foolish, hope she doesn't laugh, think I'm ridiculous. "Maybe . . . I . . . should bury it . . . Just in case."

But she doesn't laugh at me, think I'm silly. Doesn't make fun of me. She gives me a little squeeze, like I did good, and says, "What a wonderful idea."

She finds a pretty scrap of fabric from her sewing basket, all pink and soft and cozy, and we wrap it in that like it's a little blanket. And I want to make a cross, so God will know where to come and pick up the baby's spirit to bring to the new family, so I get two little branches from the tree outside and we cut them to the right shape with scissors, and I fasten them tight with red yarn. I glue glitter and silver confetti stars to it, and it looks so pretty. And while I do it, make the preparations, I feel sad for the baby, but glad too. And my heart feels so full and heavy and light all at the same time.

When I've got everything ready, Cindy and Joseph say they'll come with me, but I don't know, I feel like it's somethin I need to do by myself. And they understand.

I go out by myself. It's dusk, shadowy, almost night, but not quite. I can still see.

I decide to plant her at the base of the oak tree in the back yard. The one I got the branches for her cross. Bury her among the roots.

The ground is real hard. Frozen, difficult to dig up with Cindy's tablespoon, have to chip away. Do it though, takes a long time, but I do it. Manage to make a big enough of a hole, then I put the baby, or at least, what I think might have been the baby in it. Place it in tenderly, stroke it with my finger. Real gently, cause it's so small, even with the blanket wrapped around it. Then I put a cherry lifesaver in that I'd been keepin in my pocket. I give it to her so she'll have a treat to nibble on while she waits for God.

Wish I had some flowers, but then, when I give it some thought, I realize that wouldn't have been good, cause I never would have been able to chip away a hole big enough to accommodate flowers. I would have been chippin away until May for sure.

And I wonder what they do, how they bury whole grown-up people when they die in the winter. Not so bad, in Oakland, but if you were plannin on dyin in Chicago, you just had better wait until spring. Until the ground had thawed. Better flowers then too. You'd get a way prettier funeral.

But I have no flowers, which is a blessin and a curse, but what can you do? Have no flowers, so I put the crumples of frozen dirt back on it, fingers, clumsy, numb with cold. Patted it down. Stick the cross in, but it keeps tippin over, finally I prop it up with three little rocks and that holds it pretty good.

I say a prayer. Thank God for my second chance, for givin my baby a second chance too. Ask him to find her a good family this time, a lovin family. A family like the Salyns. A family like that. And then I say, "Amen." And cross myself even though I'm not Catholic. I cross myself, cause it seems like the right thing to do.

Then, even though it's cold, dark outside. Moon disappearin in and out from behind clouds. And the wind blowin chills through my body, makin it rattle and shake, whippin my hair, snake like, across my face, into my mouth, makin me make little *plah* noises spittin it back out. Even though it's cold, the wind whirlin in off the lake, freezin me to the bone. The clouds, flyin fast, like a witch on a broom, thick veined clouds, so that at times, even with the moon behind them, you can still see the glow shimmerin through parts of it, and blackness through the rest. And so, even though it's this kind of night, I lie down on my back on the hard frozen ground, lie down beside my baby's grave and we look up at the sky. The old oak tree's arms makin black lace patterns overhead.

We look up at the clouds, the moon, glidin across the night sky, the occasional star, winkin in and out, playin hide-and-seek. We look up at the beautiful sky and breathe in long. Cold air, searin the lungs. Breathe in long, and deep. Full of thanksgivin.

And later, when I go back inside, all hunched over and shiverin from the cold, Cindy makes me a pot of tea. Constant Comment tea. And I drink it with her, put milk and sugar in it. We drink it out of Christmas mugs, mine has a smilin snowman with a carrot nose that bumps into my chin if I'm not careful. And the hot tea feels good, comfortin, cupped in my hands, warm wet steam envelopin my face when I tip my head to take a sip. It feels good to sit there and talk with Cindy like I'm a grown-up.

We talk about God, his wisdom, his goodness, and that maybe he gave the baby to another family, but maybe he saved it too. Maybe he decided to save it for me, for a later date, when I'm big. When I'm grown.

That's one of the things Cindy says. That's one of the things we talk about, sittin at the kitchen table, sippin tea, nibblin on Scotch shortbread.

And now, lyin here in bed, snug, warm in my bed, the chill gone from my bones. Lyin here thinkin over everything we talked about, I feel so much better. Cause you know, I was kinda worried that maybe I'd killed the baby with all of my bad feelins.

But she says I didn't.

I'm so relieved! I can't even tell you! Didn't have to have a baby! Didn't have to get an abortion! Can't tell you what a relief! I was so worried about that baby. If I was gonna be a good parent? How I was gonna take care of it? Feed it? If I was gonna be able to still get an education? Doubted it. Especially with my mama kickin me out. Didn't know how I was gonna manage. Couldn't work, couldn't legally get a job until I turned fifteen, almost three years away! That's what the girls in the home said. So how was I gonna support it?

I gotta tell you, it gave me a lot of sleepless nights. Worryin, worryin about that baby.

But now? It's like God has given me a second chance at life. Like God still loves me, hasn't given up on me! It's like God has said, "Here, Gemma, another chance. Don't screw up!"

And I won't! I'm gonna go to school! I'm gonna work so hard! I'm gonna get straight As. I'm gonna try to be a good person, and help other people. Gonna try to be like Cindy. Good like that! A kind sort of person. One that does good in the world.

God has given me a second chance and I'm not gonna mess up! I swear it! I swear it on all that is holy! You'll see! I'm gonna do big things with my life.

·—▶·

That was a total waste of a day. Started off bad and didn't get better. Waiting around to get his day in court, locked in a cramped holding cell like he's a rabid animal. And then when they finally got before the judge, Hazen's "attorney," *Mister* Partap, didn't do anything. Just rustled through his disorganized reams of paper he carries around in that beat-up briefcase of his, and that's another thing, he should get a new briefcase, because that one, frankly, is an embarrassment. It's beat up, tired out, and inspires no confidence whatsoever. Got his lunch in there, for Christsake! No kidding. Hazen saw it with his own two eyes. Fucking squashed egg salad sandwich wrapped in Saran wrap rolling around with the paperwork. And Hazen's sitting there thinking, "This is my attorney? This is what's gonna make the difference between prison or walking free?" And he wanted to reach over and pop the guy. Would have if they weren't in court.

Partap wanted him to plead guilty! Said he might be able to get him a shorter sentence.

Needless to say, Hazen told him where to shove it!

"Not guilty, your honor!" Hazen said. Threw the "your honor" in, Partap hadn't told him to say that. But Hazen, he's smart, he knows how the game's played. Figured it was a good touch, soften the judge up, show him a little respect, no criminal here. Gave him a little smile, like they were at a Sunday barbeque, a baseball game, passing on the street in front of the pharmacy. That kind of smile. But the guy's obviously not very sociable, didn't smile back, just looked down at his papers, tapped his right forefinger on his desk a few times and then set the trial for February first, provided there's a courtroom available. February first! Fifty days away!

"Do you mean to tell me that I have to stay in that county jail for fifty goddamned days!"

"That's about it," Partap said, packing up his briefcase. "Unless you or your family can come up with the five hundred grand." Superior snot-faced shit. Five hundred thousand dollars bail! Who the hell's got money like that?

— ◆ —

Guess what? Another good thing happened. I made a mistake! Cindy hadn't just signed me out for the holidays. She'd signed me out for good! I get to stay for as long as I want!

Forever if I want, until I'm all grown up! That's what she said! And you know the funny thing. I'm happy, right, I'm so, so happy, and yet I was bawlin like a baby when I found out . . . I just started bawlin. Jumpin up and down, smilin so big, bawlin like a baby. And Cindy, she started cryin too, and we're huggin each other. It was great! It was just great! I get to stay forever. They want me to stay forever. And not just Cindy, Joseph too.

I know that, cause I asked. Did it when Cindy was gone, so he wouldn't feel the pressure, like he had to be nice or polite or anything. Told him I understood that takin on an almost teen, someone who's had some challenges, is past the sell-by date, isn't what most people would want to do. Told him I understood if he didn't want me to stay, no worries. Not to feel bad. That I wouldn't tell Cindy, I'd just go away, make a life on my own, would be fine. Lived on the streets before, it's not like I'm a baby, can't take care of myself, so no obligation. That's what I told him. All of it comin out faster than I'd practiced in my room. Just came out, a rush of words, like a water balloon hittin the pavement.

He seemed kind of startled at first, looked around, like he was hopin Cindy was still here, and I was talkin to her. Cause he's kinda quiet, lets her do most of the talkin. But I wasn't talkin to her, I was talkin to him. She was long gone.

"Oh . . . um . . ." He cleared his throat, tipped his head down so he was lookin at me over the top of his readin glasses. "It's . . . It's fine by me," he said. "I'm . . . I'm happy for you to stay."

That's what he said! "I'm *happy* for you to *stay*." Those were his very words! Can you *believe* it? It's so great!

And the weird thing is, I had *no* idea they were gonna be my foster parents! None! Just thought it was for the holidays! Thought they were bein charitable, had no idea that they *wanted* me! That they chose me out of all the boys and girls in the whole world that needed, wanted a home. They *chose* me! And not only that, I was *past the age*! I was *pregnant*! And *still* they wanted me!

Makes me feel all humble, and good, like I got a belly full of warm cocoa.

I didn't really realize it, but after he said that, the "I'm *happy* for you to *stay*," I was just standin there beamin at him. Wearin the biggest damned smile.

"Well . . . ah . . ." Joseph cleared his throat again, looked embarrassed. "So . . . ah . . . anything else?"

"No," I said. "Nothing else." And I went to my room so he wouldn't think I wanted more flattery. Gotta say, though. Sure made me happy. Glad I screwed up my courage to ask him. Lay on my bed, lookin up at the ceilin for a long time after our talk. Lyin on my bed, with its ruffled girly bedspread, thinkin over his words. Playin them over and over in my mind. Say them out loud, softly so he won't hear me, but loud enough so I can hear them again, dance around, fill the room.

And you know the coolest thing of all? I've been here for almost two weeks, and he hasn't tried to touch me once. No once! Not my top, or my butt or nothin! Hasn't tried to stick anything in me either, nothin!

Just nice. Nice and kind. And he's always losin his glasses. It's funny. He's always misplacin them and I help him find them, cause he's a bit absentminded, like a befuddled professor, or an eccentric scientist. Bumblin around, always readin, has zillions of books, and he doesn't mind if I read them. "Go ahead," he says, wavin his hand toward the bookshelf. "Be my guest, help yourself. Books are for everyone to enjoy. Think they get lonely if they aren't shared." Says things like that. Cozy things.

And so I read them. Wash my hands before I get one down, treat it with care. Let him know, see that I appreciate it. And we spend the days like that. Readin. Him in his armchair, me, curled up on the sofa like a cat.

And around midday, I get up, stretch, make us some lunch, cause when he's readin or caught up in his research, he has no idea of time. Would probably starve durin the day if it wasn't for me. Doesn't even know he's hungry until I put it right before his nose. And then, he mumbles, "Thank you, dear . . ." He calls me "dear." Like I'm dear to him. Makes me feel good. "Thank you, dear," he says, and then he eats, eyes still buried in his work, nibblin from the outside in, tiny little bites, turnin his sandwich round and around like a little mouse. Doesn't eat this way at dinner, when he's not workin. Don't think he's aware of it. That he eats this way when he's thinkin. It's funny, endearin. I turn away so he won't see me smile, get self-conscious.

And sometimes, it's really funny. You know how I help him find his glasses. Well, yesterday, he thought he'd lost them. "Where in the tarnation are my darned glasses?"

He says these made-up swear words cause he's tryin to be a good role model. Tryin not to swear around me. That makes me smile too. Him and Cindy, tryin so hard not to swear, cause they have no idea! Really, they have no idea, the kind of words I know.

It makes me smile at night, thinkin it over as I lie in my

bed, them goin through all that trouble to not say words I've heard, said myself, a million times. All this effort to protect my delicate ears. But it's funny. It kind of rubs off, cause now I'm tryin not to swear too. I figure if they can do it, so can I. And you know what? I think it's a good habit to get into. Cause you really don't hear fancy people cursin up a blue storm.

So anyway, he was sayin, "Where in the tarnation are my darned glasses?" Gettin all frustrated, and I looked up from my book and guess where they were? He thought they were lost, lookin all over for them, and they were stickin right out the front pocket on his shirt! They were right there, waitin patiently. We sure had a good laugh about that one. Told Cindy when she got home, and she laughed too.

"Good thing you're here, Gemma," she said. "It's a good thing you're here." And she ruffled my hair, her smile beamin down on me like warm toast and jelly.

· ◄ ·

He's in isolation. They put him, an innocent man, not only in jail, but in fucking isolation! Like he's some kind of freak. Wearing some pansy orange jumpsuit. An orange jump-suit, so everyone in the whole county jail thinks he's a freak. A faggot, some sort of sexual deviant.

It's an outrage! He pays his taxes! He pays his dues! And for them to throw him in here, on circumstantial evidence. On some hearsay by a demented twelve-year-old . . . It's an outrage!

He's gonna find out, he's gonna find out who the sena-tor is. Who the damned senator of the state of Illinois is!

Give him a piece of Hazen Wood's mind! How dare they? Locking up innocent men. Incarcerating peace-loving, law-abiding, men! Find out who the senator is. Give him a piece of his mind. Tell him he'd better change his policy or he'll be losing Hazen Wood's vote. Better look into this outrage they call the penal system!

It's inhuman! Locking him up like an animal. Fucking eight-by-ten cell. Minuscule TV, no cable! Hard mattress! Food sucks! Tastes like somebody crapped it out and dished it up. Damned well sucks! Gonna be a skeleton by the time he clears this mess up. Gets out of this freak house.

And to top it all off, the straw that's breaking the camel's back. They've stuck him in an orange jumpsuit! Why the fuck did they have to do that? Should be in blue, like the rest of the population! Should be able to go out in the yard, with the rest of them. But no. He's stuck in his cell all day. No one to talk to. Can drive a man mad. Stuck in the silence of his own brain. Too much time to think.

"For your own safety," they'd said.

His own safety? He's stuck in here with a bunch of perverts! A bunch of faggots and freaks! Makes him sick just to look at them.

Told his lawyer that they'd made a mistake. Put him in the wrong jumpsuit, have him segregated, isolated. Told his lawyer that, and the asshole just laughed. First time Hazen had ever seen him so much as smile.

"What's so funny?" Hazen demanded.

But it didn't deter him. Mr. Partap, Mr. Richard-tight-ass-Partap just kept laughing, swiped at his eyes behind his Coke bottle glasses.

"That would be good," he said. "That would be good. I'd like to see that. Throw you in there with the general population."

"Yeah," said Hazen. "I want a blue jumpsuit like everyone else."

But the Partap putz isn't listening, he's back rustling through his papers. Ignoring him. The asshole's ignoring him.

So Hazen slams his fist down on the table. Slams it down hard. Makes Partap jump.

"Did you hear me? I *want* a blue jumpsuit. If I gonna be stuck in here, due to *your* incompetence, at least I should be dressed in the appropriate color."

But Partap, just looks at him, over the top of his papers. "Don't be an idiot," he says, face tired, bored. "They'd eat you for lunch."

· — ·

We put up the Christmas tree. A real one. We bought it at a Christmas tree lot. They had tons of trees. Millions of them. And we stomped around in our boots and winter coats . . . Did I tell you I have a winter coat? Yeah, I got one. Cindy's sister gave us one. Gave us a whole bunch of clothes. She has a daughter who's eleven, one year younger, but she's taller, bigger than me, on account of my bein so small for my age and everything. Anyway, Cindy's sister Camille had a bunch of extra clothes lyin around. Her daughter had just gone through a growth spurt, couldn't wear them anymore, didn't fit. And some of these clothes, almost brand-spankin-new! Beautiful too! Fashionable!

It's a weird feelin actually, cause I love these clothes, and want to show them off, but I'm kinda nervous about goin to school here. Don't know what I'm gonna be walkin into. Kids might not like me, I sound different, have a different accent from the people around here. They might think I'm weird, odd. Might gang up on me, like the kids at my old school did on José. Don't know.

But maybe, wearin these fashionable clothes, maybe they'll give me a chance. Think I'm normal, one of them.

Been tryin on outfits the last few days. Tryin to decide what to wear the first day of school. Lookin in the mirror. Lookin hard. Studyin myself real close, right up bright light harsh. Lookin so my nose is almost up against the mirror, foggin it up, and even lookin that close, that careful, lookin for any trace ... I gotta say, other than my dumb hair, and a few little belt buckle scars you can barely see, could be chickenpox scars for all anybody would know. Lookin up close ... I don't think, and I could be wrong, but I don't think there's any way anybody could tell, by just lookin at me, about all my troubles.

Unless, of course, they saw one of those stupid missin child posters. Unless they saw one of those. Paid attention.

I hope not. I really, really hope not.

Maybe Cindy would let me change my name. If I changed my name they wouldn't know it was me. Maybe that would help.

Hope nobody's seen the posters. That would suck, That would not be good.

Too bad I like learnin so much. Otherwise, no problem,

someone recognizes me, figures it out, no problem, just quit school, walk out the front door and never come back. Walk out, hit the road, sayonara, baby.

But I can't. Even if someone figures it out, things get tough. Gotta stick it out. Got my plan. Promised God, promised myself. Have been given a second chance. Gonna make somethin of my life. Gonna get a higher education. Gonna go to college. And if I'm gonna do that, I gotta work hard, get a scholarship. Gotta get straight A's. Can't expect Cindy and Joseph to pay for everything. I'm already a strain, a financial strain, not that they'd admit it, but I know about these things.

So it's kind of a mix of feelins. I'm scared to start school, but I also can't wait. Good or bad, I just want to get started. This not knowin how it's gonna be is gettin to me big time.

Tryin not to be negative, to think positive. "Yay!" I say to myself. "I get to go to school here. Wear my new clothes. Make lots of friends. Get to work on my plan!"

That's what I tell myself. Do a pretty good job. Sometimes I actually convince myself. Can't wait to get started, like those racehorses on TV. You know, all stompy and snorty, kickin at the stall door, the little latch door that needs to be lifted before they can bolt out, run like the wind. That's me. Chompin at the bit, ready to go. Not kickin at the stall, though! Not doin that!

Yeah, sometimes I get like that. Excited, like school, life, everything's gonna be good now. And then other times, I want time to stop, slow down. Don't want to have to deal with the future. Just want to stay here, happy and safe. Don't want to go to school, leave Joseph and Cindy. Just want it to stay Christmas forever.

Anyway, enough about that. Let me tell you about the tree. We got a beautiful Christmas tree. Must have looked at about a hundred trees for sure. Pullin 'em up, turnin them this way and that. Noses red, fingers, toes goin numb. Feet stompin. "Feels like snow." Everyone's sayin it. "Feels like snow."

And I stomped my feet too. Slapped my hands together. Said, "Feels like snow," too. Just like an old pro. "Feels like snow. Uh huh. Yep, feels just like snow."

Said it to everyone I met, so they'd know I live here. So they'd think I'm an old pro with this snow stuff, this weather. "Feels like snow," face matter of fact, knowledgeable, like snow's just a matter of time. Everyone was sayin it now! Everyone! So snow must be comin! And even though I act all casual, the fact is, I can barely sleep with the excitement of it.

We looked at lots and lots of trees. Tested them out, buried out faces in them, breathin in their scent. We looked at hundreds of trees and then we found it. Actually, I was the one who first discovered it, but I'm sayin "we," cause I don't want to brag.

We found the most beautiful Christmas tree any of us have ever seen! It was just the right size, shape. Had just the right feel, smell. But, most importantly of all, it had that Christmas magical feelin that only special Christmas trees have. That feelin that just calls to you, swirls around you, promisin miracles and happiness and happy-ever-afters. And this tree we found . . . *It had it all!*

So naturally, we bought it right there on the spot. Bought it, brought it home, tied it to the top of our car. Had to leave the car windows open a crack for the rope to go through. Tied it down good. Then Joseph drove us home, nice and slow, so the tree wouldn't fall off. And once we got it inside, set it up, we decorated it to kingdom come!

Partap is gone. Mr. Richard Pompous-Ass Partap is officially gone. "A family emergency . . ." Hazen was told. "A death in the family . . ."

Bullshit! He's gone cause Hazen got rid of him, plain and simple. He told that "Mr. Richard Partap." Hazen Wood told that idiot. Showed him who was boss. Made him sit up and take notice. Partap may have thought he was just dealing with another shmoe, but he had another think coming. Thought he'd get Hazen to agree to waive his right to a "speedy" trial. Like who the hell are they kidding? Fifty days in jail? Not to mention all the time he spent in their hospital bed, recuperating from the goddamned bullet holes Chicago's finest blasted into him, with no just cause.

"You . . . want me . . . to sign this?" said Hazen, being oh-so-civil. "And why, might I ask?"

"We want to wait, put the trial off as long as possible . . ." Partap would have kept talking, blathering on. Pontificating fool. Would have kept talking, but Hazen, he wasn't feeling in a listening mood. Had listened and listened. And for what? To what end? To end up rotting his life away in jail?

"Wait. Back up a minute." And the guy, the poor putz,

he actually flinched at Hazen's tone. Must have known then something was coming.

Hazen spoke slow, distinct. "Let me get this straight. You want to *wait*? Put it off as *long as possible*? You want to play casual with my life?"

"Listen. It's in your best interest—"

"Fuck you!"

"Look, you go to trial now, you've haven't got a shot in hell. The kid's holed up with Detective Salyn and she's not going anywhere. They've got DNA. Granted, it's not conclusive, but they've got it. They've got witnesses. And they've got the kid. And what do I have? What do I have to work with? I've got you. An asshole who not only *did* everything he's accused of, but he actually doesn't have a problem with it. That's what I've got. And I'm supposed to try and get you off? I hate my job!"

At first Hazen was stunned by the ferocity of Partap's outburst. Didn't think he had it in him, just sat there, looking at him.

"Wow," Hazen said, cause what the hell could he say? The guy's flipping on him.

They sat there for a bit more, nobody talking, and just when Hazen was starting to feel a modicum of respect for the guy, Partap apologizes.

"Look, I'm sorry, I was out of line. The baby was up all night. Colic." Partap massaging his temples, forehead like he had a headache coming on. And that's all well and fine, but they need to get down to work, figure out a strategy.

"That's okay," Hazen said, being generous, getting the ball moving. "That's okay, man. Look, that's something we have in common, I'm gonna be a father too. And that's why it's real important I get out, see. Got family to attend to."

But the personal touch wasn't working. Partap looked like he just took a slug of sour milk.

"Whatever . . ." he said. "The thing is, the best thing to do is stall. Hope Salyn gets tired of the kid, sends her back to Oakland. Gotta try to draw it out, maybe their witnesses will die or forget. If we really get lucky they'll lose the DNA. Don't count on it though. What we're waiting for is a shot in the dark."

"Uh huh," said Hazen, and he was trying to be calm, keep on track, but it wasn't working. He could feel his neck going red. Felt the rage building up. Partap playing God with his life. "I see. You want to wait. You want to wait for a 'shot in the dark.' That's what you want to hinge your defense on?"

And when Partap's Adam's apple bobbed in his scrawny little neck, and he started nodding his stupid gargantuan turnip head, like that was a reasonable plan, something in Hazen just snapped. "A *shot* in the dark? *Are* you out of your fucking *skull*? *Jesus Christ!* You don't give a *crap* about *me!* My *life.* You just want me to *sit here*, twiddling my thumbs, *rotting* my life away, sit here, waiting for a '*shot in the dark*'? I don't think so!"

And Partap wanted to speak, Hazen could see that. Opened his mouth to, but Hazen came down on him like a fist of fire. A fucking fist of fire. Grabbed him by his little pansy button-down shirt. His Brooks Brothers cheap imitation pinstripe shirt.

"Now you *listen* to me. I've been reading up. Yeah, that's right. I *can* read. And I know my rights. I know my rights, *asshole.* Now I've tried with you. I've tried to be patient. I've been a saint. But no more. I want my trial. I demand my right, as an American citizen, my right to a speedy trial. Do you know what that means? Huh? Do you? That means no, I will not, I will *never* waive my rights to a speedy trial! You got that? You *got* that, *asshole*?" And by that time Hazen was shaking him. Shaking him like a scarecrow. And the guard had to come in, drag him off. "You got that! You *got* that, asshole! No way in *hell* I'm *waiving* my rights!" And then Hazen couldn't see Partap anymore, cause the door had swung shut, two more guards had arrived and had wrestled Hazen to the ground.

So that's the true story. That's the real one. Not some "family emergency." Partap's "mother" didn't have a "heart attack." The wuss was scared of him plain and simple. And even better than that, the new guy, Partap's replacement, he's sharp. He's real sharp. Not some sad sack court-appointed attorney. No way, not for Hazen Wood, he's the man. And apparently he's got, according to the guys on his cell block, one of the best, one of the finest lawyers in the country. Mr. Samuel Levy, that's his name. A Jew, not that it bothers Hazen one bit. He's not prejudiced, hell no. He'll take a Jew any day of the week, not to dinner mind you, but as a lawyer, they're the best. Smart, sneaky, wily, little bastards.

What happened is, this Levy guy apparently had been following Hazen's case on the news and decided, on a whim, to take him on.

"What about payment?" Hazen had asked him. "I'm broke, you know . . ."

"Don't worry," Levy had said, his hand waving away

the question like it was no big deal. "We'll work something out." That's the kind of man Mr. Levy is. A class act, even though he's a Jew. A triple A class act.

- ◆ -

Cindy got a phone call from the station. Had her all worked up. Slammin the pots, the cupboard doors all around the kitchen. Joseph said it was best not to go in when she was like that. "Just give her ten minutes and she'll calm down." He said. So I didn't go in, stayed where I was, sittin in the livin room. Just sat there, pretendin to read my book, watchin the clock they got on the mantlepiece out of the corner of my eye. And ten minutes came and went, and she was still bangin, so Joseph went in. She was mad, I could tell, was tryin to keep her voice down but it was risin just the same. She was yellin about a Samuel Levy, and swearin, and sayin things like "blood-sucking, ambulance chaser," and "Why . . . why . . . why!" And I could hear Joseph's voice, calmer, soothin, couldn't hear everything, just a few words here and there, floatin to me, like "TV" and "publicity" and "It's not the end of the world." And when he said that, Cindy started yellin again about "You don't know!" And "This guy is good! Really, really good!" And goin on about all the cases that he's won. And then all of a sudden she started cryin, soft, like she's tryin to hold it in. I wanted to go in and comfort her, but I didn't want to intrude, cause maybe she would have been embarrassed me seein her like that. So I just stayed on the sofa, like I was a mummy, not movin, barely breathin, and I could hear her sayin, voice all choked up with tears, "It's not fair . . . It's just not fair . . ."

- ◆ -

The nightmares keep comin. Can't seem to get rid of them. Keep vistin me every night.

Gotten so bad that I'm nervous about goin to sleep. I like my bedroom durin the day. It's all cozy and pretty and homey. But when it starts to get dark, I find all kinds of excuses not to be in there. Readin a book, comfy on the sofa, drinkin tea in the kitchen, want to watch TV, doesn't matter what. Well, actually, that's not true. Don't want to watch anything scary. Can't. Makes me too nervous. Nothin with killin in it, or shootin or people bein mean. Even hokey shootin shows, like John Wayne, cowboys and Indians. Can't even watch those. Get too scared. Only seem to be able to watch happy things. Happy-ever-after shows.

And you know, honestly, even if I could watch them, James Bond and things like that. Even if they didn't make me so scared, I wouldn't. And that's the truth! I mean sheesh! Why would I do that? Pay good money to get scared? That's the stupidest thing I ever heard of! Life's scary enough. And when life's not bein scary, my imagination is scarin the crap . . . I mean . . . ahem . . . the "heck" outta me!

Bein scared, I'm sorry, but that's just not my idea of a good time!

Nightmares comin back, night after night. Wake up screamin, and Cindy comes in, comforts me, strokes my head until I go back to sleep. I'm glad she does, chases the night terrors away, but, I feel bad too. She doesn't complain, but I know I'm tirin her out, cause in the mornin, Cindy's shoulders are slumped down, and her head is practically buried in her coffee cup. She wasn't wakin up like that when I first moved in. Now when she gets her body up, goes to the sideboard to refill her mug, her legs are movin so slow, like she's havin to push her body through invisible sludge. Movin her way around the kitchen. Dark shadows under her eyes.

Wish I could get on top of it. Stop keepin her awake with my tomfoolery. Wish I didn't have such bad nightmares comin to me in my sleep.

And when I'm not dreamin about him, about Hazen Wood. When I'm not havin nightmares about him, then I'm dreamin about my mom. Dreamin about her shape-shiftin, comin back to get me. At first I'm happy, so happy to see her. And then she shape-shifts, shape-shifts into a monster, and she's tryin to kill me. And I can't fight, and I can't move, and I have to kill her or I'll be killed myself, but I can't. I can't. It's like I'm petrified, like I'm petrified rock and everything in me is yellin "RUN! SAVE YOURSELF!" But I can't move. Can't run. Am tryin to call out, but it's like my vocal cords are underwater, in slow motion. And I'm tryin to move my mouth to make noises, to let her know that it's me! Her daughter! But it's not workin and she's laughin and laughin, head tossed so far back I can see all the metal fillings in her teeth. And she's got a big knife and laughin like it's real funny and stabbin this huge bloody knife down at me.

And then I wake up. At that moment, I always wake up, and my face is all wet from cryin and my heart is makin my body rock cause it's beatin so hard.

That's the moment that I wake up, right before the knife slashes through my forehead.

I hate those dreams.

And it's like, when it starts, when those dreams start, it's like your brain remembers it from before. Starts out normal enough, my mom comes into my room to ask me somethin. Starts out normal enough, but your brain remembers, doesn't remember quite what, but it remembers, and your stomach drops and your mouth has that metallic feelin like you've been suckin on a handful of change. Your heart starts racin and you have that trapped feelin like you're in a runaway car that's headin straight for a brick wall and there is nothin you can do about it.

Hate those dreams. But at least I don't wake up screamin, callin out, from my mom dreams. At least I don't wake up the whole house with those dreams like I do with the Hazen dreams. The trunk dreams. At least I don't do that.

Just lie there, heart poundin, still cryin. And then I start thinkin about my mom. My real mom, not the shape-shiftin one. Wonderin if she misses me. Worryin that she's gonna come get me. A part of me, wishin she would. Wantin her to want me again. Or at least call me once in a while, make sure I'm okay, act like she cares. Not that I'd go with her ... At least, I don't think I would. But I want her to want me. Want me just a little. Want her to wish she hadn't been so mean, leavin me here, losin her rights. Want, wish, she'd have just a little bit of regret.

And sometimes, when I can't shake the dream, can't shake it, her tryin to kill me, wantin me dead, I turn on all the lights. Walk around the room. Walk quiet so I won't wake anybody up. Walk around, blanket wrapped around me, cause they turn the heat down at night to save electricity.

I try to outwalk the dream. And sometimes it works and after an hour or two, I can crawl back to bed, go to sleep.

But sometimes it doesn't. Just doesn't work, outwalkin it, and then I have to keep all the lights on and do somethin else. So I write.

I write poetry now. I haven't told anyone. Keepin it secret. Started that night I had the miscarriage. Didn't know it was gonna be a poem. Just started writin and it helped, felt good, came out as a poem. Don't know if it's any good, my poetry. Just know that I need to write it. Write about things. It releases things somehow. To write it.

So sometimes, if the dreams won't go away, and walkin won't work, I just get out my pen, get out my paper, and I write. Just keep scribblin until mornin light starts to come up, just a hint, scarin away the blackness. And then, when I see the light start to change, the first tinges of gray creepin in, it's like all of a sudden, my body gets heavy, my eyes get tired, and I crawl back into bed and go to sleep.

— • —

Detective Sheffman's here, at the house. We weren't expectin her. In the middle of dinner, when her car drove up. Doesn't seem to be a social call, her wearin her suit and all. Not here to see me, though. Doesn't seem to be here to see me, to ask me more questions about Hazen, about Buddy.

"Cindy, I need to talk to you," she said as she banged through the kitchen door. No "Hello." No "Oh, what are you eating? Can I have some?" Didn't even seem to notice the food. "I need to talk to you," she said to Cindy, face like a brick wall. "You too, Joe."

They got up, no questions, me sittin there at the table, chicken leg stickin out of my fist like a question mark.

They filed out, moved out, like it was a dance or somethin, no need for words, everybody knowin the steps but me. Out they went, food left on their plates to get cold, mine too, appetite gone.

When I first saw Detective Sheffman drivin up the drive, I thought that she was here to see me, being the investigatin officer on my case and everybody bein so tense about this new Levy guy. Thought she was here to talk to me some more. But she wasn't.

She's holed up with Cindy and Joseph in his study. They're talkin real low, so even with my good ears, even though I'm sittin real quiet in the kitchen, which is right next door to Joseph's study, sittin real still, eardrums turned on high, I can't hear a word they're sayin. Just a low murmur. That's all I can hear. Different tones, I can make out Joseph's rumble, Cindy's voice, Detective Sheffman's. But no words, like writin on a chalkboard when you rub your forearm over them, you can see that they were words, you can see that, they're just too blurry to make out. That's the way they sound, blurry words, impossible to make out.

I just listen to the rise and the fall of them. Hopin the words aren't about me, knowin they probably are. Somethin bad about me, somethin I've done wrong. Don't know what, but I know it's somethin bad. And there's nothin I can do about it, no way to defend, explain, whatever it is. They're in there, I'm out here. All I can do is hope. Fingers crossed, toes crossed, legs and arms crossed. Hopin, talkin to God. Prayin they aren't sendin me back . . . tired of me . . . Too much trouble. Prayin hard.

And then, in the middle of all that prayin I hear the study door open, and I uncross everything real fast and act like I'm still eatin my dinner.

"Gemma . . ." I hear, and I look up. Cindy is in the kitchen doorway, brow furrowed, face drawn. "Gemma honey, Bonnie . . ." She pauses, glances around, like she's tryin to settle herself by lookin at solid things, tangible things, the refrigerator, the stove, the sink. Only for a moment and then she looks back at me, "Ah . . . we'd like to talk with you, honey."

I put my chicken leg back on my plate, wipe my hands on the napkin, get up from the table, walk toward her in the doorway, slip myself under her arm. Into the crook of her arm, like she's a mother bird and I'm her baby robin. All safe and protected. I feel her stiff body soften, and we walk like that, her arm around me, back to the study.

Joseph's at his desk, his hair, rumpled, like he's been runnin a hurricane through it. "Hello, dear," he says, he tries to smile, but his mouth won't cooperate.

Detective Sheffman is standin in front of the empty fireplace. Hands behind her back, like she's warmin herself, like she hasn't realized there's nothin in there.

"Gemma," she says. I'm used to her voice. When I first met her, she scared me, was so abrupt, brusque, so different from Cindy. But now I'm used to it. Don't take it personally. It's just her way. "We were having a discussion and weren't sure what we should do. Sit down," she waves at the sofa. "No need to stand, this might take a while."

I sit on the sofa. Cindy perches on the arm of it. Doesn't look comfortable, looks nervous, as if she might take flight at any moment. I want to tell her it's all right. But I don't know if it is, so I don't do anything. Just sit there. "Any-way," continues Detective Sheffman, "we decided, since it involves you, that it is only fair we let you in on it. And ultimately, let you make the decision as to how you want to proceed."

The room's quiet, the clock's tickin. The house shifts, creaks.

"Okay . . ." I say, nod my head.

There's a pause. Like everybody's holdin their breath. Then Cindy clears out the silence. Her voice perfectly calm, matter of fact. Like if I wasn't lookin at her hands, givin her away, I would have thought she was talkin about some-thin unimportant, like whether Tide or Cheer cleans clothes better.

"Your mother called the police station, Gemma. She was trying to get ahold of you."

"She has no rights," Detective Sheffman cuts in. "It is totally up to you if you want to talk to her."

Cindy continues, as if Detective Sheffman hadn't spo-ken. "She asked where you were."

"We didn't tell her," Detective Sheffman again.

"What . . . what does she want?" I say, playin for time. Cause I know what she wants. My belly knows. Feel like I'm wrapped in cotton gauze. Layers and layers of cotton gauze. The kind they use for operations and injuries to soak up the blood. So removed from myself, my mouth, my body. Like I'm sittin up in the corner of the ceilin watchin myself on the sofa be calm and rational and ask questions.

"What does she want?" my mouth says.

"She wants you to come home." Cindy again, eyes, face, worried.

"You don't have to." Detective Sheffman's voice is brusque, almost angry. "It's totally up to you. Don't even have to talk to her if you don't want to. She has no rights whatsoever. The courts have taken away all rights she had over you when she walked out that door and stranded you here in Chicago."

And I'm hearin everything, with that faraway noise, like I'm listenin through a keyhole.

"Is Buddy still there?" I hear myself ask.

I see Cindy nod. Eyes watchin me, sad, dark.

Detective Sheffman snorts. "Yeah. He wants you home too." She looks at Cindy, jaw set, like she'd like to punch Buddy on the nose. Like she knows about Buddy too, even though I still haven't spoken a word about him to anybody.

And the image of that, Detective Sheffman sluggin Buddy with his big beer belly, sluggin someone she's never even met. Walkin up to him, "Hi, how do you do? I'm Detective Sheffman," and then *Pow!* Smacko on the nose! Right on the old noggin! And the image of that, cause Detective Sheffman looks real powerful, even if she's a woman. She's all muscles and might. And Buddy . . . Well, let me put it this way . . . Buddy is kinda soft. Squishy, like uncooked bread dough. Soft and clammy.

And the image of that, him goin "Ooff!" Flyin backwards, clutchin his nose. Well, it has me bustin up. Bustin up laughin, even though I know I shouldn't. Know this is serious. Know this is absolutely no time for laughin, But I can't help it, it's bubblin, burblin, tumblin outta me. Won't stop. And they're lookin at me, seem shocked, like they don't understand, can't figure out why I'm laughin. And I want to stop, but I just can't help it.

"I'm . . . sorry . . ." I'm sayin, chokin on spit, on words, on laughter. "I'm so . . . sorry . . ." But even though I'm sorry, the laughter won't stop. Laughin so hard that it hurts bad, like someone is poundin me hard in the gut, over and over, poundin into me like the butt of a machine gun. It's that kind of laughter. The outta control, hurtin kind, and the tears are comin too. "I'm sorry . . . I'm sorry I'm . . . laughin . . . I'm sorry . . ."

Cindy gets up, wraps her arms around me, holds me. "It's okay," she says, to each of my "I'm sorry's."

"It's okay . . . It's okay . . . Gemma. I'm right here . . . I'm right here . . . Don't worry, you're safe . . ."

She holds me until the laughter stops and it's just cryin.

And after that, she still holds me. Takes me onto her lap, even though I'm big. Wipes away my tears, her hand smooths the hair outta my face, while Detective Sheffman and Joseph clean up in the kitchen.

And when I can finally get words out, I tell her about Buddy, my promise to my mom, how my mama knew about Buddy, the things that he did. And when I tell her all this, I start cryin again and she holds me. And by the end of my story, she's cryin too.

· — ·

All cried out. Tired of cryin. Tired of all this sadness and tears. Said good night, off to bed. Too tired even for bad dreams. Off to bed, Detective Sheffman gone. Left now.

Haven't called my mom. Don't know what to do. If I even want to call her or not. Stomach, twisted in knots. Belly hurts whenever I think about it. Wish she hadn't called. Wish they hadn't told me. Left it up to me to decide.

"Sleep on it," said Joseph. "Take your time. No hurry. See how you feel. Maybe you'll have more clarity in the morning." He says this kind of thing, practical, pragmatic. "Maybe you'll have more clarity in the morning." Very Joseph.

Cindy tucks me in. "You okay?" she asks.

And I say, "Yeah . . ." I'm tired, but I don't want her to leave me just yet. "Cindy?"

"Uh huh?"

"Why'd you take me in?" I say, cause I want to know. Need to know. Not sure why. Want to know, I guess, that she likes me too. Likes me a little. That I'm not just a charity, a good deed. Need to know if they regret it. Havin me. Signin me outta McLaren's Hall, askin me to stay.

"Do you regret it?" I say, not able to look at her, look down at my bedspread, smooth it out with my hands. Smooth out all the folds, all the wrinkles. Make it all smooth. "Do you regret takin me in?"

Kind of embarrassin to ask, but I need to know. Will help me decide what to do, about my mom and all.

Don't want to be a burden. Like Joseph and Cindy too much for that.

Not pregnant anymore. That's one good thing. That's one good blessin. But still, Ms. Finnegan is right, twelve's a difficult age. And given all of my troubles, how I stole from them, and lied, and how I'm always actin weird and cryin, havin stupid nightmares and everything, and then tonight, laughin inappropriately.

Cindy sits down on the side of my bed.

"I'm a lot of trouble . . ." I say.

She takes my hand in hers. "Gemma," she says. I don't

look up, too nervous. "Gemma . . ." And she tilts my head up, hand under my chin, so my face, my eyes are lookin directly at her.

"Not, for one moment." She pauses, eyes searchin mine. "Not for one millisecond have I, or Joe, regretted taking you in," her face, her voice, so serious. "Okay?" she says.

I nod my head. Feel like a big weight has been taken off of my shoulders. Feel like the elephant just got off of my chest and I can breathe again. Cause part of me, back in Joseph's study, with Detective Sheffman and all, part of me was worried that they were lettin me choose cause they didn't want me anymore.

"Oh good . . ." I say. "I don't regret it either." We smile at each other. It's quiet. A cozy quiet. I can hear Joseph movin around in the kitchen, finishin up the dishes.

"Now . . ." says Cindy. "The second question . . ."

She looks out the window. Nothin to see, not with the bedside light on. Can't see the moon or the trees, or the glow of other houses, not with the light on. Just looks like blackness, like a sheet of black glass, shadowy reflections of us, mirroring our moves, playing out, like ghosts of the past. But I don't tell her about our ghost images, or that it's pointless to look out the window at night, when the light's on. Figure she probably knows that. I don't say anything. Just wait for her to speak.

"Why did we take you? Well . . ." She looks back at me, like maybe she can find the words she's searchin for in my face. "It's a little more difficult to explain. Not so clear cut. I guess the easiest explanation is that you reminded me of myself."

"I did?" I say, wantin her to elaborate. Pleased to think that I'm like her. But she just nods. So I say, "How? When?

When did you realize I was like you?" I like sayin it, hearin it out loud, that I'm like her.

"Well . . ." she says, and I can tell by the way she says it, that she's gonna tell a story, so I snuggle down, settle in for a story about me and Cindy, and how alike we are.

"It was almost instantaneous actually. The first time I saw you, getting out of that gray Dodge Intrepid. I felt a connection. You, a skinny little bundle of clothes, and you looked so scared and small and beaten down. And he was grabbing for you, and I don't know, it was like this enormous surge of protective power roared through me, and I'm not sure how it happened, how I got to you so fast. But I was damned if I was going to let him get away with you." And she laughs, rememberin, and I laugh too.

"I was scared," I say.

"Me too," Cindy says. "Me too. Didn't even know you, but I was terrified that we'd lose you."

"I didn't notice you, didn't know where you came from. Thought I was supposed to go to the buildin."

"That was the plan. The plan was to get you safely into the building, and then apprehend the perpetrator. But when he reached for you, everything changed. We were scared he was on to us, grabbing you. Worried he was leaving with you as a hostage. Maybe we'd get him, maybe not. But the thing was, especially with the risk that he was on to us, you'd be in more danger. And that was just not a chance I was willing to take."

"Where were you?"

"Behind the navy blue sedan, two cars away from you. I was the shopper fumbling with my keys, the trunk, my packages. Bonnie was teasing me about it, said it was like I thought I was Superwoman or something, that I literally flew, vaulted over the trunk of the car next to you, had you in my arms before he had even blinked."

"I didn't see you."

"No."

"I felt you, but I didn't see you," I say.

And I remember Hazen. I don't talk about it, but I'm rememberin Hazen. His face, his breath, the smile on his face right before it all happened. Remember bein yanked backwards, away from the car. I remember the noise, the yellin, everybody yellin all at once. Hazen flyin backwards, his car door burstin open, from the impact of the bullet hitting his body, arms outstretched like he's still reachin for me, still gonna grab me. I remember peein my pants. Blood spurtin out of his side. I remember him hittin the pavement, lookin confused, not sure what's happenin. Callin to me, tryin, even though he's shot, to get me. I remember that.

"I remember what you said," I say. "You told me your name. Told me you were Cindy. That I was safe with you." And I nestle in close, to remind myself, cause Hazen's on my brain now. I try to keep my mind from him, turn it to other thoughts. But sometimes, Hazen sneaks up on me, grabs ahold of me, won't let go. And when I think about Hazen, it always makes me feel a little . . . I don't know really . . . a little creepy, I guess. Makes me feel dirty, like I'm a bad, yucky person. A bit like that, and a bit like I'm comin down with the flu or somethin, kinda like I get chills and nauseous all at the same time. Feel like that. Guilty too. I feel guilty, like it was all my fault.

And I keep havin dreams that he's comin back to get me.

And he's mad, real mad. I keep worryin that they're gonna let him outta jail, cause he's good at talkin, he's good at convincin. I get scared they're gonna listen to him, let him out, and he's gonna come and get me again. And this time, cause he's mad, this time, he's not gonna be so nice.

I nestle in closer. "I'm glad you're a police officer," I say, cause my heart's started runnin away again, all this thinkin about Hazen.

"Me too," Cindy says. "Otherwise, I never would have met you."

She smiles at me, and I try my best to return it. Hard, though, his angry face still stuck in the center of my forehead.

"And what else about me reminds me of you?" I say, partly cause I want to know, and partly to change the subject, get my mind off him.

"Well . . ." she says, "you remind me of me, a long time ago."

"Really?" I say. "Why?"

I see thoughts, images, tumblin across her face. I wait. When she starts talkin, she's pickin her words careful, like she's walkin barefoot across a minefield.

"I . . . I also had challenging times . . . difficult times . . . like you," she says.

"When? What?"

"When I was little."

"Really?" I say, and I can't quite believe it. "You did?"

"Uh huh."

And then she told me. But I'm not gonna say. Not gonna tell what happened to her. She told me cause we're close, cause she knows she can trust me. She told me, and that's as far as it goes. But I gotta say, I had *no* idea. I never, *ever, ever* would have thought that she'd had such a difficult time growin up too. Made my heart ache. Her own flesh and blood. And she was younger than me. Way younger when it started. I'm not sayin what, let me just say, he's lucky he's already dead.

But Cindy, she says that our challenges are the very things that have made us who we are, that give us our strength, our compassion, our endurance.

She kept sayin "us," "we," "our," but I don't know, to be honest, I don't know if I have those qualities. Cindy does, but I don't know about me. I'm pretty mad a lot of the time. Feel sometimes like a downed electrical wire, snappin and arcin and tryin to destroy everything in my path. Like Cindy's father, when I heard about that, what he did to her, I didn't feel no compassion or forgiveness in my heart! I wanted to destroy the son of a bitch. And I'm sorry I'm swearin, but I gotta let it out somehow, cause I'm tellin you, I just don't think I can keep it inside.

"What are you thinking?" she said.

And I told her what I was thinkin, how I was feelin about her dad.

"I know," she said. "I feel the same way about Hazen. But we just gotta keep working on letting it go. We have to leave it in the hands of the law. Hope that the courts are able to do what is just."

And I asked her but what if? What if the courts fail? They do sometimes. What if Hazen gets out? And what about her father? He didn't go to jail. So what then? I mean, shouldn't we just go out and get them? Knock their blocks off?

But she said no. That then they'd win.

"But how? They'd be dead," I said. "That would be good."

"But you'd be in jail, and that wouldn't. No. The best thing that we can do is to try and live a good, fruitful and honorable life. To walk right in the world. That's the only thing we have control over."

And I want to do that. I want to be that. Like Cindy. Make the world a better place. Don't want them to win.

I told Cindy that, and she said, "Good." And then cause we had finished our talk, and Joseph, he needs some cozy time too, she hugged me good night, Cindy, my new mother. She hugged me, kissed the top of my head. Tucked me in, nice and cozy. Pulled the blankets up around my shoulders so I'd be warm. Never had anybody do that. But Cindy does. She tucks me in every night. Cozy and clean in my new flannel pajamas.

Tucked me in, turned out the light. Left the hall door open a crack, just like I like it, so the night terrors can't get me.

And I lie on my bed, thinkin about her, what we talked about.

Cindy says that the person you are, the person you become, is a choice. She says that good things and bad things happen to everyone, and it is how you meet them, these challenges, what you learn from these experiences, that makes you who you are today, shapes who you'll be tomorrow.

And I try to think about bein like that, all good and honorable. But I can't help it, I just keep on thinkin about her father. How I wish he was alive so I could kill him. Kill him slow and horrible. Crack open his skull, pee on his brain. I'm a bad person, I guess, cause I think about doin that and it makes me feel good.

I think about Cindy too. About how she's got a gun and knows all kinds of fancy self-defense stuff, and yet, she didn't do it. She didn't kill her dad. He died of old age. Went out to get the mail from the mailbox. Came back, told her mom that he felt a little funny, sat down in his favorite armchair, and died. Just like that. Nice and peaceful! And I wonder how God could have let him have such a peaceful death. Such a bad person! Shouldn't he have had some horrible disease, where he had to suffer long and slow, like he made others suffer? And I just don't understand it. Don't understand God sometimes.

And I asked Cindy, "Aren't you mad? Aren't you mad that he didn't suffer? That God let him die so nice? Doesn't it make you mad?"

"What would that accomplish?" She'd said, head tilting slightly to the side. "How would that change things? He's dead, it wouldn't affect him, and I'd be walking around carrying it." And I guess I know what she means, but it's a lot to get my mind around.

I lie there in bed, room dark, the moon smilin at me, castin a pattern of the oak tree on my wall so I won't be alone. And I can hear the rumble of Joseph's voice, Cindy's voice softer. The water is runnin, probably brushin their teeth, and I listen to them talkin, bumpin around their bathroom, gettin ready for bed. And it's comfortin, these night noises, these gettin-ready-for-bed noises. So different from the bedtime situation at my mom's house, what with all the fightin and the drinkin and Buddy comin in. So different.

But I'm here now. I'm here. I breathe in deep. Cindy and Joseph down the hall. I can see out of the window now, the air fresh and cold. Can see everything, the night sky, the moon. Can see it all now that the bedside light is off. And as I watch, I can see, right before my eyes, the stars twinklin on, one by one, fillin the sky with their brilliance.

I lie there in my bed, and I think about Cindy and me. Her life, my life. And I think about the fact that if Hazen hadn't stolen me, I never would have met her. And if her dad hadn't been such a jerk, maybe she never would have seen her in me and me in her. And I realize that if these two bad things hadn't happened to us, then I wouldn't be lyin right here, in this wonderful, cozy house, with sweet-smellin sheets, and comfy flannel pajamas with fluffy, big-eyed kittens on them, all tangled up in blue balls of yarn. And when I think of all these things, all my anger, my madness, it just melts away. Melts away like an ice cube on hot cement. Just melts away, and I am tremblin, so full of thanksgivin. Cause it's like my body, my whole room, the whole house is near explodin with blessins. Everything hummin and vibratin and my heart is filled up. It's just filled up, burstin wide open with Hosannas.

CHAPTER SIX

He dreamt of her last night. Woke up hard. Thinking about how good she feels. His baby growing in her belly.

Woke up, thinking about forgiveness, compassion, and happy-ever-after.

She messed up, just a kid, for Christsake. The doctor probably put her up to it, the busybody doctor. Knew he'd made a mistake the minute Gemma disappeared into that building. It was a mistake to send her to a woman. Should have gotten a man. Then none of this would have happened.

Should have gotten a male doctor. What was her name? The bitch. What was her name?

And he reaches, reaches into the back of his mind, rummages around.

Dr. Fries. Dr. Janet Fries. That's it. Bitch. One more person to take care of. One more person to clean up once this mess is over.

But not Gemma. Not his Gemma. Changed his mind on that. Just a kid. Didn't realize what she was doing. Poor messed-up kid. What good would that do? Getting rid of her. Who would that help? And besides . . . And this makes Hazen laugh. Besides, his crazy cock would never forgive him.

Been awake for forty-five minutes at least, and the

thing's still stiff as a board. Demanding, insisting he deal with it. So he does.

Would like to take his time, but there's no privacy here. Any asshole with a uniform on can look in, come in, whenever they damned well please. Can just sally on in, don't need a reason to pay you a visit, rip up your room, destroy it. No reason. Just for the hell of it. Just to mess with your mind.

He used to fight them, but not anymore. Does no good. Just get the crap beaten outta you, cause they like that kind of shit. They like trying to control you. Smug little pricks. They just come marching in with their riot gear, bunch of sissies! Won't fight fair. One on one. Hell, two on one, and it'd be worth it! But no way.

You try to fight, you try to resist, hell, even if you're only talking the talk, in they march. Like marionettes! All geared up. Bring at least half a dozen assholes to knock you to the ground, beat the crap outta you, and then on top of that you lose privileges.

Yeah, he used to fight. Hazen Wood. He used to fight. Not anymore. Nope. Just sits there, lets them do their inspections. Lets them rip the place apart. Just sits there planning. Cause this jail thing? This isn't permanent. Not with Mr. Samuel Levy on the case. The guy's *brilliant*. Fucking brilliant! Putting together one hell of a defense. Got a way of twisting things, saying things that makes Hazen shout with laughter, just at the sheer pleasure of being in the room with somebody who is so skillful. It's like Hazen's watching a magician at work, things Partap had said were insurmountable obstacles, and Levy's just keeps coming up with ways to make them disappear like smoke. Hazen Wood, he's as good as free. They got nothing on him. Not really. Nothing.

So he can afford to sit, let the guards strut around, tear up his cell. He just sits, calm as can be. Doesn't rise to the bait, cause he's gonna be outta here soon. This is just a pit stop. This is just a rest stop until he fixes his flat tire and gets on with his journey.

Gotta think about the future. When he's outta jail. A free man. The baby's gonna need a daddy, Gemma too. They're both gonna need someone looking out for them. Someone to take care of them, feed them, bathe them. Gonna need someone to make sure their hair is brushed. Gotta get out of this place, take care of Gemma and his baby. Hope it's a girl. A little baby girl. A little baby girl just like Gemma.

That would be great. That would be fantastic! Then just when Gemma starts getting too old and saggy, starts to lose her appeal . . . Voilà! Baby Gemma's right there to take her place. Perfect. Life's gonna be perfect.

Gonna have to wait for a while, lie low. Let the authorities forget about him, move on to someone else, and then he'll strike, claim what's his, get his family back together again. First order of the day is to clear up this mess, the smear on his name. Straighten out this little misunderstanding. Might even sue the Chicago police department for aggravated assault, use of a deadly weapon, bodily harm. Because, as Sam pointed out, correct procedure was not followed. Maybe they'll slap a lawsuit on Chicago's finest, smug little bastards. Yeah, that would be good, that would be real good. It would pay for Levy's bills, and might even be a little left over for Hazen. A little nest egg to start a new life. With a new baby coming, he'll need it.

—•—

It snowed last night. And let me tell you, it was the most beautiful thing I ever saw.

Joseph was the first one to notice. We were eatin dinner, Cindy was talkin, tellin us a funny story about her and Eric "on the job." That's what they call it when they're at work. "On the job." I think it's a police thing.

Anyway, I was payin attention to Cindy, listenin to her story. That's how come I didn't notice right away.

Now Joseph, he was listenin too. But maybe he wasn't listenin as hard, cause all of a sudden, he got this little smile on his face, and he said, "Gemma . . ." right in the middle of Cindy's story, cause he knows, heck the whole world knows how long I've been waitin for snow. "Gemma . . ." he said. "Look outside."

And Cindy stopped talkin and I stopped listenin and we both turned and looked, and lo and behold, there was snow!

Little snowflakes driftin down, floatin down from the sky.

Wouldn't probably have noticed them, if the porch light hadn't been on. But it was, and we did. And I was on my feet. Feet jumpin me up and down!

"Can I go outside? Please? Please? May I be excused?"

And they said, "Yes." Laughin at the expression on my face.

I ran outside, lookin up at the sky. Could feel the snowflakes, dainty little fairy kisses on my face. And I was delirious with joy. I started dancin. Dancin a wild, mad, crazy woman jig. Dancin with the snow, face turned up to the heavens, arms outstretched wide. I heard Cindy call out, "Gemma! Your coat!" And I didn't want to stop my dancin, my celebration, but I didn't want to disrespect her either, so I ran back to the door, where she was standin, my coat in her hand, Joseph's arm around her shoulder. Both of them smilin, and I put on the coat, my legs still dancin their joyful jig. My smile so big it felt like it might split my face in two. Right in two, like a ripe melon.

Then, coat on, and I was back in the yard, dancin like a wild woman. Whoopin and hollerin, whirlin with the snow. And next thing I knew, I heard Joseph say, "What the heck!" And he came out on the lawn with me, and he started hollerin too. Wavin his arms, dancin around, leapin up, clickin his heels together like he's Gene Kelly, and Cindy's doubled over, laughin so hard she's gotta clutch at her belly to hold it together. And we were yellin, "Come on! Come on!" And Joseph was laughin, a big goofy grin on his face. "Come on!" he said, with an extra fancy twirl. "It's so much fun!" And so Cindy came out too, and we danced! We danced a wild, wonderful, snow dance.

The neighbors' outside light came on, they watched us, noses pressed to the window. Joseph yelled, "Come on! Join the fun!"

But they didn't. They stayed in their nice warm house, shakin their heads, thinkin we'd gone crazy for sure.

We danced a little more, but it wasn't quite the same. Didn't have quite the same "joie de vivre" with someone watchin. So we gave one last whoop for good measure and then rushed back inside, shiverin, teeth chatterin, and snowflakes clingin to our hair like little icy stars.

Joseph made a big roarin fire in the livin room. We huddled around it, tryin to warm our bones up, and then I got the good idea to have a marshmallow roast! So I asked Cindy if we could, and she'd never thought to do that before. To have a marshmallow roast inside. But, after she'd thought it over, she said, "Well, I don't see why not . . . Just be careful of the furniture." So I ran outside and got us some marshmallow roastin sticks, hard to find straight ones, all the tree's branches were bendy. But I broke off the straightest ones I could find and brought them back to the kitchen, scraped off the bark, sharpened them good with the kitchen knife. And then we roasted marshmallows in the livin room! It was perfect. Marshmallows, family, a roarin fire, and *snow* fallin outside, and Joseph said it looked like it was gonna stick.

It was a perfect, beautiful night.

This mornin, when I woke up, at first, I didn't remember. Knew there was somethin, but my mind wasn't awake enough to know what it was. And *then* I remembered! I looked out the window and, oh my. You have *never* seen me get dressed so fast in all my life!

I put on two of everything for warmth. Two pairs of pants. Two pairs of socks. A sweater and a long-sleeved shirt. Two of everything, cause last night, it was real fun, but I gotta tell you, I did get cold!

So two of everything. Then I ran into the kitchen, got my coat from last night. Had left it on the kitchen chair. Don't normally do that, leave my things lyin around helter-skelter, but last night, I was so excited, I guess I just plumb forgot.

"I see the snow hasn't lost its appeal," says Joseph dryly from behind his paper. He's wearin his pj's, robe and slippers, and his hair is stickin up every which way.

"Yep," I say jauntily, as I stuff my feet into my black rubber boots. Have to push a bit, wrestle my feet in, on account of my wearin two pairs of socks. "Wanna come?" I say hopefully, although I know it's unlikely, he looks pretty sleepy and he is still in his pajamas.

He laughs. "No . . ." he says, a little ruefully. "Sorry, last night's frolic should do me for the next twenty years. Could barely get my old bones out of bed this morning." He tousles my hair and goes back to his paper and coffee with sugar and cream.

"Have fun!" he says as I go out the door. "Make a snowman for me."

So I do! I make a snowman for him, and one for Cindy, and one for me. I make three snowmen! I make them standin together on the front lawn like a family. I make smiles on their faces with bendy twigs, and I use carrots for their noses, just like all the pictures you see of snowmen! And I dig through the snow, and I find little round rocks for their eyes and buttons.

I make one of the snowmen smaller than the others. I make it a girl snowman. I make it look like me. And I make Cindy's snowman look like the mommy one, and Joseph's one look like the daddy. And I make them happy! So happy. And I put them so that everybody who drives by our street will look at them and say, "Look at that! A family of snowmen. A mommy and a daddy and a little girl. And look at that! They're all smiling. A happy family must live here."

I'm clever! I place them where the world can see them, but we can too! I place them so we can see them when we're sittin on the sofa in the livin room.

You want to know how I managed this?

I figured out that if I put them where I could see the sofa, see it from outside, then that meant that when I was inside, sittin on the sofa, then I'd be able to see the snowmen!

Snow's so fun. And when I finish with the snowmen, I make a snow angel, and then I have a snowball fight with a tree. That wasn't quite as much fun as the other stuff. Hope the snow stays until school starts, cause I bet it's fun when you have other kids to play with.

And then after all that, I just flop back, "plop" and lie in the snow. Just lie still, watch the snowflakes driftin down. Everything, so beautiful. The trees, the branches, the fences, the roofs, even the old metal garbage cans coated, covered in snow. A thick, white blanket. Mufflin everything, makin it quieter, more still. Like magic has happened, and everything, the traffic, the trees, the birds, everything, is just holdin its breath. Just a quick little intake, like an "Ahhh . . . perfect . . ." It's that kind of feelin. An "Ahhh . . . perfect . . . Snow . . ."

- ◆ -

In my bed, thinkin about the day, the snow. Feelin somehow, like the snow comin, somethin about it, feels like a sign, another sign. Like God's talkin to me again, talkin to me, sayin, "I've given you this fresh start, this clean slate.

What are you going to do with it? Which path are you gonna go down, Gemma? Which path?"

And I think about my mom, my one in Oakland. I think about her wantin to talk to me. Wantin me to call. And me, puttin it off, not callin. I think about that, and I feel bad, cause I know what I want. I know already. I know how I feel when I think of goin back, and I know how I feel when I think of stayin. Two totally different feelins.

And it's hangin over my head, this whole callin thing. It's present even in the real fun times. It's like wearin a sweatshirt that has mildewed. No matter what you do, try to ignore it, put perfume on, powder, wash it a million times, nothin will work. That sickly sweet, mildew smell will just follow you around, smellin everything up. Nothin you can do except take the sweatshirt off and throw it away. Cause it's gonna stink no matter what you do.

So I get up off my bed and go to the livin room. Joseph and Cindy are sittin on the sofa watchin this show about the migration patterns of the polar bear. Looks sorta interestin, like if I wasn't all scrambled about my mom, I probably would have sat down and watched it with them. Standin in the doorway, watchin them watchin the show, and Cindy looks up. "Hi, honey," she says. "Did you need something?" Cause I'm just standin there, tryin to pull the words out.

"I ... um ..."

Joseph looks at me too now. "What's up, Gem's?" He clicks the remote control at the TV, turns it on mute.

"It's okay ..." I say, feelin embarrassed. "I just ... um ... I'm ready to call my mom is all. No big deal. I just ... ah ... thought it would be a good idea to ... to call. You can watch your show. I . . . I just wanted to know if it was okay. You know. Okay to use the phone?"

"Oh sure . . . That's fine. She'll . . . she'll be real happy to hear from you," Cindy says.

"If you like you can use the phone in my study," says Joseph. "It'll give you a little more privacy."

"Oh thanks . . ." I say. "That would be great." My stomach is tied in a million knots. "I'll go do that." And there's no more reason for me to keep standin there, so I make my legs walk me into the hall. Don't get to his study. Get too scared. Come back to the livin room. The TV is still on mute, and Joseph's arm's around Cindy now. They are talkin in hushed tones, can't make out what they're sayin. They stop when they see me.

"Wasn't she in?" Cindy says. She looks all tense, nervous. Way different than when I left a few seconds ago. Looks like she's about ready to cry or somethin. Joseph's arm is around her, and I feel like I walked into somethin private. A private conversation.

"Um . . ." I say, and I'm embarrassed to ask, especially now that they seem to be havin a talk and everything. But I don't know what else to do, and I've already interrupted them anyway, and this should only take a minute or two. "Um . . . I'm sorry . . . I didn't mean to interrupt . . . But . . . um . . . The thing is . . . I haven't called yet . . . See, I'm . . . I'm kinda scared . . . Scared to call . . . And I was wonderin . . ." My dumb, stupid eyes start to cry. Can't help it. Hope they don't notice. "And . . . I . . . I was wonderin if one of you would mind . . . holdin my . . . holdin my hand when I call?"

And Cindy, it's like she's stuck for a moment, like a fly on sticky paper, like she wants to get up, but her body won't let her. Just for a moment, and then she leaps up, Joseph too. And she's huggin me, comfortin me.

"Oh, sweetheart! Of course we will. What were we thinking? Do you want one of us? Both of us?"

"You sure you don't mind? I know you're busy."

"Gemma," says Joseph, "we were watching a TV show. How important is that? If you need us, all you have to do is ask."

And so we walk to Joseph's study, the three of us. All holdin hands. Have to walk slightly sideways in the hall so we all fit. We get to his study. They let me sit in his work chair, the wood one with the armrest and the swivel bottom. The one I have longed to sit in ever since the first time I saw it, and twirl it round and round and round.

But I don't. Even though this is my first time in it. I don't for two reasons. One, I'm not particularly in a swivelin mood. And two, even if I did feel like swivelin, I wouldn't, cause this is just too important for that.

I breathe in, out. Can feel Cindy and Joseph behind me, their hands restin on my shoulders. Can feel their love, their strength, pour into me, like they are anchors. Have anchored me to the earth, are holdin me safe here, so I don't just fly up, float up, disappear into the night sky. Cindy and Joseph are here.

I breathe, I pick up the phone. I dial.

Funny, feels odd, punchin out my old phone number. Known it for years. Called it six, seven, eight times a day that first week I was in McLaren Hall. Sometimes more.

Listened to it ring. Listened to the operator askin her if she'd accept my call. Listen to my mama say, "No."

I dial the number, and the odd thing is, I have to hesitate. Not quite sure for a moment, what my phone number is. Have to think, pull it up, out of my past. It comes, only a split second of a pause, and it comes back to me. Nobody would have noticed it. Nobody but me.

And I find this strange, somethin like my old phone number, that was so totally ingrained, such a part of my past, my life for so many years, can just slip away like that. Disappear, evaporate, like it never existed.

I dial the number. Listen to it ring. My palms slick, slippery wet, with nerves.

It rings once. Twice. Three times. She picks it up.

"Hello?" she says, her voice husky, low, like maybe she and Buddy were right in the middle of goin at it, and I don't know, it's like I'm paralyzed or somethin, cause I don't say anything.

"Hello?" A little more impatient this time, like if I don't speak soon, she's gonna hang up.

And I gotta say, the chicken part of me would like that. She hangs up. There. I called her. Did it. Done.

But I don't do that. Discharge my responsibilities like that. Cindy wouldn't do that. She'd call, say why, explain, face to face. Or in my case, phone to phone.

"Hi Mom . . ." I say, voice soundin all weird to me, like someone sucked all the sound out of it. Sounds like wind blowin through a crack in the window.

"It's me," I say. "Gemma . . ."

"Gemma!" And my mama, she sounds like she's scramblin, either sittin up from lyin. Or grabbin a chair and sittin down from standin. Movement of some kind or another.

"Gemma! Jesus Christ! Thank God! Do you know how hard it's been tryin to get ahold of you? It's like tryin to deal with the fuckin Gestapo! I miss you, baby. When are you comin home?"

And my hands are sweatin, my back too. And my throat, my throat's all closed up.

"I'm . . ." My heart is hurtin bad. Hurtin just hearin her voice. Hurtin with the hurt I'm gonna have to do. "Mama . . ."

"Yes, baby?" she says.

"Mama . . . I'm . . . I think I'm . . ." Try to suck in breath. "I've decided I wanna stay here." I've said it. I know I've said it. Can feel it ricochetin back and forth along the phone line. Vibratin, buzzin, hangin in the air, gobblin all the oxygen.

I've said it. Told her. Got it out. Cindy, Joseph's hands calm on my shoulders.

"I see," my mom says after a pause. Voice cooler. Not so friendly now.

There's another long pause. I don't speak. Don't know what to say. Underarms clammy. Don't know how to fill the space now. Half expected her to hang up on me. She does that a lot. Hangs up on me. But she doesn't hang up, and I hadn't figured out the conversation beyond that point. Didn't expect there to be one.

"Look, Gemma . . ." Her voice tired now. Like she's all worn out. Like life's just too exhaustin. And I feel bad.

"Look, Gemma," she says. "I know you're mad. I know

I hurt your feelings. I know you're scared. But the thing is . . . The thing you gotta understand, Gemma, is that I forgive you."

And I'm thinking, "You . . . what?" Tryin to catch up. But Mama, she's still talkin, not hearin my brain.

"I forgive you, Gemma," she's sayin. Well, her words are sayin anyway. But the sound of it, the tone of her voice, that's tellin me a whole other story.

"All that stuff you did with my Buddy. All that sneaky two-timin stuff you did . . . I forgive you. And that's a hell of a lot to forgive. But I'm tellin you right now, that I forgive you all of that, and I want you to come home . . . I want you to come home where you belong. We'll let bygones be bygones, okay? How's that sound?"

And honest, I didn't expect her to want me. To try to talk me into comin home. Didn't expect her to talk about Buddy, has always avoided the subject. Don't know what I expected, but I didn't expect this. Got no answers for this.

"Why?" I say. That's it. Real dumb response. That's all I can come up with? "Why?"

"Why what?" she says, a tinge of impatience, like she's got somewhere to go, somethin to do, and I'm just bein difficult by bein so stupid.

"I . . . I don't understand . . . Why?" The words just aren't comin out right. "Why . . . Why do you . . . want me?"

"Gemma . . ." she sighs. I can hear the match. The inhale, long and deep. Can hear her as she blows out a thin stream of smoke through her lips. Can hear it. Hear her smokin. Can just see her in my mind, puffin on her cigarette, wavin the smoke away. "Why do you have to make . . ." sucks in again, ". . . things so complicated? All the time, every-thing . . ." exhales, ". . . so complicated. Why?"

"I . . . I just want to know."

There's another pause. Then she talks, like she's removed from her voice, like she's pissed off that I've asked her, like she's tryin to cover it up, but I've known her all my life. I can tell.

"Why do I want you? Well, let's see. The house doesn't feel the same. I miss you . . . Sometimes . . ." She snort-laughs through her nose. "No, seriously, I'd like to have you back. And besides, you not being here . . ." sucks on her cigarette again. "It's makin things real hard down here. They're askin all kinds of questions, wantin to know why? Things like that. Just think it'd be easier all around if you were back."

And her voice, it has that slightly blurry, slurred qual-ity it gets when she's been drinkin too much. And I re-member how she kissed me on the forehead and then left me at the police station. I think about her on the phone, choosin Buddy. In the Howard Johnson Motel, knowin about Buddy. Knowin and not sayin, not carin.

I think about all of this and I say, "No." Just like that. "No. I love you, Mama . . . But . . . I'm not comin home." Just like that. Calm and firm.

And she starts yellin. Yellin and screamin. Callin me all kind of foul words, but I just listen for a while. Just listen, and then I hang up. Her voice gettin smaller and smaller until the phone receiver is restin back on its body and the phone is hung up.

- ◆ -

Had another bad dream about Hazen. A real bad one.

· ▬ ·

They had me hang a Christmas stockin. Which seems kinda funny, cause I haven't had a stockin for years.

I tried to tell them, didn't want them to think I was tryin to get free stuff, pullin the wool over their eyes, pretendin I still believed in Santa Claus. Didn't think that would be right, you know. Wouldn't be fair, honorable.

"You have to hang a stocking," Cindy insisted. "It's Christmas Eve."

"But . . . You see the thing is . . ." And I was right in the middle of tryin to explain, but then, Joseph, he cleared his throat. "Ahem . . ." he went, and then, made all kinds of weird facial gestures behind Cindy's head, so I knew he wanted to talk to me private.

We snuck off to the kitchen, leaving Cindy holdin the stockin in her hand. And he explained to me, reminded me about Cindy. How she'd always wanted to be a mother, never had the chance. Never got to be Santa, or the Easter Bunny. Never got to hide Easter eggs or fill stockins. How much it would mean to her, how much fun it would be, for her to pretend. That of course they know that I'm too big. But would I mind pretendin? Make it seem more Christmasy. It would be fun for Cindy if she could do that.

I said okay. I acted a bit reluctant, so he'll know I don't really believe. Felt a little foolish pretendin, but I felt excited too. Like in pretendin for her, it almost made it real. Made me feel like just maybe Santa really did exist. Even though I know he doesn't.

We hung my stocking above the fireplace, put my name on it with a tag of paper that I decorated on. Drew three little snowmen, and a candy cane and a Christmas tree. And GEMMA written right in the middle. It looked pretty.

We put out milk and cookies for Santa, never done that before. Milk and cookies and a carrot for the reindeer.

Then, when all the Christmas Eve preparations were done, I gave them a hug good night and went to bed.

Was hard to fall asleep. Was excited. Real excited. Could hear rustlin of packages and paper in their bedroom. Whispers and footsteps up and down the hall. Could hear little bumps and thumps and muffled laughter.

Felt like Christmas! Really felt like Christmas! The old-fashioned kind that you read about in books. Cocoa and gingerbread, that kind of Christmas. And just as I was driftin off to sleep, I thought I heard jingle bells and a faint "Ho . . . ho . . . ho . . ."

I'd swear I heard it, even though I know I didn't. Cause honestly, even though I'm pretendin for Cindy, I'm way too big to believe in Santa.

So I figure, it must have been my imagination playin tricks on me. It does that sometimes. Must have been my imagination playin tricks on me, makin my Christmas even more magical.

• ◄ •

We had a most beautiful Christmas. Nobody got mad or drunk or yelled. It was just great! And best of all, Cindy and Joseph loved what I made for them. They really did. Cindy cried when she read the poem I'd written about her and me, and that night we had our talk. She cried and then she hugged me and hugged me, read it all over again, and cried some more.

"Thank you, honey," she'd said, holdin it to her chest. "Thank you, Gemma." And then she showed it to Joseph, and he cried too. Not a big cryin, just had to take his glasses off and wipe his eyes.

"Beautiful . . ." he'd said. "Beautiful . . . You've got quite a talent, Gemma."

And I felt proud. Happy. Glad they liked it so much.

Joseph, he liked his present too. I gave him a picture I did of him when he was writin.

It looked good, had gotten it pretty right. Hair tumblin forwards, glasses fallin off his nose, brow furrowed. Fingers pushin against his temple, makin the skin rumple, like he's tryin to force the words to come out of his brain and onto the page.

I'd drawn it hurriedly, sketched it in. Snuck-drew, when he wasn't lookin. Had the paper hidden in the book I was pretendin to read. Drew it fast, the basic bones, then took it back to my room to finish. Took a long time to get it just right. To capture the Josephness of him.

Think I got it, though. Cause he threw back his head and laughed when he saw it. And Cindy said, "Oh my!" Ran and found a frame for it. Right then and there. Smack dab in the middle of openin our presents. A real nice frame and we put the picture in and she set it on the coffee table, right by the lamp with the pretty birds painted on it, so everybody who came into the house would see it, and admire it!

I'm glad they liked my presents, cause I was worried about them.

Thought I had everything under control, but then, a few days before Christmas, Joseph offered to take me Christmas shoppin. I told him no thank you, I already had Christmas presents, that I'd made some. But then, right as I said it, I felt worried, like maybe they weren't good enough. Like maybe I should go Christmas shoppin. Like maybe they'd rather have store-bought ones. And I was just about to say I changed my mind, that I'd rather get store-bought ones for them, when he said, "Oh great! Homemade! That's the very best kind of Christmas present to get. Something that has been made, with your own hands and love. Boy oh boy, I can't wait until Christmas!" And he looked so enthusiastic that I didn't say anything. Didn't say maybe I'd better go Christmas shoppin. Didn't want to burst his bubble.

So I left it at that, and I'm sure glad I did, cause they really loved my Christmas presents.

And I loved theirs! Oh boy, I really raked it in! I got a sled for sleddin! And Joseph says he's gonna take me! And I got mittens! Good ones! Nice and warm. Waterproof too. Gonna be way better than wearin Joseph's old wool socks on my hands. And I got candy and all kinds of cozy knickknacks in my stockin. A Santa Claus Pez, where the little square candy comes outta his mouth, and a little soft stuffed reindeer with a red nose, so soft. So soft you just wouldn't believe it. Just can't stop rubbin it on my cheek. Cindy likes to feel it too, all soft and cuddly against her cheek. It was funny, the reindeer was the first thing I saw. His head was stickin outta my stockin. Right out of the very top! Like he was curious, wanted to see what was goin on with the world, to check out the house, the Christmas tree. Pokin outta of my stockin, right next to a big candy cane. And there was an orange in there and nuts too! Nuts in their shell! I'd always wanted to try those. Safeway always had them in the store around Christmastime. Big bins of them. But I could never get my mom to buy them. Said they were too expensive, too messy. "A pain in the ass to open," she'd said.

So I got some real nuts! And Joseph said they have a nutcracker in the kitchen, so I'm gonna crack them later.

And I got a new hairbrush and it works real good, makes my hair all soft and fluffy, and float around my face cause of static cling. And I got real pretty hair clips, and a new toothbrush. And there was nail polish in my stocking. Pale pink, with a pearlish tinge to it, sorta that soft, foggy color, like my old abalone shell. I got all kinds of great stuff. Real girly-girl stuff. Nice. Made me feel all . . . I don't know . . . fancy, I guess. Special. And . . . last but not least . . . I got a new top. It was rolled up in the toe of my stocking. Rolled up and tied with a red ribbon. And it's real pretty. Gonna wear it for my first day of school.

. ➤ .

Levy had dropped by that afternoon. Unexpected. An earlier court date had opened up, did they want it? Apparently, some poor sucker had been iced in the yard, so there was a vacancy. January third.

The odd thing was, Hazen had been wanting, waiting to go to trial, and here was an opportunity to get there sooner. Get it over and done with, and his first impulse was to say no. Found himself scared, hands shaking like a goddamned junkie.

"Ah . . . forget it," Hazen found himself saying, trying to sound nonchalant. "Why don't we just leave it where it is?"

"We could," Levy had said. "But the thing is the kid. She's in a good environment right now, the longer she's there, the more stable she might become. Less traumatized, everything not so fresh, close to the surface. This might make her harder to intimidate, not as malleable. On the other hand, it might backfire. She might be the kind of kid where time makes her less reliable, gives leeway for her story to shift. I don't know, it's an either-or situation. So I thought I'd run it by you. You know the kid, what do you think? We've got to give them an answer by two. Now, we have several choices. We could take this new opening. We could stay with the original court date of February first. Or you could, and yes I know you've told me you don't want to, but I must mention it again, because it is a viable option. You could waive your right to a speedy trial. We could draw this thing out, take our time, and hope everything unravels for the defense. The kid gets cold feet, they lose witnesses, et cetera. The third option would give us more time to prepare, but it also gives them more time as well. There are no easy answers. What do you want to do?"

"If we draw it out, I waive my rights, do I have to stay here?"

"Yes."

And just then, it was like a curtain parted and everything seemed clear. This date opened up for a reason. It was a sign. God thought it was better to go sooner. Didn't want Hazen wasting his life away in jail. He wanted this thing resolved, wanted Hazen to take his rightful place as father, husband, and provider.

"Let's do it." Hazen said. His voice strong, impressive. "January third it is." Felt good about it. Righteous. Made the decision. Took the plunge.

But now it's night, and he's lying on his bed and Manuel, a skinny Hispanic boy is sobbing next door. And there's something about the sound, that's messing with Hazen's head, and the kid won't shut up. And it's pissing him off, cause it's making him feel small, the sound of all that weeping. And he's worrying, wondering if he made the right decision. Sleep impossible, because Hazen's got all kinds of scenarios ricocheting around in his head and none of them are good.

— ◆ —

Bonnie came over last night. A social call. Came with her girlfriend, Lisa.

I'd never met Lisa before. Actually, I didn't know that Bonnie, you know, Detective Sheffman, was gay.

But she is, and Lisa's her partner. They've been together for ten years, so that's something.

I like Lisa. Like seein the two of them together. Gives you a whole different perspective on Bonnie too. She laughs a lot when Lisa's around, doesn't look so stern, so much like an angry bulldog.

Lisa's real pretty. She's short, has sparkly eyes and curly dark hair, and she wears red lipstick. Not the red, red my mama wears, more of a bright cherry red. All spadang and shiny, like life's real excitin. I like it. I think maybe, when I grow up, I'll wear that color of lipstick.

And you know, you'd think it would be weird, seein two women, like husband and wife, all in love and everything.

You know, how all the kids talk about that kind of thing at school. Like it's the worst, most disgustin thing ever. But it isn't. Doesn't feel weird or nothin. Once you get your mind around it, feels fine. Certainly doesn't feel like anything "bad." Seems natural. Like, of course Bonnie would be with Lisa, they're so cute together, make a great couple. That's the kind of thing you think.

Anyway, they were over last night. A social call mostly, but then at the very end, Lisa asked me to show her my snowmen. They were mostly melted, but I took her outside anyway, and when we came back inside, Cindy and Bonnie were talkin business.

Apparently Hazen's lawyer has changed the date for the trial. Guess he's allowed to. We'd thought it was going to be a while before I had to go to court. Not until the beginnin of February. But apparently it's gonna be in eight days. On January third. I'm kinda nervous. I'm gonna have to see him in eight days. I'm kinda scared. Hope I do okay.

Anyway, everything's changed. We were gonna go to Navy Pier, have a family day and see this beautiful indoor botanical park. Then we were gonna take a ride on this enormous hundred-and-fifty-foot-high Ferris wheel. That's what we were gonna do.

But instead, stupid stinky pants ruined everything and Cindy and I are gonna have to go over to the D.A.'s office instead. And he's gonna go over some stuff with me. Gonna run me through some stuff. Not sure what that means, but I can tell everybody's a little nervous. Wonderin what Hazen's side has, why they're rushin it.

Cindy says we'll go to Navy Pier another day, to celebrate after this is all over, and that there's nothin to be worried about. That everything's gonna be fine. But I don't know, she looks real worried to me, and everybody's actin very skittery.

- ◆ -

On the way back home from the D.A.'s we stopped at the beauty parlor. Not only did we stop, but we stopped for *me*! I'm tellin the truth! We stopped for me! An extra holiday treat that Cindy and Joseph had planned so I could get rid of my stupid, dumb, stinky, two-toned hair! And believe me, when I say my hair looks bad . . . you have *no* idea.

My old hair is growing back in, and the stupid dyed brown hair is growin out, so it's like my head is a badly striped sweater, all jaggity, and crooked, and yucky lookin.

And another thing, whenever I look at it, at my hair, it reminds me of him. Of Hazen. Of what he did to me.

I avoid lookin in mirrors, store windows, fountains. Anything with a possible reflection. Cause you never know when the sun's gonna burst out from behind the clouds and make what seems to be an innocent window into a reflection of what you don't want to see. Have to keep my eyes movin around pretty fast, don't let them settle on anything that might morph into a mirror.

But now, after today, it's gonna be gone. All gone. It'll be like it was before Hazen Wood ever came into my life, stole me, did all those things. Can't tell you how good that feels.

The beautician, Sharon, when I first came in, she said "Oh my . . . What happened to you?" But Cindy and I, we didn't tell her, just smiled and Cindy said, "She'd like to go back to her natural color."

And Sharon the beautician said, "I should hope so. Whoever did your last hair color deserves to be shot. Hmmph . . ." She sniffed through her nose, runnin her fingertips through my hair. "And I have to say, I'm not too impressed with the haircut either. Looks like it was done with a hacksaw."

"Just about," says Cindy, cause she's heard the whole story. "Just about . . . Anyway, do you think you can fix it?"

"I'll try." And then Sharon gets me outta her chair right fast, takes me in to the back room. Makes me hustle, cause she doesn't want anybody to come into the shop and see me. Doesn't want them to think I got my last hair job there.

She washes my hair in a special hair-washin sink. Has a fancy chair, which tips way, way back into the sink with a hole cut out, carved into it, for your neck to fit in. And it doesn't sound good, sounds uncomfortable when I describe it, but really, it actually feels quite nice. They put a folded towel around your neck to cushion it.

The water comes out of a special hair-washin sprayer hose. Kinda like the sink cleaner hose Cindy and Joseph have on their kitchen sink. But this one has a bigger head, flatter, rounder. And the water that comes out of it feels so good. It's so warm, like a warm waterfall, swishin all over your head. And she's, the beauty shop lady, she's talkin and talkin, nonstop talkin.

I can't tell if she's talkin to me or Cindy. Can't really hear what she's sayin too good, on account of the water. But I just say, "Uh huh . . . Uh huh . . ." every now and then, just in case, so I won't hurt her feelings if it's me she's talkin to.

"Uh huh . . . Uh huh . . ." I say, and she scrubs, massages my scalp. Uses lots and lots of shampoo. Can't see it, but I can feel it. All thick and luxurious.

And she rubs and scrubs and I feel like a cat, feel like purrin. Feel like a fine lady. A fancy lady, gettin my hair done in a real live beauty parlor. And Cindy sits in the chair beside me, and we smile.

CHAPTER SEVEN

Today's the big day. He's gonna see her. See his Gemma. Set the record straight.

Feels good. In fighting form. Gonna make those fuckers sorry they ever set eyes on him. Gonna burn the Chicago police! Today's the day he gets vindicated! The day Hazen Wood walks out of here a free man. And it's gonna feel good!

First thing he's gonna do, is get himself down to Denny's. Get himself a big meal. Steak. Yeah! A New York steak, medium rare. That's what he'll have. A steak with the works. Mashed, no, baked potato, sour cream, bacon bits, butter. Lots of butter, maybe a little bit of those green things, what do they call them? Chives, yeah that's it, chives. Get himself a sprinkling of chives. Cheesecake for dessert, strawberry sauce, whipped cream. Wait, maybe he should save that, save the dessert for when he's back with Gemma. Eat it off of her. He likes to do that, did that in . . . Where was it? Eugene maybe? That was good. Best cheesecake he'd ever had. It was a big mess afterwards. But Sweet Jesus, it was worth it!

Gonna see Gemma today. Wonder if she's showing yet? Gonna see his sweet baby doll Gemma.

— ◆ —

His mother's here. His mother! Who told her to come? Who the hell told her about this? Shit! The bitch! Sitting there so sanctimoniously. So piously, with her little Bible. Playing her long-suffering mother part oh so well. Two-faced hypocrite! Fat cow! Who the fuck asked her to come?

Then, the answer to his question, dickhead Levy gets up and goes to her, shakes her hand. "Thank you so much for coming. Your support means so much to Hazen."

"Like hell it does . . . stupid cow," Hazen mutters.

Levy was out of line on this one. *Out* of line. Should have talked to Hazen about this. Should have given him a choice. He doesn't want that old hag here. Shit. Not that he cares, of course. It's just looking at her face makes him want to puke. Stupid cow.

And what pisses him off even more is the fact that he's a grown man. Full grown, and he's still scared of her. Scared she's gonna cuff him along the side of his head and tell him he's a screw-up. Finds himself trembling at the sight of her.

And at the same time, there's something about her, seeing her, sitting there, supporting him, that undoes him, and he finds himself having to fight real hard not to cry.

In the courtroom, in his goddamned arena where he's supposed to conquer the world, and he's got tears in his eyes. Dumb bitch! Levy should have asked him if he wanted her to come.

· ✦ ·

Drivin over to the courthouse. Wearin my new clothes we bought the day before yesterday in the shoppin mall.

It was fun shoppin, lookin at all the clothes, pickin out

my new pants, pale blue with a little thin belt. Nice pants. A top to match, long sleeves, white, with a blue butterfly on the front. A pale blue butterfly with spots of pink and yellow on her wings and she's got her wings stretched out wide like she's just gettin ready to fly.

Love my brand-new clothes. Love them. We had such a good time shoppin. Everything was fine, laughin and jokin. Buyin the clothes. But then, when we were leavin, goin out of the store, this really embarrassin thing happened. I don't know why, I mean I know he's in jail and all, but as we were goin out of the store, a bunch of people pushed by, and I don't know . . . I thought I smelled him. You know how I have a real sensitive nose. Well, I thought that I smelled Hazen and I kinda freaked out. Thought he was comin to get me. Guess I started screamin and cryin. Don't remember it so well. Don't want to. Kind of embarrassin. I remember grabbin on to Cindy, not bein able to let go. Remember that. Remember her tellin me over and over, "He's in jail . . . He's in jail, sweetheart . . . It's okay . . . You're safe . . ." I remember her sayin that, calmin me down, the two of us pickin up our bags off the floor, me keepin my eyes down. Tryin not to look at anybody. Hope nobody from my new school saw me actin so weird.

And of course Hazen wasn't there. Nowhere to be seen. Just freaked out for no reason. Passed somebody who smelled like him is all. How embarrassin.

And now, drivin to the courthouse, and the car, it seems to be travelin faster than usual. Time too. Goin fast. Want to slow it down, to have a little more time to calm, get ready. The car's goin too fast. Gettin there too soon. Not ready to see him yet.

Bein brave though. Not carryin on. Bein like Cindy. We're talkin about the weather, my new school that I start the day after tomorrow. We're talkin about things like that. Both of us. Me too. We're chattin all normal like, and I wipe my palms on the sides of my pants, not the front. Dry them off on the sides of my pants so the sweat stains won't show.

The car swings into the parkin lot. We're here. Car turns off. "Are you okay?" Cindy asks, cause I'm shiverin slightly even though I got my coat on. My winter coat that Cindy and Joseph got me. I feel my lips, my teeth shakin. Can't stop em. They're just shakin on their own accord. Not cause I'm scared or anything, cause I'm not. I'm not a cry-baby. I'm strong, real strong. They're just shakin that's all, clatterin a bit.

"Are you all right? Do you need to wait a moment?"

"No, no, I'm ready," I say, and I smile my lips so she won't worry. Teeth still rattlin together, hopin she won't notice. But I don't know, the smile doesn't seem to do it, so I pull open the door handle, like "let's get this show on the road." Get outta the car. "I'm ready," I say, lookin at the courthouse, and there are lots of grown-ups millin around in front, TV cameras, and flash bulbs.

"Oh . . . no . . ." says Cindy. Cause she's lookin at them too. But I don't think it's so bad, somethin to focus on. Don't know what they're there for, but if I focus on the excitement over there, I won't have to look at her. Don't wanna look at her. Don't wanna cry.

See, this fear hit me back there, hit me like an old greasy dishrag to the face. Just back there in the car. Slammed into me unexpected like. When she turned the car off, asked if

I was all right, if I needed a moment, somethin about the expression on her face, got me panickin. Hit me bad. This slap of fear, slug to the gut, threatenin to pull me down, under. Not that these panic attacks are so bad, I mean, no problem, I can deal with them, it's just I wasn't expectin it, is all.

"Wow. A lot of steps," I say, and I can hear my voice, it's higher than usual, more crackly. Cindy moves to hug me, but I move away. Don't want to hurt her feelins, but honestly, I don't think I can take it, kindness right now. Might break me, splinter me into a million pieces. Move away. "Better get goin," I say. "Don't wanna be late." Voice soundin like someone else's.

. ▬ .

Waitin. I'm waitin now. Am in a little room. We got through the crowd in front. They were pushin, yellin, sayin things. Got through them, though, and now I'm here. In this room. The walls have pale green paint on them, not pale green like Easter, or delicate or anything, it's more like somebody took some vomit green paint and thought maybe it'd look better if they mixed some white in it. Or maybe the paint's so ugly cause the painter got a good deal on it. Was able to buy it cheap. Or maybe they paint these waitin rooms in back of courthouses these colors to depress you, make you feel like the world is comin to an end for sure.

The paint's been put on thick, globbed on, like my grandma's old lipstick that she'd accidentally left out in the sun. Melted. Wouldn't roll up or down. She had to scoop it out of its container with an old Popsicle stick. Used the Popsicle stick to smear it on her lips. She said it looked just fine. But it didn't. Went on just a touch too chunky, not all smooth and silky, not all glossy like my mama's.

My mama, her lipstick always looked pretty. Didn't matter if she was passed out drunk on the livin room floor, her red lipstick was always in place.

Once when I was little, and she was passed out but good, I ran my finger over her lips, I did it real soft, gentle, so she wouldn't wake up, and she didn't, and a little bit of her lipstick came off on the tip of my finger. She didn't wake up, so I leaned in close and placed my mouth on her mouth, like I was her boyfriend. I laid my lips on hers and tasted my mother, and she tasted of gin, and vomit and cigarette butts. I did it gentle, soft, sneaky, and she didn't wake up. Didn't matter to me that she wasn't awake. Didn't matter. Is one of the first kisses I remember gettin from my mama. But I'm sure she kissed me lots. Probably kissed me lots when I was a baby.

And after our kiss, I dragged a kitchen chair into the bathroom, it was hard work cause I was small then, but I managed. Got it in there, stood on it in front of the mirror, the sink. Looked at myself for a long time. At my reflection, tracin my mouth, gentle with my fingertip, so I wouldn't take any of it off. Lookin, feelin different, feelin loved, my mama's crimson lipstick, stainin my lips.

But enough of that. Not gonna think about my mama now. No point really. Things are what they are, and I should count my blessins. How lucky I am. And I do. I count my blessins every night, a million times a day. I know how lucky I am. I know how blessed.

I'm just a little scared now. That's all. Just a little scared. Worried somehow everything's gonna come undone. Unravel. Like a sweater with a slipped stitch. Everything's gonna come undone, the last four weeks gonna get pulled out from under me, gonna vanish like fog comin outta my mouth. Worried that he, you know, that Hazen is gonna figure out a way to trick them. To fool them. Get me back. Kinda worried about that.

Hard to keep my mind off it, sittin here in this room by myself. Cindy's in front now. Cindy's in the courthouse where the trial's gonna be held. She's sittin with Joseph. He came here earlier, brought his cell phone. Came here earlier so if there was a delay in our case or somethin, he could let us know. Didn't want me to sit here in the courthouse any longer than was necessary. And I'm glad they thought of that. Cause already I feel like I've been sittin here too long, like a cat wearin someone else's skin. All prickly inside, like I'm gonna jump right out of it. Nervous like. Heart bangin away. Scared. I'm scared now. Can smell him. Feel like I can smell him all the way from here. Scared. Tryin not to move. Tryin to keep my legs from runnin me outta here. Am hummin little songs to take my mind off it. Off him. Hummin anything I can think of, radio songs, lullabies, Christmas carols, the "Happy Birthday to You" song. Just keep myself hummin. Keep my mind busy. Keep it off of him.

"Are you going to be okay?" Cindy had asked when we got to the little room. The room I was supposed to wait in. Wait until the bailiff comes to get me, to bring me to the judge. "Are you going to be all right here by yourself?"

And I nodded, acted all nonchalant. "Oh yeah . . . Sure, no problem. You go get a seat."

She hesitated, and I knew she was thinkin of stayin,

and I really wanted her to. But that was short-term wantin, cause the thing is, you see, I also wanted her in the courtroom, needed her there, and I was scared they were gonna run outta seats. Or all the close-up seats would be taken and she'd have to sit behind a pole or somethin and I wouldn't be able to see her. I don't know why, I just feel safer with Cindy around, like Hazen can't get me, won't be able to get me so easily.

She's got her gun. I made sure she brought her gun. Had her check a million times before we left the house. "You got your gun?" I'd said. "You didn't forget your gun? Didn't take it off when you went to the bathroom?"

And she said, "Yes, Gemma, I have my gun." She was real patient with me. "But you don't have to worry." She said. "You're going to be safe in the courtroom. Even if I wasn't there, you'd still be safe. He'll be shackled, he'll have a guard, he won't be able to get you." But I still had to check before we go out the door, make sure, see it with my own eyes, her gun, secure in place. All metal and polished wood, hidin in that sling under her jacket. Her jacket Christmas red, so I'll be able to see her easy.

I'm grateful she's here, Cindy and Joseph. Glad I have somebody, not goin through this alone. My mama's not here, not comin.

I called her, asked her if she was comin, but she just sniffed, said, "Don't see why I should."

We didn't seem to have much to say to each other, all my words stuck in my mouth, none comin outta hers. So I told her I loved her, hung up.

Don't know. Really don't know what's gonna happen there. If I'm ever gonna get to see her again. My mom. If she's ever gonna want to, now that I chose to live with Joseph and Cindy. Sometimes, lyin in bed, I wonder about that. If we'll hook up sometime, me and my mama. Maybe later, when I'm grown, no longer such a burden. Wonder if she'll want to see me then? I'm hopin she will. I'm hopin she'll learn to love me, forgive me, let go of that tight grippin in her heart. Maybe she has. Maybe she has already, just doesn't know how to show it. Too messed up by Buddy. Stupid, dumb, asinine boyfriend. His fault this all happened. Stupid jerk.

Who knows? Maybe my mama does love me, maybe she always has. She just doesn't know it, that's all.

Anyway, enough of my mama. The reason I told Cindy to go get a seat, is cause it was a question of which was worse. Keepin Cindy here, and risk her not gettin a seat in time, or toughin it out. Sit here by myself for a few minutes, how hard could that be? Then for sure, she would be there, in the courtroom for the worst part, the scary part, the part where I have to see him again.

Didn't want her to go, but it would be worse if she didn't. So I smiled, made like I meant it, like I was calm, cool as a cucumber. "No, really, I'm fine, really," I said noddin and smilin, not lookin her in the eye. And I hope it doesn't count as a lie, cause I'm really tryin hard not to do that. Don't think it was a real lie, more like a white lie, a "No, your haircut looks real pretty" kind of lie.

She wasn't goin to, but I made her leave. And now I'm here by myself, tryin to keep my mind busy. Tryin not to think about him sittin two doors down.

Cause really, there's nothin to be scared about. He can't get me. Can't get me now. They've got a guard on him.

Cindy pointed him out to me when we arrived. Saw the guard sittin outside Hazen's door on a metal foldin chair. Saw him. He had a gun, not hidden under his jacket, it was out there on his hip for everyone to see. A gun and a badge too. Looks strong. So Hazen can't get me. Can't get out of that room. There's a guard at the door with a gun, there's bars on the window, and the windows in these rooms are real high up, and small too. He wouldn't be able to fit his head outta that window, let alone his stupid mean ass, even if the bars were gone he wouldn't be able to do it. No, he can't get me. I'm safe here. Cindy told me. I'm safe here.

I'm safe. Keepin my mind busy, have hummed all the songs I know. Gotta start from the beginnin again. Don't know what's keepin them. Cindy said it wasn't going to be long. Don't know what's keepin them. Sweatin, hands sweatin, clock on the wall, tickin so slow.

The D.A. came in. Said hello. Made sure I was okay. Asked me if I wanted a soda from the Coca-Cola ma-chine down the hall. I said no. Was scared it would make me have to go to the bathroom. Don't want to have to go into the bathroom. What if Hazen's goin to the bathroom. What if he had a soda, and he has to go to the bathroom at the exact same time as I have to? That wouldn't be good. I mean, maybe the guard wouldn't go to the bathroom with him. He might find that too disgustin. Maybe Hazen would get to go to the bathroom by himself, and the wom-en's bathroom and the men's bathroom are usually right by each other, right side by side. And if I was goin to the bathroom and he was goin to the bathroom, he might see me, grab me, and that would be that.

So I tell the D.A. no. No, thank you. Can't remember his name. A long complicated name that twists around itself. Don't remember his name. Cindy would. Cindy remembers everybody's name. She's real good at things like that.

"No, thank you," I say. I don't take a soda, even though I like them. Even though they're a treat. Don't want to have to go to the bathroom.

Maybe I should have said yes, though. Could have saved it for later. Afterwards, for a reward, when it's all over. Could have drunk it on the way home, in the car with Cindy. Could have shared it with her, I would have too. Maybe I should have taken it, Cindy probably would have liked it. Be nice to give her a treat for a change. Give back. Darn. I should have said yes. I should have gotten root beer. Cindy likes root beer, me too. Root beer would have been good. A&W. That would have been tasty. Darn. I should have said yes.

Wonder how long it's gonna be? Wonder how long I'm gonna stay in here? Wonder if he'll be in the courtroom when I'm there, when they're askin me questions?

Cindy says that he will. That he most likely will. That I'll be able to see him, and not to let that throw me. "Just tell the truth." That's what she says. "Just tell the truth, answer the questions, truthfully and honestly, and you'll be just fine." "Judge Phillips is nice," she says. "He's an honorable, fair man. You're in good hands with him. I'll be there, Joseph too. We'll be right there in the courtroom. So if you get nervous, or scared, all you have to do is look at us. We'll be there, loving and supporting you. I'm going to wear all red so you can find me easily. We'll be there, look at us if you get scared. We'll keep you safe. Don't worry. You'll be able to see Hazen, but he can't hurt you now. You will be safe."

That's what she says, over and over. "You will be safe."

And I'm glad she says it. Makes me feel better. Calms my tummy a little. Say it to myself when I'm not hummin. Say it to myself. "You're safe . . . You are safe, Gemma . . ." Say it over and over. "He can't hurt you now. You are safe . . ."

Heard a door down the hall open and shut awhile back. Heard footsteps goin down the hall. Don't know if it was Hazen or not. Heart poundin so fast. Didn't know if it was him. Could have been, came from the right direction, the direction of his room. Another door opened and shut, further down the hallway. Could have been him goin into the courtroom. Hope so. Hope it wasn't the guard takin a coffee break, goin to the bathroom. Don't know.

Waitin, hands twistin. Waitin in this room.

More footsteps, comin closer, closer, and I'm holdin my breath, cause I don't know, maybe just a secretary, or someone who works here, walkin by. But maybe not . . .

Maybe Hazen's guard did go to the bathroom, and Hazen's scoutin, roamin the halls lookin for me.

Someone knocks on the door, on my door. *Boom . . . boom . . .* Sounds like that, big and hollow. Makes me jump, jolts me up, like white-hot light shootin through me.

I don't answer, sit still, don't move.

Boom . . . boom . . . the door goes again.

I hear a man. "Hello . . ." Doesn't sound like Hazen, but I stay put, stay quiet, barely breathin just in case. Pretend the room is empty, nobody here.

The door swings open.

"It's time," he says. It's not Hazen. It's the man who works for the court, standin in the door. Can't remember his name. Names aren't seemin to stick now, don't know why. Remember his face, though. Know it's okay to go with him. Cindy introduced me to him when we came in. Told me that he would take me to the courtroom.

It's time now, and all of a sudden I don't feel so good. I stand up, but I'm shakin, it's like I got the flu. I stand up, tryin to look normal, walk to the door, gotta remind my lungs to breathe in, force my throat to let the air pass.

"I'm ready," I say, and I'm tryin to smile, but I don't know if it's workin, feels like my face is so stiff, gonna crack with the effort. But luckily, the man doesn't notice, he's already headed down the hall.

Hazen must already be in there. His guard isn't in his chair anymore. Hazen must already be in the courtroom.

And my body's shakin. I can't stop it from shakin. It's shakin all over.

"You're safe," I say, walkin, walkin down the hall. "You're safe . . . you're safe . . . you're safe . . ."

• ➤ •

They bring her in. They bring Gemma in. And she's walking that hunched-down walk. That walk she does when she's trying to act invisible. And it's funny, brings back memories, makes Hazen smile. Makes him smile for the first time in this whole damned charade.

Walking all scrunched up. Face, so pale, like all the color was vacuumed out of it. Pale, translucent, beautiful. Scared. He can tell. Eyes hurt, confused, vulnerable, violet shadows under them, like bruised flowers, must not be sleeping good. Must be worrying about him. About Hazen Wood, her man. Feeling bad, guilty about sticking him in prison. Probably didn't realize the consequences of telling, of opening her fat yap to the doctor. Gotta teach her that. Gotta teach her not to do that, when he gets out. Too dangerous, running off at the mouth like that. Gotta teach her, let her know, for her own good. For her safety.

They futzed with her hair. Frou-froued it up. But that's okay. Looks good. Back to its normal color, so that's good. Doesn't seem to be showing the pregnancy yet. Looks good enough to eat.

He tries to get her to look at him on her journey to the witness stand. Wants to smile at her, let her know there are no hard feelings, that he's okay, that he forgives her. Wants her to look at him. But she doesn't. Just follows the bailiff, looking down at her sneakers.

She raises her right hand, says the oath, voice barely above a whisper. Wouldn't know she was talking if he hadn't seen her lips moving. Had to lean forward, strain his ears to hear her, hear anything. Miss her voice, that soft delicate voice she has, miss the soft hitch, the slide of it.

Her hand, the uplifted one for the oath, is trembling slightly. She looks terrified.

And Hazen, he feels this surge of outrage. That the police are putting her through this! The insensitive assholes! Using her, forcing her to testify, putting her through this, when it is obvious she doesn't want to be here. It is obvious that this is just too much of a strain on her. The child is pregnant, for Christsake, they should just leave her alone!

He turns to Levy, cause as much as he likes seeing her,

he cares for her, for her health even more. "Is there any way to get her out of here?" Hazen whispers. "I don't know if the poor kid is up to it."

"Yeah . . . She looks bad . . . That's good," Levy whispers back. "This is your chance, Hazen. This is your best shot. If you can get her not to talk, do it. The ball's in your court. It's Showtime."

"What?" Hazen whispers. "What are you saying? You want me to scare the kid?"

"Yeah, that's right. Scare the hell out of her. We've got to break her down in order to get you off. Have to discredit her. I'll have a better shot at it if you have her intimidated." And while Hazen's surprised that Levy would suggest such a thing, he's gotta give him credit. It's a good idea. Might help. Cause the prosecutors, they're putting a real messed-up spin on things, painting him as a monster. Doesn't know where they get off making up that crap. And he feels for Gemma and all, but this is war, and in times of war, a man's gotta do what a man's gotta do.

— • — • —

I can see him. Tryin not to, but it's hard. It's really hard. Whenever the D.A. moves, shifts his weight, I can see a part of Hazen. A flash of him, way worse than seein all of him at once, gettin it over with. And the D.A.'s askin me questions, and I want to answer, but my mouth's not workin, glued shut. Lockjaw. A wordless freak. A mummified sack of dry bones and dust. Fossilized. Everybody, lookin at me, whole courtroom, full, waitin. Gotta, wanna speak, do like we practiced. The D.A., askin me questions, things I know the answers to, things we rehearsed over and over in his office, but everything's clenched shut, and all I seem to be able to do is shake my head, yes or no. Mouth won't talk. Body starts rockin, won't stop. We rehearsed this over and over, what I'm supposed to say, and now I'm messin up. I've let him down, the D.A. I know it. His words are kind, gentle, but I can see the impatience, the frustration in his face, and that just makes it worse. I want to speak. I do, but no words are comin out.

The D.A., he walks back to his table, shakin his head like he's pissed, sits in his chair with a thump. Exhales hard. His hand slides under his glasses, massages the bridge of his nose, elbow on the table for support. My heart, so loud in my ears.

The other lawyer jumps up. Hazen's one. Firin off questions. But it's hard to hear him. Hard to focus on what exactly he's sayin. He's not blockin Hazen from my view. He's not standin where the D.A was standin, he's stridin all over the place, and Hazen, he's sittin right in front of me, a little to the side. But there he is, can't miss him, no matter how hard I try. His lawyer pointin at him, gesturin at him, poundin the table with his fist right in front of where Hazen is sittin. Impossible not to look, even though Cindy said not to. Don't want to see him, but he's sittin at a table right in front of me. Starin at me. Eyes fixated on me, like he's a dog and I'm a bone. Almost don't recognize him at first. His hair's longer, greasy. Looks like he's not so keen on bathin now.

Looks different, but his eyes let me know was him. The way he's lookin at me. That's how I know for sure.

He's wearin an orange jumpsuit. Must be prison clothes, cause I've never seen him wear orange before. Got short sleeves. Can see the dragon tattoo he's got on his arm, the fire-breathin dragon with the spiky tail that curves up and around his muscle. Try not to look at it, but I can see it jumpin. Always does that when he's mad. When he's gonna hit me. Can see it jumpin, like it's dancin on hot coals. See his tattoo jumpin. Don't look up, don't look at his eyes. His eyes, they freak me out. It's like I can tell what he's thinkin, and none of it's nice. Don't look at his eyes.

And I am shakin, my whole body, tremblin like a leaf. A leaf in a windstorm that's about to fall off. And I'm back in that trunk. That urine-soaked trunk. The smell, closin in on me, gaggin up my throat. I'm back in that trunk, no clothes, tied up, unable to breathe.

And I'm scared. The way he is lookin at me. My belly racin all outta control. Feel like I'm drownin all over again.

I'm tryin to hang on, but I'm panickin, like that day, that time he found me in the dumpster. Hot and cold, heat and ice, runnin, rushin through me. "I'm drownin . . ." I think. "Drownin . . ."

Hand risin to my throat, tryin to clutch in air, and his lawyer, Mr. Levy, I think that's his name. He is askin me all kinds of questions. Dirty, filthy questions, and Hazen's lookin like he's likin it. Smirkin at me. And Mr. Levy, he's talkin about bad things. Things that I did. How I begged Hazen to have sex with me . . . And I did . . . I did do that, and I want to explain, that yes I said those words, those words that he quoted, but Hazen had a knife, he was makin me say those things, beg for it or he would cut me! I want to explain about those things, get my mouth open, but Mr. Levy doesn't let me. Cuts me off, moves right on, on to the next subject. Says this was not a case of kidnappin. This was a case of mutual consent. Granted I was underage, but I was a whore. That's what he said. That I was a whore. Makin me out to be a cheap whore, sayin I did it for money. That I was just a cheap sex-driven nymphomaniac. Twistin my words, twistin the circumstances. Gettin things, lies like that out before the D.A has a chance to yell out, "Objection!"

And all those people lookin at me. Like I'm a freak, an oddity in the zoo. Embarrassin. Humiliatin, for Joseph and Cindy to hear what I did. The things I did to survive. And Bonnie's there and Dr. Fries. Even Ms. Lindstrom came, is hearin this. And it feels real bad, cause after our blowup, after I yelled at her, she was gettin nicer and I was startin to like her. And I know they must think all these lies this lawyer is tellin are true, the real deal. I mean, why would they believe me? My side of the story? I'm just a kid. And here's this guy, this grown-up in a suit and shiny shoes, why would they believe me?

I'm cryin. Don't want to, but I am. Can't help it. Them all here, listenin to all these horrible things about me, and the worst part is, some of them, when you twist it around that way, some of them are true. And I feel like I'm a squashed bug, bein sucked down the toilet with all the other crap and the shit, and nobody cares. Good riddance, flush her down.

I'm drownin, hand scrabblin, tearin at my throat, tryin to talk, to explain, tryin to breathe. But when I manage to get any words out, Mr. Levy just twists them back in on themselves, crams them back down my throat.

And I am done for. This is it. I'm well and truly dead, when I hear a noise. A throat clearin. Loud, pure like a bell. A church bell, callin me home, callin me to mass. And I follow that noise, that bell, that cough. I follow it to Cindy, all dressed in red, and she smiles at me. Doesn't look re-pulsed, disgusted by me, the things that I did. She smiles at me, face clear, like cool fresh water. And smilin at me, she lifts her right hand, and gently knocks on her heart, just a gentle tap, like she's testin a watermelon. Just a gentle tap. A love tap, a heart tap. And my sobs, still comin, but my throat loosens up, can let go of it now. Take my hand away from it now. My throat loosens up, and even though I'm cryin, I know I will talk now, for her, for me, for all the other girls out there, girls like us.

And Hazen, he's lookin at me like he's still got that knife at my throat. Tryin to force me to do as he wants. Bend me to his will. Control me, train me, like the good Gemma dog he had before.

He is tryin with his look to gag me again. Silence me again. Bound and suffocate me with his stinky cut-up under-wear! And I feel this rage swell up. A huge enormous wave of it, and I want to stand up. Stand up and scream, bellow, "No!"

Want to roar it out.

But I don't. I look at Cindy. Settle myself in Cindy's face. Calm my heart to beat like hers. I don't bellow. I don't rage. But I do talk. I stop cryin and I talk. I speak. I tell the truth. And I don't let Mr. Levy stop me. I answer Judge Phillips's questions. And I tell him more. I tell him all the things the D.A. and I had talked about. I answer Hazen's attorney's questions, I don't let him twist my answers. I keep talkin even when he tries to shut me up. I tell the truth. I try to keep the tremblin out of my voice. I answer all of the questions. My voice, it seems so loud in the si-lent courtroom. So quiet now you can hear the buzzin of the overhead lights. And I feel like I'm yellin, but I guess I'm not, cause the judge, Judge Phillips, keeps leanin forward, hand cupped around his ear, "I'm sorry, Gemma, could you speak up just a little?"

I tell my story. I tell it all, tryin to talk loud, but voice barely raspin above a whisper. And I can feel his rage. Hazen Wood. I can feel his rage crashin over me in waves.

But I keep on swimmin, I keep on tellin, I keep on talkin until I've finished. Until there is nothing left to tell. I keep on tellin until I reach the shore.

And when I've finished talkin, I know I've done well, cause Cindy is smilin at me, noddin her head. And Joseph and Bonnie and Ms. Lindstrom, they're all smilin at me, and I try and smile at them with my shaky lips.

I don't look at him. I don't look. I never want to look at him again.

And Judge Phillips says I am done, and he smiles at me too, not a big smile, just a tiny upturnin of his lips. Almost didn't see it, didn't know it was a smile, his eyes clued me in. Dark and compassionate.

Then the bailiff comes to get me, to take me out of the courtroom, and I'm glad I am done. Get up from my chair. The witness stand. That's what they call it. I get up, and that's when it hits me, the flu. Hit me like a ton of bricks fallin on my head. Perfectly fine, and then bam! Have to hold the handrail for a second. Legs all wobbly. Vision blackin out, like a TV screen, shuttin off in slow motion. First the outer edges black, like a picture frame, and then it's like the blackness bleeds inward, until there is only a little pinprick of vision, of light left, and then that goes too.

"Are you all right?" the bailiff says. The one who was supposed to guide me out of the courtroom.

I nod, but I have to stay there holdin the handrail for a second more, until my vision comes back. And then I walk my wobbly, rubber legs out of the courtroom. Keep my back stiff. Don't look back at him. Hazen. Don't look even though I can feel him tryin to make me. Don't look back. The big door swingin shut behind me.

And it's like the door, the door closin makes the flu hit me even harder. The nausea. And it must be some terrible horror of a flu, some powerful, instantaneous flu, cause I have to run fast to the bathroom. Scared I won't make it. That I'll barf all over the fancy, shiny hall floors.

When Cindy finds me, I'm still crouched over, dry-heavin into the toilet, all vomited out, but my body won't stop tryin to expel the poison. Clutchin the toilet bowl for dear life.

Odd the things that can be comfortin. The smooth, cool, porcelain of a public toilet. Now who would ever think that would be comfortin? But I'm tellin you, I would have rubbed my cheeks on it to cool off if I didn't know what people use it for.

So that's where she finds me. On my knees clutchin the toilet bowl, don't care how filthy, who peed in it. Don't care. Hunkered over it, tryin to throw up, dislodge this horrible feelin in my throat, in my gut.

"Oh, honey," she says as she kneels down beside me, helps me get up. Washes my face with cool wet towels. Paper towels soaked in water. My hands, my wrists, the back of my neck. "You did well, Gemma," she says. "You did real well."

"What's gonna ha . . . happen?" I ask, even my voice

wobbly. "What's gonna happen now?" Can't let go of her arm, can't help it. "Are they gonna . . ." I feel dizzy. I feel so dizzy. "Are they gonna let . . . let him out?"

"We don't know yet," she says. "We'll have to wait and see. You did a good job."

She tilts my chin up and I can see that she means it and she smiles at me, love in her eyes.

"We were so proud." She smooths back my hair, helps me get it out of my face. "So proud of you, Gemma."

And when I feel well enough, we walk outside to the car, to the parkin lot. Street lamps, just flickin on. Not dark yet. But they're lightin up so they're prepared. Ready for the night.

ACKNOWLEDGMENTS

I'd like to thank Charlotte Sheedy, for pulling Gemma out of a pile of short stories and insisting that she was a novel. For her constant support and encouragement these last fifteen years.

Claire Kirch, who stuck with me and Gemma through all kinds of weather. Started out a publicist, ended up a friend.

Karen Shatzkin, who rescued Gemma from the bad guys.

Mike Nichols for a very good idea.

I'd like to thank Ken Freeman, for his friendship, encouragement, and invaluable assistance, especially for the patience and time he took from his very busy schedule to answer my millions of questions

Christianne Hayward, Emily Naylor, and the teens and parents at her Vancouver Young Adult Kidsbooks bookclub. Thank you for your help, input, and belief in this book. I might not have had the courage to take this route had it not been for you.

I'd like to thank Kyle Hunter, Maria Manske, Wendy Holdman, and Mary Byers at Syren. It's been a real pleasure.

My friends Dawna and Diana for your help and friendship throughout the process.

And last but not least, my family: Don, Emily, David, Will, and John. I love you all.

Meg Tilly is the author of the critically acclaimed novel *Singing Songs* (Dutton, 1994; reissued by Syren Books in the fall of 2006). Formerly an accomplished film actress, Ms. Tilly is best known for her role as Chloe in *The Big Chill* and the title role in *Agnes of God,* for which she won a Golden Globe for Best Supporting Actress in 1986, as well as an Oscar nomination. Ms. Tilly lives with her family in British Columbia, where she is at work on a children's book, *Porcupine,* to be published by Tundra Books (Canada).

Fifty percent of the author's royalties from the sales of *Gemma* will be donated to organizations serving children who are victims of abuse.

The following organizations may be able to refer you to help if you (or others you know) are in an abusive situation.[1]

JUSTICE FOR CHILDREN
2600 Southwest Parkway, Suite 806
Houston, TX 77098
713-225-4357
jfcadvocacy.org
Advocates for children's rights

SIDRAN INSTITUTE
200 East Joppa Road, Suite 207
Towson, MD 21286
410-825-8888
sidran.org
Nonprofit that supports people with traumatic stress conditions

NATIONAL ASSOCIATION TO PROTECT CHILDREN
46 Haywood Street, Suite 315
Asheville, NC 28801
828-350-9350
www.protect.org

NATIONAL SEXUAL VIOLENCE RESOURCE CENTER
123 North Enola Drive
Enola, PA 17025
877-739-3895
www.nsvrc.org

CHILDHELP USA
Hotline: 800-4-A-Child (800-422-4453)
National child abuse hotline

NATIONAL CENTER FOR MISSING & EXPLOITED CHILDREN
699 Prince Street
Alexandria, VA 22314
800-THE-LOST (800-843-5678)

NATIONAL RUNAWAY SWITCHBOARD
800-621-4000

---

1. Please note that inclusion here does not indicate endorsement of this novel on the part of the organizations listed.

To order additional copies of *Gemma*:

Web: www.itascabooks.com

Phone: 1-800-901-3480

Fax: Copy and fill out the form below with credit card information.
          Fax to 763-398-0198.

Mail: Copy and fill out the form below. Mail with check or credit card
          information to:

          Syren Book Company
          5120 Cedar Lake Road
          Minneapolis, Minnesota 55416

Order Form

Copies	Title / Author	Price	Totals
	Gemma / Meg Tilly	$15.95	$
		Subtotal	$
		7% sales tax (MN only)	$
		Shipping and handling, first copy	$ 4.00
		Shipping and handling, ___ add'l copies @$1.00 ea.	$
		TOTAL TO REMIT	$

Payment Information:

__ Check Enclosed   __ Visa/MasterCard
Card number: Expiration date:
Name on card:
Billing address:
City: State: Zip:
Signature :   Date:

Shipping Information:

__ Same as billing address   __ Other (enter below)
Name:
Address:
City: State: Zip: